A Year in the Life of
TheManWhoFellAsleep

A Year in the Life of
TheManWhoFellAsleep

Greg Stekelman

First published in Great Britain in 2006 by Friday Books
An imprint of The Friday Project Limited
83 Victoria Street, London SW1H 0H
www.thefridayproject.co.uk
www.fridaybooks.co.uk

British Library Cataloguing in Publication Data.
A catalogue record for this book is available from the British Library.
ISBN 0 954 83184 5

Designed and produced by Staziker Jones
www.stazikerjones.co.uk

The Publisher's policy is to use paper manufactured
from sustainable forests.

I'd like to dedicate this book to my mum and dad; my sisters, Dina and Rachel, and my girlfriend, Carmen.

Acknowledgements

Many thanks to Paul and Clare at The Friday Project for having faith in me. And thanks also to everyone on the message board and all the strangers and friends who emailed me via the website.

Foreword

Themanwhofellasleep lives in a mythical London. It's not the London of Big Ben and the Houses of Parliament. It's not the London of Notting Hill, café lattes and Fresh & Wild. It's the London of ceaselessly sprawling suburbia, of ghost tube stations and dilapidated newsagents. And polar bears.

And it's the perfect backing for this novel, because it's a London that doesn't work. It's a city of cancelled trains, exorbitant rents and early closing shops. It's a city that is falling asleep. It's a city with a dead whale floating down the Thames.

This book is about finding your own reality. Not in an airy-fairy way; I'm not talking about running home from the disco and hiding in your bedroom. It's about understanding that you can find mesmerising beauty or horrifying squalor around every corner. London is a city with 10 million different faces, and any one of them could be an assassin, a lover, a Greek God or an angry postman.

And the jokes!

There's an Englishman, Irishman and a Scotsman, trapped in a jail cell. Eventually they all starved to death.

And perhaps that's what's uniquely striking about the book. Normally, jokes only work because they're inconsequential – no harm is really done. *A Year in the Life of TheManWhoFellAsleep* is funny because it serves up a double dose of misery when you're expecting a punchline; and then just when you're comfortable with urban misery, Jesus wanders on the scene, drunk and lonely, complaining that his dad never writes to him.

Such dreams are these. Spaced-out and sumptuous. I suspect that if I ever met themanwhofellasleep, I'd want to give him a slap and tell him to wake up. And move to Brighton.

Julie Burchill, Sussex 2006

January 1st

The doorbell rang. I looked at my alarm clock. It was 3a.m. I closed my eyes and pretended I hadn't heard it. It rang again.

I put on a pair of jeans and answered the door. It was Jesus. He looked terrible. His hair was unkempt and there were grey bags under his eyes. He stank of whisky.

'You had best come in', I said.

He sat down on the sofa and I put the kettle on. He stared shamefacedly at his bare feet.

'What's wrong, Jesus?' I said. 'It's not like you to ring the bell at this time of the morning. You're normally so considerate.'

'I… I… I can't say.'

'Is it your dad? I know he gives you a hard time about dying for our sins and everything.'

'No', he scrunched up his face and sobbed. 'It's not him. It's you.'

I didn't say anything. I made two cups of coffee and handed one to him.

'I love you', he said.

'Of course you love me', I sighed. 'You're Jesus. You love everyone.'

'No… I mean, I do love everyone, but it's different with you.'

I approached him and put my hand gently on his shoulder. He pulled me towards him and pressed his lips against mine. I felt his straw-like beard against my jaw. I felt his tongue trying to prise open my teeth. I pulled away and wiped my lips against my sleeve.

'Jesus. I like you. You're a good kid. You've got a big future, but I don't like you like that. I don't go for Messiahs.' He didn't say anything.

'You can sleep on the couch', I said. I climbed the stairs and went back to bed. I was going to have to have a quiet word with God.

Upstairs, in the darkness of my bedroom, I could hear his muffled, uneven snoring.

I am
the man
who fell
asleep

January 2nd

I awoke to find myself in a new room. I was lying in a white bed, staring at white walls. The room slipped in and out of focus, and the base of the bed seemed to be shrouded in a thin white mist, like a carpet of dry ice upon the floor. I stepped out of the bed. I found that I was wearing a thin paper smock, the kind that patients in hospital wear for operations. I do not like smocks and I wanted to change clothes, but there were no items of clothing in the room.

My feet unsteady, I opened the door and left the room. I found myself walking down a long white corridor of indeterminate length. I could not see the end of the corridor; it seemed to stretch and curve beyond my vision. I walked on. The corridor was bare, but on one side there were windows. I glanced out; there was a sea of gravel, grey and uniform. No other buildings. No people. No sounds. Just the fog in my head and the mist around my ankles. I don't know how long I walked. My mind wandered. I couldn't remember anything. I could only think of certain colours and smells and sounds, echoing around my empty head: it must have been the drugs.

Finally, the corridor came to an end. There was a single door of dark mahogany. I knocked. The door was opened by a smiling middle-aged man, wearing a suit and a doctor's white jacket. He welcomed me in and offered me a plastic chair. I sat down, self-conscious in my smock.

'Hello', he said. 'How are you today?'

There was something odd about his face. He seemed to be wearing a fixed smile, like a cheap plastic mask, and when he spoke, his lips were not in sync with his voice. He was a badly dubbed character.

'Ummm… I'm OK. How did I get here? Where am I?'

'You don't remember?' he raised an eyebrow. 'Well, I suppose that's natural, given everything that's happened.'

He spread his hands upon his lap and smiled beatifically: 'You've been in an accident.'

'No', I protested. 'No… I don't know what I'm doing here. I don't know why I'm wearing paper clothes… I don't know… but I am sure there's been no accident. I'm fine.'

He smiled again, and his smile seemed to drift around the room, independent of his face. 'Trust me. You've been very ill. You've been asleep for a very long time. One day you'll be better.'

'Who are you? What's your name?'

'I am Dr Gepetto.'

'Dr Gepetto? Is that a joke? What are you going to do? Turn me into a real boy?'

'What?' he asked.

'Gepetto... Pinocchio... He wanted to be a real boy. He was sick of being wooden.'

'I am afraid I have no idea what you are talking about', he said.

His smile continued to swim around the room and I started to feel giddy and sick. I could feel the bile rising in my throat and looked around the room to see if there was a bathroom attached.

'We should get you back to bed,' he said, then he pressed a buzzer on his desk. I don't remember what happened after that.

Now I am back in the bed, and the room is dark. I don't know what is happening, but I am writing it all down. Don't panic. All will be revealed, of that I am sure.

Now the room is spinning and I am finding it hard to stay awake...
I am asleep. Ignore what I just wrote. It isn't important. Wipe the slate clean and take a deep breath. Then read on.

January 4th

Some of this journal is true. And some of it is false. Half-truths. Lies. Exaggeration. But then, some of the greatest works of human art are lies. I'm sure you'll agree that this journal is such a beautiful work of art that it elevates my lies to a greater truth. That is the purpose of art, afterall.

The journal will take you on many strange journeys. Some of them will be exceedingly dull, but you must stay patient. There are many clues. Piece them together and step back and you will see a complete vision of my existence. You will laugh, you will cry; you will believe a man can fly. It may not make much sense, but that is God's fault, not mine. In his infinite wisdom, God has created life without reason, and it will take a better man than me to put the reason back into life.

The journal will span a year of my life. This is because the stationery shop only sells one-year journals.

As a man of some importance, I am often contacted by celebrities, philosophers and International Aid Agencies. It's not as glamorous as it sounds, but I will include details of such meetings regardless. Since I do not own a camera, I will illustrate some entries with my own illustrations. Keep hold of the illustrations – some day they may be valuable. Additionally, where I have found posters, drawings and receipts that are of relevance, I will include them in the journal. This is a free service. There are no hidden charges. Do not read the fine print.

Of course, much of my real journal is not included within these pages. The real journal is far too dangerous for public consumption. It is buried somewhere in the Midlands.

January 5th

Let's skip the preliminaries. You know what goes on in a journal. In fact, let's skip the whole journal. Here's a rough breakdown of my year:

Winter

It is winter. There is no snow. It seldom snows in winter anymore. My inner child is disappointed, but he's been disappointed since I turned 16 and started growing chest hair. Always ignore your inner child – he grew up to be you. You know better than him.

It is winter and crowds huddle at bus stops, stamping their feet and shuffling along cold seats. London Underground stations are flooded and apologetic guards redirect passengers at Kings Cross to nearby Euston Square. A thousand commuters dig out mobile phones and call work to say that they will be late. Lines form outside coffee shops as skinny lattes are wrapped in tissue paper and cardboard and delivered to desks, where young fathers brush sleep from their eyes and adjust their novelty ties.

It is winter, so I do nothing. I hibernate and lick my fur. I check my email and ponder a thousand revisions to an unwritten story that is floating around my mind. My afternoon is punctuated by the hourly click of a kettle boiling and the cough of a cigarette outside the front door. Winter, winter, winter. I am frozen in time. My doctor prescribes bugs in amber.

Spring

Spring. Spring in the air, if you feel like it. It is spring. You know the routine: Renaissance! Rebirth! Crocuses fight their way through damp soil and greet the sunshine. The frost in the mornings gives way to mist and mildew. Adventurous Londoner men experiment with T-shirts and receive the unwelcome stares of women in business suits. An advert on the side of a bus suggests that the sun is shining, and we should bathe ourselves in Diet Coke, but it's drizzling on the bus and faces are pressed against tired glass, staring at a traffic jam in Crouch End.

It is spring. I hack up phlegm and donate it to Cancer Research. My doctor tells me to exercise and I smile and tell him I've started jogging. The record jogs and I start the paragraph again.

It is spring. I shave off the winter beard and am amazed at my youth. My face never quite matches my age – it anticipates the future and remembers the past, but can't quite remain in the present. Couples push prams up hills and I have to pinch myself to remember that my peers are parents, not babies. The council pulls up daffodils that a local gardener has planted on their soil.

Summer

London is unsuited to summer. The Underground melts into a chocolate smear, and secretaries gather on mossy landfills to bronze themselves in their lunch hour. Buses sink into wet tarmac and angry drivers gesticulate and shout at the elderly. Blackberries grow bitter, then sweet, and hang, plump and inviting on thorny tendons. In a small café an overhead fan cools coffees and sticky buns, and builders strip to the waist to expose pierced nipples.

It is summer, and I sweat my way through three shirts before it rains for a week and the cricket is cancelled. I fear the long summer evenings, when the night does not arrive on time, but hurries into my bedroom late, late, late and bearing no gifts. I resent the ever-present offer of sex. Girls wear short skirts and expose flat stomachs and I smile vaguely into the middle-distance, stabbing a voodoo doll of myself that I found in a skip.

Summer is full of threats and promises. Sunshine, sex and stinging insects. I try my best to ignore all of it. I remember that I am not part of the human race just yet. I am a brand new species and totally genetically redundant.

Autumn

Autumn in New York. Golden leaves in Paris. No. This is not the romantic autumn of jazz songs and Woody Allen movies. This is autumn in north London. A steady downpour of grey rain and gleeful insects. The flowers have blossomed too soon and are washed into the kerb. The days shrink and are parcelled into 8-hour packages, to be shipped off to God knows where. Night falls at 5 p.m. and I decide against leaving the house. It is a relief, truth be told. There is a pressure that never leaves me: the pressure to socialise, to fuck, to laugh with friends. It is a relief when those pressures fade. They are nothing to do with me. They are not my own desires. They are some American TV executive's idea of a good time.

It is autumn again. Time flies when your head is in the sand.

You can stop reading now, if you want, but you can't ask for your money back unless you've read the whole book.

January 6th

I used to be so cold-hearted. I used to be a selfish brute. But I have seen the light. I was blind and now I can see. Life is shit, but it's OK. Shake hands with fate and get on with it.

Today Jesus came round for brunch. We had coffee and croissants. We read the papers in silence. I did the Times crossword – the general knowledge one, not the cryptic one. Cryptic crosswords are beyond even my powers. I am not Roger Moore on an oil rig.

After brunch we played chess. He was black and I was white. It was a little frustrating, since Jesus didn't know the rules and kept on randomly moving the pieces instead of playing properly. I forgive him. He has especially low self-esteem, so I smiled and encouraged him and told him

he was playing very well. He's taken enough knocks over the last few thousand years. The last thing he needs is any grief from me.

After he had 'won' a few games, he suggested that we play for money. Cheeky bugger. Of course, I accepted.

January 9th

I am an artist. I am a pilot. I am a Renaissance man.

Work on my sculpture is going well. I have encased the model in brass and clay and she looks incredibly lifelike. Her face is a poignant mask of fear and agony. I think this latest piece will speak to everyone. Art should be universal. I have no interest in art that speaks only to the chattering classes – art must be bold and decisive, like a hungry fox in a dustbin. I want to make statements that reduce the world to spasms of alarm.

Good news seldom lasts for long. This morning, as I walked alongside the dewy grass in the park I noticed a police poster enquiring about the disappearance of my model. Apparently, she was a local student, and her parents are very worried about her. I doubt they are fans of my art.

Why are people so negative about my artistic endeavours? It says a lot about the state of contemporary Britain. Everyone is a critic.

So, today I spent the whole afternoon wandering around north London (someone *must* do something about the price of travelcards!) removing the police posters. The things I do for my art.

January 11th

By my bedside there is a glass of water. Perhaps it is tonight's water, fresh and clean. Perhaps it is last night's water, dead and stale with a dry film on the surface. It doesn't matter. I have battles to fight.

I have seen him again. I don't know his name, but I can never forget his face. I see him sometimes, following me home from the shops, or hiding behind a tree in a wide avenue. I don't know who he is and I don't know what he wants. But he's been with me for years now... this strange alter-ego who disappears and reappears with the seasons.

He is a tall, thin man, with pitted skin and bony cheeks. And though I get older, he does not seem to age. He always looks the same. Perhaps he is more than just one man... perhaps he is a father and son team, intent on haunting me throughout the generations.

Who knows what he wants? I am ashamed to say that I don't even know for sure that he is real. He could be a metaphor or an allegory or even an old-fashioned hallucination, but he has always been there. When I was a child in dungarees, when I was a teenager in stonewashed jeans, he was there, lurking. He never tries to make contact, he just follows me. Sometimes I go months without seeing him, but he never quite slips from my mind. He inhabits the corners of my subconscious, colouring my days and creeping up behind my motives.

I call him my Shadow. It's melodramatic, but I can't think of a better word. He is half-light and insubstantial, and he disappears with the oncoming night. I only see him during the day.

I have never tried to approach my Shadow. I do not know what would happen if I spoke to him, but I am sure no good would come of it. He may not be an enemy, but I am sure he is not a friend. Anyway, I am scared of shadows. For many years, I tried to avoid casting any form of shadow... I would only leave the house at noon, when the sun stood directly overhead and my shadow fell directly beneath me.

But enough of him. I do not want him to sour these early entries. The journal must be a happy place, full of jokes and banter and momentum. And joy. Lots of joy.

January 13th

I meet lots of pop stars. It's because they are lonely and cling vainly to men of substance, such as myself.

This afternoon Simon and Garfunkel came round for tea. I say tea, but I didn't have any tea, so I gave them mugs of hot water with a splash of lemon-flavoured washing up liquid. It's the lemon that adds my trademark 'zing'.

Things do not appear to be going well between Paul and Art. There were frosty silences and bitter glares between them, and I suspect that Paul deliberately sabotaged the harmony as they sang me 'Bridge Over

Troubled Water'. Paul looks very old, like a hardened walnut, and seems to have shrunken to the size of a small child. I had to help him into his chair as he couldn't reach it on his own. By contrast, Art seems taller than ever, although he is terribly skinny and his halo of frizzy hair makes him look like a lamp post glowing in the twilight.

I think it would be fair to say that the afternoon was a disaster. I had served only two fondant fancies. I ate one and Paul and Art bickered endlessly over who would eat the second one.

In the end I settled the dispute by eating it myself.

January 15th

There are 275 tube stations and 12 tube lines in London. The network runs from Amersham in the west to Upminster in the east, from Watford in the north to Morden in the south. It used to extend all the way to Blake Hall, but no one ever used that station, and it withered away like a maimed limb.

There are 417 escalators on the tube, and all of them are broken, or so it seems. The deepest station on the network is Hampstead, which lies some 59 metres below ground level. This is ironic, since people who live in Hampstead are among the shallowest in London.

When the London Underground first introduced escalators in 1911, there was great public outcry about safety issues. To reassure people, a man with a wooden leg – his name was Bumper Harris – was employed to travel the escalators and prove that they were safe. It is not known if Harris lost his leg in an escalator-related accident, but I think it is likely. After all, more people die each year on the escalators of the London Underground than are killed by handguns in America.

I have always had a love affair with the Underground. What is more musical than a garbled tannoy announcement? What is more dramatic than the sudden rush of hot air that precedes a train's appearance on a platform? There is something magical about it. Even when you are going somewhere, you feel as though you may be going nowhere. And when you're going nowhere, you sense that somehow you may still be moving in the right direction.

The Underground is safe to me. It is the safety of mildew and decay. Sadly, I fear much of life: from milkmen to safety matches and Manila envelopes. I inhabit a world of barely-contained fear. If a man looks at me sidelong in the street or a woman laughs too loudly in a pub, I look away. The only safety lies at home. Home is safe. Home is where you hang your head. And the tube is almost my home…

That is the beauty of the tube. It allows me to travel while remaining at home. I can travel across vast distances but maintain the illusion of remaining stationary. I sit down at Wood Green and watch the stations scroll by like television, and suddenly, without moving, I am elsewhere. Holloway Road! Green Park! Hammersmith! I have traversed London, and yet all I have done is sit down.

There is another reason I love the Tube. I love it for the dark spell it casts over my fellow passengers. It affects everyone. It warps the mind. It deadens the senses. How can anyone behave normally when they are hurtling through tunnels below the surface of the world?

Amid those deep, dank platforms unruly teenagers slouch in tracksuits and mutter into their hands. Sallow-faced young women stare at their reflections and dream of sunlight above. Businessmen read *The Standard*

TUBE GOSSIP

over each others' shoulders. Secretaries smirk as they scan the daily gossip. The reception on a mobile phone dies away, as ringtones are replaced by prerecorded announcements. All signals fail.

Down there, we are trapped in lonely carriages and trapped between stations. We are held hostage to the hiss of an opening door. The Underground belongs to anyone brave enough to use it.

Throughout the journal, I will be including snippets of overheard conversation from my journeys on the London Underground. Are the conversations real? That's for you to decide. You have a brain, don't you?

Things overheard on the tube

Today's journey:
Piccadilly Line: Wood Green–Green Park

1. Why does George Lucas insist on that walnut-whip hairdo?
2. I had a dream that Chris Sutton was angry with me. He had released a folk single and I had slagged it off.
3. I'm not a misogynist. I just hate women.
4. Of course it's not Halal. It's a fucking pork chop.
5. By adding a hip-hop drumbeat to my spoken-word monologue, my peers will consider me eclectic and bohemian.
6. Oh, my boobs are falling out.
7. Nick Cave has a very long face.
8. All human tragedy is grist to your sordid entertainment mill.
9. Billy Crystal has never had a funny moment in his life.
10. My Palm Pilot fills me with a sense of infinite woe.

January 16th

Today I had another visit from a would-be-missionary. I opened the door to find a giant worm on my doorstep. It was wearing a blue porkpie hat.

'Are you worried about the state of the world?' said the giant worm.

'Do you think that the country is getting worse and that there is less love and spiritual understanding around you?'

'You're a giant worm', I said.

'Yes, you're right of course. I am a giant worm. But let's not get stuck on that. I'd really rather talk to you about the state of the world. Tell me, are you a religious man?'

'So... wait a minute... if I cut you in two, do you become two separate worms?' I asked.

'Well, yes, I suppose I would. But I'd rather talk to you about Jesus. Do you think that the love of Jesus touches your life?'

'Hang on a second', I said. 'I am going to get a knife.'

January 18th

The bloody politicians have been around the barrio again. The dustbins have been knocked over and obscene graffiti has been scrawled on the youth club walls. Windows have been smashed in pubs. Worst of all, I found this pinned to a tree.

The Greek philosophers are back on the prowl. There goes the neighbourhood. *Cogito ergo* Scum.

January 20th

The sky is brown. This afternoon I had another visit from would-be missionaries. This time it wasn't a worm.

The Jehovah's Witnesses came round for a friendly chat. There were two of them. I managed to mask my displeasure at being awoken before 3 p.m., and smiled politely. I explained that I couldn't chat to them as I had some very important business abroad and needed to leave for the airport immediately. I think they fell for it. They left me some literature to read. I ate it. It was delicious.

In the past I used to try to deal with Jehovah's Witnesses by explaining that I was 'not of their faith'. But this never worked. As soon as you show any sign of interest in any religion, be it Islam or Judaism or even Christianity, they see an opening and pounce. They tell you all about God, and Jesus, and heaven, and the possibility of an impending apocalypse. It all sounds terribly dreary.

So, after wasting many afternoons talking to them and nervously looking at my watch, I decided on a different tactic. When I saw them approaching the house, I would simply fire at them with my air rifle. It was only many years later that I discovered that this was illegal.

Religion is out of date. We live in a consumer culture. People will inevitably pick and mix from the various religions and call the result *spirituality*. I will not burden you with my beliefs. They would only make your brain hurt.

January 22nd

I know things no one else knows. It should make me great, but it just makes me an idiot.

January 23rd

I awoke early. The front garden was wet with dew and the air was fresh and cool. I felt like the first man on earth. But even at this early hour, the buses were running and bakers and bikers were straggling to work.

As I walked down Palace Gates Road I spotted something unusual: a polar bear. There are very few polar bears left in London. Most of them were chased out of the city by the GLC in the 1980s. Another reason to hate Ken Livingstone.

'Good morning, Mr Bear', I said.

'Good morning young sir', said the bear. 'How pleasant of you to greet me so cordially. No one else here has any manners.'

'Manners maketh the man', I replied, smiling. The sun was bright and I crinkled my eyes at the horizon.

'And manners also make the bear', said the bear.

'Good day to you', I said, and gave an exaggerated bow of humility.

The bear saluted me and waved goodbye.

Bears are wonderful things. Here are some facts about polar bears.

A POLAR BEAR, SMOKING A CIGAR

1. The most famous polar bear in the world is probably Minty, the polar bear that stands astride Fox's Glacier Mints. In his heyday in the 1940s Minty got more fan mail than the Beatles and the Rolling Stones together.
2. Polar bears are very sarcastic. It's not irony – it is *sarcasm*.
3. When hunting, polar bears cover their noses so that they blend in with the snowy background. Yet, this hinders them as they then have only three paws to hunt with.
4. In 1931 Hollywood was scandalised by Fatty Arbuckle's affair with Fru Fru, a (married) polar bear. Neither Arbuckle nor Fru Fru's career (she was an ice-dancer) survived the media backlash.
5. Many people assume that polar bears are mammals. They are in fact a form of wingless bird.
6. Just as Jews are often blamed for catastrophic events in the global community, so polar bears are often blamed for disaster in the arctic community. Because of this, many polar bears refer to themselves as jewbears.
7. Famous musical polar bears include Jimi Hendrix, Larry Adler, Cyndi Lauper, Jeff Beck and the man from Baby Bird.
8. In 1914 the polar bear population of London was 12. It is now 15.
9. Polar bears have the most natural rhythm of all the arctic animals. During spring and summer, polar bears often give salsa classes across west London.
10. If you are very sad and very lonely, and you think hard enough about a polar bear, one will appear beside you.

January 24th

I was sitting in a café with my friend Ned. I was eating two sausages, beans and chips and he was tucking into bubble and squeak. There was no sign of the Shadow. It was not an important day; it was just another filler day that dragged on like an opera.

Ned and I were talking about the meaning of life and I was dabbing my chips into a pool of ketchup. Café ketchup is sweet.

'You see', said Ned, clutching his glass of Coke, 'some people will tell you that the glass is half empty, and some will tell you that it's half full.'

'I know', I yawned and a chip fell on the floor.

'But what I do is stick to the facts. I will say: the glass has 150 ml of Coca Cola in it. I am not stating whether it's half empty or half full. That's *opinion*, not fact. I am not making a value judgement, I am just trying to stick to the verifiable details.'

'And you apply this to the rest of your life, do you?' I was sceptical, to say the least.

'Well, it's easier said than done', he shrugged. 'I mean... when you're talking about a can of Coke, it's one thing. When you're talking about your family getting kidnapped or your house burning down, it's something else entirely. It's hard to just focus on the facts... I suppose there's not really such a thing as an empirical existence. We can't ever really exist outside of our own perceptual contexts.'

'Still, nice chips', I said.

'Yeah, not bad', he nodded.

We always have the same conversations. They don't really go anywhere, but I like them. We debate the kind of lightweight philosophy that can only really exist in cafés or park benches or pubs. True friendships can tolerate silence, but we are not yet ready for that level of commitment.

January 25th

Another day, another free local magazine on my doorstep.

This one was baffling. It contained one page of text – a letter from the editor – and the remainder of it was glossy photos of old men in wheelchairs wearing leather gloves.

The text (in heavy black print) read as follows:

Friends, have you ever wondered what would happen if everybody on earth clapped their hands at the same time? No, I can't say that I have either. But I don't wonder about much.

Or have you ever wondered who would have won in a fist-fight between Richard Nixon and Pope John Paul II? I know that I haven't. I think only of high culture. But culture is bad. Not only do kids nowadays show their elders no respect, they don't even know who their elders are! Their arithmetic and basic counting is so poor, they actually think they are older than their parents.

So, I hear you scream, 'What can be done about modern life?'

Personally, I am very dubious about herbal remedies. I like my drugs to have a noticeable effect, be it positive or negative. I also loathe shirts that hang too long. I prefer a shirt to err on the side of shortness, although I fear that one day I may accidentally expose my midriff. Of course, they say that as women get older, they prefer hairier men, but they also say that bald men are more virile, which is untrue. Bald men are merely balder. Such things are simple. I understand complex matters, which is why I know I can depend on your trust and fidelity.

'What should I do? What can I do?' Do not ask what your country can do for you. Start small. Ask what your house can do for you. And then ask what your borough can do for you. If in doubt, do nothing. I rarely do anything. Working on the premise that the road to hell is paved with good intentions, I'm hoping that the road to heaven is paved with bad intentions. And even though my heart is filled with hatred and sin, I never actually do anything about it. This is a good thing and no doubt you are heartily pleased.

People ask me what the point of life is. 'Oh father', they cry, 'What is the point of life?' And this is what I say: the point of life is to get from A to B as quickly as possible. In this, the alphabet is possibly the greatest form of transport invented by man. But remember, the joy should always be in arriving, never in travelling. Do not dwell on the moment. Think only of the future and all pleasures deferred – remember that anxiety is your friend, your only real friend. Do not be dissuaded by positive energies. Throughout your life, you may encounter people who will tell you that you will never amount to anything. This is poisonous claptrap. The fact of the matter is that you will never amount to much – that is a very big difference.

Throughout history, man has fought man, brother has struck brother, bear has baited bear. Religions have come and gone. Yet one argument lingers like an unwanted houseguest... **bold** or italics?... **bold** or italics?

What is the best way to emphasize the importance of text? Friend, you know that I like to keep out of these matters (and am reluctant to be drawn on issues of font), but something must be said.

The magazine left me quite confused and angry. I threw it in the bin. Even there, among the dead cigarettes, I could feel it mocking me. What kind of editor was this? What kind of fool writes such drivel? Do not read free magazines.

January 26th

I awoke cold and nervous. I could feel the presence of my Shadow. I know I will not see him today, but his presence lingers.

Today I meandered around the house, killing insects. The phone rang and a message was left. It was friends inviting me out.

We went bowling. I travelled across London and found myself in an alien place, this alley of doom, populated by 16-year-olds of both sexes. All the boys looked like members of So Solid Crew, complete with weak oxide moustaches and wonky baseball caps. All the girls looked like trainee prostitutes. I wandered around the alley, fearful and agitated in unfamiliar shoes.

The game itself was predictable. The ball rolled slowly down the lane. Sometimes it hit the skittles. Mostly it slipped into the gutter. I can't see it catching on.

January 27th

What becomes of the broken hearted? I don't know. I have absolutely no idea at all.

I do have some good news. I got a letter in the post today informing me that I have been chosen to be the new portal through which the gods of Olympus may return to power on Earth.

It is all very sudden, but apparently I have been picked as the prime vessel for the spirit of Zeus himself. I'm quite pleased. I'm not sure exactly what this entails, but I'm pretty sure it will mean celebrity parties and cocaine and me appearing before supermodels in the form of a goose.

When I heard the news from Olympus I wrote to my parents to tell them all about it, but I'm not expecting much of a reply. Nothing I do impresses them. When I was at school I was chosen by my classmates to be the May Queen, and everyone in the area was very excited for me, but all my parents could say was: 'Is there any money in it?' I tried to explain that it was a great honour, and that it wasn't about money, and they just looked to the heavens as though they had heard it all before.

This could not fail to impress them, though. People are always impressed by Greek gods. Maybe it's because there are so many of them. Quantity beats quality every time.

Things overheard on the tube

Today's journey:
WAGN: Alexandra Palace–Highbury and Islington, then Victoria Line to Oxford Circus

1. I have nothing to fear but fear itself, which I fear intensely.
2. Come on! Let's get drunk. It's Tuesday... it's practically the end of the week.
3. You are all whores.
4. Chicken Kievs! I don't want any more chicken Kievs! Just leave me alone.
5. Janet Jackson has had almost as much plastic surgery as Michael Jackson but vainly clings to some sense of artistic and moral superiority.
6. Before he was gay, Elton John asked my mum to have sex with him.
7. Haha! Yes, well don't get back together with her. Do it if you want, but you know it'll end badly and I don't want you complaining about it to me. Seriously.
8. This body is just my passport in the mortal realm. It is not me.
9. George Foreman's special grills look scary.
10. It's got that 'dang-a-nanga' guitar sound.

January 28th

Today I spent the day losing money on fruit machines. Those machines, they seem so friendly at first, with their flashing lights and their funny noises, and every so often they do actually give me some money, but it never lasts. Somehow I end up leaving the pub with my pockets empty, having eaten 10 cigarettes in an hour.

Recently, I've started unplugging the fruit machines before I play. I still put my money in, but it reduces the risk that I might actually win something – basically it speeds the whole process up considerably. Life is much easier when you know what is going to happen.

Likewise, rather than buying food, putting it in my fridge and then not eating it, I have started just putting my money directly in the bin. It cuts out the middleman and I have never been slimmer.

January 29th

There is text everywhere. The world is written on in all its nooks and crannies. Always read the small print. In particular, pay attention to anything written on a box of matches.

I found the following information on the back of a packet of Lustrox matches:

(Made in Slovenia. Average contents: 40. Keep out of reach of children.)

'And Lo, a great horse will come from the sky and it will graze in the pasture of wrath!' Thus spoke the celebrated seer Michel de Nostradame in 1555.

Nostradamus was famous for his uncannily accurate predictions. Nostradamus – literally 'our dumb-ass' – was born in 1503 in Burnley to Mary and Phil Nostradamus, and had a happy, if forgettable, childhood. However, he grew up to be the most famous Nostradamus in history!

Nostradamus' notoriety has grown in recent years as more and more people become hooked on his infallible predictions. Among his most celebrated predictions were those referring to Hitler – '...and at some point in the future a man of evil will strike fear into all...' and the assassination of JFK '...a great leader will die by grass...'.

He is even credited with predicting his own death in the quatrain: 'Jesus! That thing is heading right at us. Move out of the...'. Scholars have puzzled for centuries over what Nostradamus was referring to. But puzzle is all we can do, since Nostradamus cannot speak from beyond the grave – he was killed by a runaway carthorse.'

As you can probably imagine, it was written in very small text.

January 30th

I walked into an upmarket art gallery near Sloane Square. Between the black and white photos and boxes of junk masquerading as conceptual art, I saw this delightful illustration:

The picture cheered me. It was terrible, obviously, but it made me smile. Terrible art is often more moving than great art. You should always think about how art affects you, and never worry about whether or not it's any good.

January 31st

I sat on the District Line next to a woman in big Janet Street-Porter glasses. Someone had left a copy of the *Sunday Express*. I opened it and read an interview in the middle section. It was one of those lifestyle pieces where a celebrity tells you about the exciting things they get up to on an average day:

A Day in the Life

Anton Hoffer, 32, is a leading London playwright and artist. Next year he plans to release an album of his self-penned folk songs.

'I normally wake up at about 7.30 a.m. I spend about 20 minutes staring blankly at the ceiling and silently sobbing before I get up. In many ways this period is the highlight of my day. As I lie there, I often try to plan out what I want to do with the day, and try to think of any redeeming features that might brighten up my life. So far I haven't thought of any.

Breakfast is light. I'm a great coffee lover and can't face the world before I've had my second mug of Mellow Birds. It kick-starts my day. It's 2 hours before I feel ready to get started with my work. I'm very lucky to have my partner Patricia, who is marvellously patient with me and understands the demands I'm under. She rifles through the neighbour's bins and always thinks of something ingenious to do with the food she finds. I find it amazing what people will throw away.

In my opinion, it is materialism gone mad.

My living-space is very Spartan. I like to feel uncluttered and focused. I have the corridor, which is something of a communal area, and then I have my own room, which is where the kitchen, toilet and bathroom are located. Patricia and her mother also live in the room, so it can be a bit of a squeeze, but as long as I have space inside my head, I can work fine. I am a bohemian, after all.

Last year the builders were in, demolishing the walls and smashing the windows, but even then I found that my unshakeable inner calm gave me the peace necessary to get my work done. Builders are scum.

I carry my laptop everywhere. If I leave it at home, it will get stolen. Last year I was mugged in my kitchen by the editorial staff of the **Guardian.** *They said it was for my own good.*

In the afternoons Patricia and I go to Relate. They used to give us marriage guidance but now they just tell us that life is difficult and shrug silently. You have to admire their bravery and honesty. Social workers are society's real heroes.

In the evening I like to go out walking around the parks. London has the most beautiful parks in the world, but they are often too crowded during the day. I like to sneak around the parks at night, when they are almost deserted. It makes my tummy feel all funny.

So many people take greenery for granted – the environment is one of my passions. I don't want my grandchildren to live in a polluted half-dead world. In fact I don't want grandchildren. I hate kids.

I go to bed at about 3 a.m. Kafka's anti-hero Gregor Samsa awoke to find himself turned into a beetle. This hasn't happened to me yet, but I'm still young. Kafka was a true artist. He exposed society's sordid underbelly. I like to think my own work does much the same. My latest play 'Oh Mama, I'm Turning Into a Snail' has a somewhat Kafka-esque subtext. Maybe it will be my breakthrough. I hope so. I hate myself and want more money.'

Interview by Arty Stark.

It was an interesting interview. I must contact this individual. Perhaps we shall become friends. Or even enemies. I miss having enemies. A true enemy is greater than a thousand shrugs of indifference.

February 2nd

I bought another newspaper this morning. I instantly regretted it. Newspapers should contain news, not this terrible hodgepodge of rumour and slander. I do not care who is sleeping with Darren Day. I do not want to know about a revolutionary new diet. I am not interested in the secret drug shame of a supermodel.

Why are celebrities always saying that their heartbreak has only made them stronger? Whether they have lost a baby, are suffering from a crippling drug addiction or are battling alcoholism, they are always saying that their troubles have made them better, stronger people. What is this obsession with self-improvement? It doesn't sound anything like my life. All the setbacks and mishaps I have ever suffered have made me nervous, bitter and scared. That's how it works, isn't it? Life smacks you in the face and you sob and wail and learn not to stick your head above the parapet. You do not become stronger; you become weaker. You learn fear. Bloody celebrities. Not a brain between them.

I was also disappointed by the lack of free gifts in my newspapers. Where are the free DVDs of my youth?

February 4th

I slept late and awoke to discover that I had been chained to my computer. These were not metaphorical chains; oh no, they were real, steel chains. They chafed my slender wrists and ankles. I spent the morning clutching my stomach in barely-contained panic and weeing into a plastic cup, before I remembered that I had the key to the chains in my pocket. Whenever I get drunk I end up chaining myself to something. It's my pathetic desire to belong.

Why am I so desperate? I don't really know. Dr Gepetto once suggested that I am preoccupied with the impermanence of things, the fact that things – and people – can disappear at any time. It rings true. I am always surprised and slightly relieved when I wake in the morning and find that my bedroom has not run off and that the house has not been washed downstream in a typhoon. So, to prevent things from disappearing, I chain myself to them. It's clumsy, but effective. The doctor says I take things too literally, but what other way can you take things?

I worry about Dr Gepetto. Suppose he disappears? I will be left alone with my neuroses. I must give him a pay rise. I suppose he accepts cash. I don't know. I only ever seem to see him in dreams.

February 5th

The rain comes down. It's wet and tastes of water. Damn my prosaic imagination. This will simply not do.

Today I went for a walk. I walked from my bedroom to the lounge, where I managed to crawl onto the sofa. Fortunately, I had left the television on last week, so there was no need for me to locate the remote control and switch it on. We must be grateful for such blessings. The news was on. A man in a suit was talking about a pig that was stuck in a well. It was a very moving story. Tears flowed down my cheeks.

In the end they managed to rescue the pig, although it had broken a leg. I'm sure the story serves as a symbol for something, but I can't for the life of me work out what it is.

Maybe one day I will change the channel. These decisions cannot be taken lightly. T. S. Eliot agonised over eating a peach, and he was a better man than me.

Things overheard on the tube

Today's journey:
Northern Line: Elephant and Castle–Chalk Farm

1. I am a 12-year-old boy. Why must Mum and Dad get divorced? I hate them. I wish I had a dog.
2. The Velvet Undergound are like... Kenco... and the Strokes are Mellow Birds.

3. Why don't you watch where you're going, you fat fuck?
4. A penguin beats a gazelle anytime.
5. When I woke up, the leg was gone. I haven't seen it since.
6. My deodorant offers me invisible protection, much like an odour-free guardian angel.
7. You see all these idiots in New York Yankee baseball caps. I don't get it. You don't see guys in the Bronx wearing West Ham hats.
8. Whenever you're ready, we can start harvesting your organs.
9. The film totally ignores his bisexuality. It is a sham.
10. Yoda es fuertissimo. El puede vencer a Count Dooku. Pero Jesus es aun mas fuerte. El tiene muchos poderes.

February 7th

One of the most bizarre people I know is the rock star Bono, the lead singer with fading overblown supergroup U2. Despite his hair weave and the fact that he shares a face with Robin Williams, Bono remains the undisputed king of rock reinvention. He's not really called Bono, though. His real name is Bonnhart Beaufort or something like that.

The thing I like most about Bono is his way with words. He's very eloquent. Particularly when paying tribute to the dead. Death is something that Bono understands very well, despite the fact that he is apparently still alive.

When people die, it's always very sad. But imagine how it comforts people to hear a few wise words from Bono. The beauty of Bono is that he's very even-handed in his tributes to the fallen. It doesn't really matter who has died. It could be a rock star, a poet or a politician, but Bono will often take time off from wrestling with the twin gods of irony and conviction to offer a few words of solace.

Now – for the first time in colour – I have collected together a few of Bono's most poignant tributes to people who are no longer alive.

Roy Hammersmith was a 42-year-old postman from Enfield, north London. He died in a car crash in November 2005. He leaves behind a wife, Barbara and two daughters.

'Roy brought rock 'n' roll to the postal delivery service. He wrote the postal blueprints that U2 used when we first started posting letters. Before Roy, people thought that they had to lick the stamp correctly, write the address clearly and include a full postcode – Roy threw that out the window. All you needed was an envelope and attitude. Roy Williams taught me to sing in my own voice.' – Bono, December 2005.

Andrejz Lipkin was a welder from Gdansk, Poland. He died last summer aged 83 after a long battle with cancer. He left behind many Lipkins – from sons and daughters to numerous great-grandchildren.

'Andrejz probably wouldn't have liked a rock 'n' roll guy like me, with my long hair and my earnest and pretentious lyrics. But that doesn't matter. Rock 'n' roll loved Andrejz.

Andrejz's story is your story, it's my story, it's everyone's story. It's a story of struggle, swagger, style and verve. He looked at welding the way that Picasso looked at women. He looked at welding like he looked at life – as a lover, as a fighter, as a cocksure boxer trying to open a tin of tuna with his gloves still on. Andrejz was the contradiction at the heart of a business I love – welding.' – Bono, July 2002.

Amanda Coombes lived in Hightstown, New Jersey. She died in 1998 aged just 17 when she was struck by a puck at an ice hockey game. She had been planning to go to Harvard University, where she was to major in Math.

'It's a terrible shock when one so young dies. It's so easy to be consumed by anger. I speak to God and ask him if he is testing me. He only replies cryptically by telling me that I didn't even know the girl and that it's a bit presumptuous to start mourning as though she were a personal friend. I talk to God often. I have so few peers.

Amanda ripped up the rule book when it came to Math. She looked Math in the eye and was brave enough to add when she could have subtracted, to multiply when she could have divided. She was more than a woman, she was a sister, lover and a mother. Even though she never had kids.' – Bono, January 1999.

Impressive stuff, I think you'll agree. It must be nice to know that when you die, Bono will be there to summarise you for the masses.

February 10th

Today is my birthday. Happy birthday me.

Every birthday I perform the same ritual. When I was young, my mother gave me a book of excuses. And every year, on this special day, I tear out one of the excuses and throw it in a lake.

Birthdays are really no time for celebration. I should know. I once produced my own series of birthday cards:

Birthday Cards

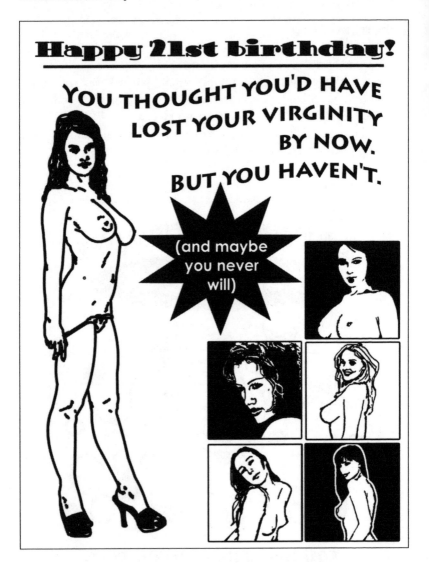

Happy 90th birthday

All your friends are dead.

February 11th

I have a nasty cold. To make things worse, I have been smoking heavily. To make things worse still, I have been kidnapped by Maoist rebels.

I didn't know there were any Maoist rebels in north-east London, but apparently there are... loads of them. My current predicament is proof of the wonderful cultural diversity that is modern London. Years ago you might get kidnapped by the IRA, but anything else would have been some exotic fantasy. Baader–Meinhof and the PLO just never happened round these parts.

Actually, my kidnappers don't seem very exotic. One is called Mark, and the other one is called Howard. They're very polite and keep me supplied with food and drink, and even Sky TV. To be honest, I'm quite enjoying it. I don't yet know what demands they've made and I'm in no particular hurry to find out. I've lied and told them that my family are people of integrity and won't be willing to pay a ransom. The flat I'm being kept in is very cushy, and I've got my eye on the spare bedroom. A lick of paint and it'll come up a treat. I can feel my life is changing. My star is set to shine.

February 12th

Freedom! Cursed, wretched freedom! Mark and Howard let me go. They didn't even have the good grace to drop me home. They just unlocked the front door and told me to go. I ended up getting the tube back home. When I got there I was disappointed to find that there was no large pile of letters ready for me. It seems my absence was not greatly noted.

I checked my e-mail. Just spam. It's very annoying. Most people get spam from strangers trying to enlarge their penis, but I only get spam from my family – I get emails from my mum saying: 'THEMANWHOFELLASLEEP – Would YOU like to have your ironing done, quicker and cheaper than you could imagine!?!'

I deleted the emails and went back to bed. My siesta lasted until morning. At times like this, what else is a man to do but sleep?

February 13th

The children sat on the floor in front of me, giggling and gurgling and shoving Maltesers into their mouths.

'Today, children', I smiled. 'I'm going to read you a story.'

They clapped and cheered and whooped.

'There was once a prince, and he wanted a princess. He wanted a really nice princess, with large eyes and soft skin. He didn't want no skanky princess.

'One evening there was a terrible storm; it thundered and the rain poured down in torrents, flooding the prince's cellar.

'In the middle of the storm somebody knocked at the town gate, and the prince sent someone to open it.

'A girl stood outside. She was soaked from the rain. Water streamed from her hair and her clothes smelt terrible. Yet despite her appearance, she claimed to be a true princess. She certainly had large eyes and a decent figure.

'A special bedroom was prepared for the princess. It was no ordinary room. There were four mattresses on the bed, and dark velvet curtains hung in front of the windows.

'In the morning, the prince asked the princess how she had slept.

"Oh, it was terrible", said the princess. "The bed was so uncomfortable – I seemed to be lying upon some hard thing, and my whole body is black and blue this morning. It is awful."

'The prince knew why the princess had slept so badly, but he did not tell her his secret.

The next morning, the prince again asked the Princess about her night.

"It was even worse!" she cried, shaking. "I feel groggy, and my body is covered in bruises."

'That night, the princess slept terribly. She had feverish dreams, and awoke early, before dawn. She strode over to the window and drew aside the curtain to watch the sun rising. Beside the curtain, she noticed a video camera. It had been there all the time, filming her! She removed the camera from the mounting and rewound the tape. Then she watched the tiny image of herself from last night, sleeping soundly in grainy black and white.

Her eyes widened in horror as the picture began to move; there was suddenly someone else in the room! It was the prince! He approached her sleeping body, and smothered her face with a damp cloth! It must have been chloroform! No wonder she felt so woozy. And then the prince left the video. But the princess wasn't alone for long. A parade of twenty midgets walked up to the bed, and started pounding her with sticks and boxing gloves and table tennis bats! No wonder she was covered in bruises.

'The princess pocketed the video and fled the prince's castle. She hurried straight to the local police station, where she showed the Chief Inspector the tape. It turned out that the prince was luring women to his castle, secretly filming them being beaten, and then posting the videos on a website called "Punished Princesses". He was making a fortune.

'The prince was instantly arrested and charged with assault. The twenty midgets were deported back to Italy, and the princess sued the prince for emotional distress and got £15 million. Then she lived happily ever after. The end.'

'More! We want more stories!' shrieked the ecstatic kids. But one story a day is enough.

February 14th

Seconds stretch into minutes and minutes into hours. Time is not on my side. Time plays for the opposition. My life is a twilight blur of shadows and fog.

I have been keeping a low profile, only leaving the house under cover of darkness. Justin Timberlake has been following me.

I noticed Justin trailing me when I got to Bounds Green station. He was mooching around by the post office, pretending to read *The Standard*. He followed me onto the train, and sat almost opposite me. He was reading a book about the history of hip-hop and muttering about his absence from its pages. However, the reading was clearly a ruse; he was much more interested in spying on me. Every so often we would make eye contact and he'd flinch and look away.

I slipped off the train at Leicester Square but Justin followed me. I made it onto the Northern Line but he was in swift pursuit, and when I got off at Tottenham Court Road I was aware he was still on my trail. I doubled-back on myself and thought I'd lost him, but somehow he ended up in front of me, his mop of dingy hair peeking at me from around a corner. I turned and ran.

Justin and I first met a few years back at the Groucho Club. Things went smoothly at first. He wanted to establish himself in Britain, but was totally ignorant of UK culture. The British tabloids like to pretend that Britain is still the centre of the universe, and so it pleases them no end to see a US celeb hanging out with Martine McCutcheon or Craig David as though these local nobodies were global superstars.

So I gave Justin a few pointers. I would hardly call myself his mentor, but I explained the difference between *Family Affairs* and *Hollyoaks,* and we explored the symbiotic relationship between D-list celebrities and the Sunday papers. Initially, everything went well, but over time Justin got increasingly obsessive. He spent less and less time with the celebrities and more and more time pressing his face up against my window, crying and begging me to let him in. He's lost it. He's a simple farm boy, not best suited to a life in showbiz.

I think that's him now. I must go. If you do not hear from me again, contact the police and tell them everything.

February 15th

In the morning I walked around Alexandra Park, taking photos of leaves and taunting the deer. They are lazy and rarely rise to the bait. Still, it keeps me busy.

I spent the afternoon spaying dogs. It's not a pleasant job. Actually, I lie, it's a job I enjoy immensely. In fact, it's not really a job, I just do it for fun. So, if your dog disappears and then reappears without its balls, it was probably me. Sorry.

February 16th

Ah, the sun mocks me. Then the rain mocks me. Weather is not my friend. The weather has struck me down, like an angry French farmer attacking an innocent British lamb. I have sunburn and pneumonia – a rare combination. I have left my house and am spending a few days recuperating at my good friend Antoine's private clinic.

The nurses have been good to me. They wake me in the middle of the night to pinch and prod me. You wouldn't get that on the NHS. They inject me each morning, with a brown fizzy liquid that looks and smells like Coca Cola. I have a sneaking suspicion it may be Coca Cola.

Dr Gepetto is here. He takes my temperature by sticking a thermometer into my ear. He sticks it quite far in. He says that my brain is cold and that it must be warmed up. He has wrapped my head in heated towels that he stole from a local Indian restaurant.

Despite all the treatment, I feel no better. I fear this is a sickness of the soul, rather than a physical malady. It is related to my Shadow, I am sure. His presence – or even his absence – affects me. I do not like him, although I do not fear him. But whatever I do, and wherever I go, I can sense him following me.

February 17th

Still I cannot sleep. I cannot wake. I feel weak. If I should die, I want this read at my funeral:

Come, my friends. Gather the lilacs and the lawnmowers. Stop the dogs with their lazy eyes and wet, wet noses. Unchain the maidens from their domestic travails. The king is dying, long live the king.

Mine have been a long hundred years. When I was born, man was on the brink of ignorance. Now, as I lie on this bed of cobwebs, man has taken a great, confident stride into the darkness of stupidity. I wish that I could be with man as he slips headlong into foolishness, but that is not my journey. My journey is a simpler one, towards a tawdry and uncelebrated end. I have smoked too many cigarettes, looked into too many mirrors, smiled at too many simpering strangers.

My father used to tell me: 'You are not my son.' I puzzled over the meaning of this statement. Years later I discovered he was not my real father and I was crushed. Sunsets come and go too casually nowadays, there is no permanence and my gums bleed too easily. Ah, I can hear the mermaids singing. I wish they would keep it down.

My adolescence was a struggle to reconcile myself to the darkness within. I knew deep inside myself that I was a man of power, but I felt powerless before maths, art, science, fruit, vegetables. The world confused me. I felt a void within me that I attempted to fill with home furnishings. It was a failure – I have never had taste, and so I erred on the side of conservatism. I shied away from love and intimacy; in my humourless stoicism they seemed like weaknesses. I knew that I would outlive love, I would conquer emotion, I would rest my flag upon the unknown regions of unknowable emotions. I was wrong, of course, but I made some money in the meantime.

Ah, jester, dance for me. You bring a poor smile to this old man's face. My beard grows old and my feet grow cold. Where is my family? Where are the melodies of yesteryear, scratched onto vinyl by the chancellor and his wife? I am a man out of time, out of space. I am out of milk, and the shops are all closed.

The servants will not gather flowers for my grave, for the flowers stopped growing too long ago. Ah, man should never have descended from the trees. Evolution is making a monkey of me, if only my old foe Darwin could see.

Things overheard on the tube

Today's journey:
Northern Line: Archway–Kings Cross, then Hammersmith and City Line to Shepherd's Bush

1. Fair maiden, may I offer you a crisp?
2. He has the flattest head of anyone I know.
3. There's an Arsenal in Argentina, an Everton in Chile and a Liverpool in Uruguay.
4. Are you sure you're meant to stick it up your arse?
5. I'd give it three stars. Out of a hundred.
6. Stop! Enough knickerbocker wisecracks!
7. I never know what they mean by 'smart casual'.
8. Madonna raps like Mr Plow.
9. There were these three guys calling each other niggers, but they were all white.
10. How the hell did that baked bean bloke get to the snooker finals?

February 19th

I am back from the hospital, although I am sure I have not totally recovered. This morning I awoke groggy and confused from a vivid dream. I cannot remember the details of the dream, except that there were fried onions and a young boy searching endlessly for a left shoe.

The shower is broken. Curse all pipes and washers! The world's problems will one day be solved by plumbers. Can you think of any global situation that could not be improved by decent plumbing? I cannot.

The world was once all water and plumbers still sense their atavistic importance in the grand scheme of things.

I splashed my face with brown water from the sink and settled down on the sofa to read the papers. Not newspapers, just any papers that I could find: adverts for credit cards, Indian takeaway menus, bank statements, an old copy of *Which Lawnmower?* magazine. It is important to keep abreast of the issues of the day, to occupy one's mind.

After reading for a while, I washed my clothes and even managed to find some fabric softener. The Greek gods smile upon me; I know that soon they will visit me in person. I have arranged the stolen ashtrays in my bedroom to form the Holy Signs. This morning I coughed up a cigarette butt that I must have swallowed last night – one of the dangers of smoking in bed. But these are trifles, minor complaints. I must steel myself. Soon the Holy Ones will come and will tell me if this year's harvest will be bountiful.

Hush! I hear the rustle of magazines and yoghurt pots... that unmistakable smell of yeast... I think they are coming now!

February 20th

It turned out it wasn't the gods. It was a stray tabby cat. We shared a tin of Whiskas and talked about the old days. I love nostalgia.

February 21st

We writers are strange creatures. We do not communicate with our peers. Rather, we communicate with history, with the vast pantheon of literature. We lift symbols and motifs from long-lost Uruguayan novels. We write pointed ripostes to authors who died 200 years before we were born.

With this is mind, I was much alarmed to see a headline in my local paper: 'Young actor aims to bring Kafka to life!'

This is a worrying trend. Reanimating the corpses of dead writers is a dangerous affair. I have only just recovered from my debacle with the rotting carcass of James Joyce.

Like many men, I mistake metaphor for reality. It's probably hormonal. Women are graced with bodies that constantly change and are thus blessed with an intrinsic understanding of metaphor.

February 22nd

The phone keeps ringing in the night. When I answer it, it is the speaking clock. The clock swears at me, which seems out of character. He's normally so polite.

'At the third stroke, the time sponsored by ******* will be 3.15 a.m., you fucking idiot.'

Mysterious events in the world of biscuits!

This morning I opened my biscuit tin for a snack. All appeared normal. The Ginger Nuts were dry yet crunchy, the Hazelnut Choc Chip Cookies were moist and satisfying, but someone had tampered with the Bourbon Creams. At first glance all appeared normal, but it soon became clear that someone had prised them apart, removed the chocolate filling and sandwiched them back together. The perfect crime.

February 24th

I have a confession: I am part of a conspiracy. I belong to an obscure group of individuals whose aim is dark and nefarious. It is not Opus Dei. It is not the Bilderberg group. Don't try guessing. You won't know it.

This loose band of free thinkers and intellectual mavericks is known as The League Against Narrative.

League members are dedicated to eradicating the scourge of storytelling: the insidious myth of cause and effect, the lie of moral justice, the erroneous conception that there is progress, growth and conclusion. These are the demons that destroy our existence.

The life of the modern man is haunted by this myth of narrative. We believe our lives are like books or films and that we are owed a concrete beginning, middle and end. We expect social introductions to lead somewhere; we wait for conversations to reach a climax... we live in the disappearing shadow of a thrilling denouement. But of course, our lives are wretchedly free from narrative. We go nowhere. For every step forward that we take, we wander down a dead end or a blind alley. We stumble from day to day believing that the passage of time indicates movement. But it is simply another day.

The League Against Narrative is totally committed to the annihilation of these false gods. We will open the eyes of the people: we will show them that we are going nowhere.

Things overheard on the tube

Today's journey:
Piccadilly Line: Wood Green–Hammersmith

1. My lucky number is 28. Hence, today is my lucky day
2. The rooftops of north London have a strange and inexplicable beauty.
3. Should I shave my crabladder?
4. Everyone nowadays is a pervert. What happened to old-fashioned boring sex?
5. That busker will destroy me.
6. No. I wasn't saying you smell bad. It's musk. It's manly.
7. We're gonna get drunk, we're gonna have a fight and then we're gonna get a shag.
8. I think you'll find that everything you've ever done is overrated and rubbish and you're going to die in a piss-filled ditch.
9. Martin Amis is certainly cleverer than Kingsley ever was, but his work is so self-consciously self-conscious. It makes me anxious.
10. History will vindicate me.

February 25th

Such strange dreams are these. I dreamed that I was a short, hairy man living in Bounds Green. I was poor and ate takeaways. I smoked too much and coughed throughout the day. My bedroom was covered in dust and fluff, the detritus of a shallow existence.

I awoke in my cave, glad that it was just a dream. Just a terrible dream...

February 26th

I met the CIA agent at the British Museum Restaurant. I was finishing off my Olde Norse pudding when he arrived. I recognized him from his fedora and carnation, and he spotted me thanks to my faded CIA T-shirt.

The CIA owe me. A few years back I let them use my house as a base when they were staking out some local kids who had been illegally revealing the end-of-season cliff-hangers for some American sitcoms.

We exchanged passwords: he asked 'Are you my contact?' and I replied with 'Yes, I have requested aid from the CIA and you are my agent.' They really need to come up with new passwords.

He sat opposite me and ordered an Egyptoburger. He slid a dossier across the table.

'Everything you need is in there', he smiled. 'And remember, if you get caught you don't know anything.'

'But I know loads of things', I replied. It was the truth.

A flash of annoyance passed over his face. 'Well, can you pretend you don't know anything?'

'I suppose so', I shrugged.

And suddenly he was gone. He hadn't even touched his burger.

I rushed home, the dossier hidden in my sports bag. I had requested that the CIA look into my Shadow and inform me if he was real, and if so, if his intentions were dishonourable.

I hurriedly opened the dossier and my face dropped. There had been some mistake. The dossier comprised a short story of total irrelevance. For the purposes of accuracy, I am repeating the story here:

Neil sat in the car. It was dark and his glasses were misty. He took them off and wiped them on his sleeve. Outside, the drizzle was falling more lightly. It looked like the night would be clear, even if it remained unbearably cold. He opened the glove compartment. There was a Lion Bar and a can of Coke. He took a bite of the Lion Bar and then rewrapped it and closed the glove compartment.

The car park was nearly empty. At the other end there was a white transit van. It looked filthy and someone had written 'Clean Me' in dust on the bonnet. There was also a blue Renault Megane parked alongside him. Every 5 minutes its alarm went off, which annoyed him – it was like a fitful sleeper who rises in the middle of the night, angry and confused, waking up the rest of the house.

He knew that the car park would soon fill up. He'd been here before. He knew what would happen.

He always arrived at the car park early to get a good spot. For him, that was half the fun; the build-up, the anticipation, the rituals before the event. He enjoyed the knowledge that he was sitting alone in a north London car park as dusk approached, while his friends were in pubs, talking about football, or lying in bed with their girlfriends, talking about holiday plans and mortgages. They all assumed he would be at home, watching television. But he was here in the car park, waiting for it all to happen. He felt a thrill in his stomach.

He twirled the knob of the radio. All dance music and ragga from local pirate stations. Then he hit the news. They were talking about the death of some former Tory MP. What did any of it have to do with him? He spun the knob and landed on the inane banter of a radio phone-in. An angry man was saying that no one understood the sacrifices that America was making to ensure global safety. The radio host was half-heartedly playing Devil's Advocate. 'My God', thought Neil, 'these people are idiots'.

Another car arrived at the car park and parked almost opposite from him. It was a Nissan Micra – green or grey, he couldn't tell. The headlights dazzled him and then died. He blinked and waited for the glow behind his eyes to fade. He listened to the radio and waited. But nothing happened. No one emerged from the Micra and both cars faced each other in silence.

This was Neil's fourth time. The first time had been in a car park in Brixton; he had enjoyed the evening, but it had taken him nearly 2 hours to drive home afterwards. So he searched the internet for a location closer to him; somewhere in north London. He had stumbled upon the car park, just 5 minutes away from his flat. He liked the incongruity of it; it was a drab, dull location that he had passed a thousand times, and it had never occurred to him that it was anything other than an ordinary car park. He smiled. He knew that he had spent so much of his life with his eyes closed to such things. It was only in recent months that something had stirred within him, and he had opened his eyes and seen the world anew. He felt as though he had been handed a key that gave him access to a whole new world, a world that lay alongside the normal world of men but was always hidden to those who could not see it.

Now the car park was filling up. A red Ford Cortina parked next to him. He wondered if it was Sandra's car. He hadn't been to last month's event, but he had seen her twice in November. He liked her. He liked the fact that she talked to him as though he were an equal; without real affection but without contempt or false friendship. He was tempted to wind down the window and take a closer look to make sure it was her, but he knew it would be better to sit tight and wait.

He looked down at the pile of papers that lay on the passenger seat. He had printed them all up from information on a website. If it was Sandra in the Cortina, he would give her the papers. He secretly hoped she would be impressed. He fumbled above his head and switched on the light. He flicked through the papers and then re-read the sheet on the top of the pile. The information was broken down into a series of Frequently Asked Questions:

What is Godding?
The term 'Godding' refers to either having or observing a religious experience in a public or semi-public place, usually outdoors. Sometimes voyeurs join in with the religious experience, but usually they just watch from a nearby location.

How did Godding start?
Godding has been getting a lot of attention lately, but people have been

doing it for many years. Recently, with the advent of the internet, mobile phones and messaging, it is easier for Godders to find one another and arrange meetings.

Why is Godding so popular?

It's fun and it's forbidden. People love to watch and be watched having religious experiences. There's also an element of challenge and adventure in finding a good Godding spot and seeking out an exciting encounter.

What kind of people go Godding?

Couples into religion are usually in their 30s to 50s, though some may be older or younger. Observers are usually single men, often disenchanted priests or rabbis. Most Godders are middle class, and most lead quite average lives apart from their unusual 'hobby'.

Where are the best places for Godding?

Godders mostly choose open-air, somewhat out of the way places, often in or near country parks. Car parks are also quite common congregating spots, and occasionally cinema halls. The best locations are hidden away from the public, but still easily accessible.

I don't have a car. Can I still go Godding?

Many Godding activities revolve around cars, as couples do like to discuss religion in cars and often go to locations that are somewhat remote. However, it's quite possible there is Godding activity in your area that is accessible by public transport. Check Godding sites and Godding groups for info.

Why has religion been driven underground? Why can't I just talk about religion in public?

You are free to discuss religion where and when you want, but it comes with a certain risk. Belief and faith are no longer considered polite subjects for conversation in most communities. Godding is popular because it allows the anonymous observance and discussion of religious experiences without fear of judgement. Most Godders would never discuss religion with friends or family, but crave some secret spiritual fulfilment.

Neil put the papers down and looked outside. It was raining harder now, and he switched on the windscreen wipers. The car park was nearly full. There were about 20 cars. Some had their headlights on and some had their engines running, but most were silent and static. The drivers sat in darkness, waiting for it all to kick off. He could feel the tension and excitement rising within.

He looked over at the Cortina. It was definitely Sandra, but Philip wasn't with her. She was alone in the car. Good. Maybe later he would continue his discussion of the Holy Trinity with her. The guys at work would laugh at him if they could see him now. But they weren't here now. He was. And he felt alive.'

I didn't understand the story. It had nothing to do with the Shadow. And yet, perhaps that was the point. Whatever it meant, it pointed towards a man with hidden hopes and dreams, trying to understand himself and the world around him.

Perhaps it's not a dead end, just a different route to my destination.

February 28th

I have awoken from my coma!

According to the doctors, I was in my coma for 2 days. Apparently, I choked on a peach stone and lost consciousness. I didn't know you weren't supposed to eat the stone. What a terrible waste.

This is how I awoke:

Me: 'Ugh... how long have I been asleep? What year is it?'

Dr Gepetto (yes, he's back): 'You've been in a coma for 2 days.'

Me: 'Ohmigod! It's 2023! I've been asleep for 20 years! My youth! Gone... my looks... all gone!'

Dr Gepetto: 'No. Listen to me. It's not like that. You were only in a coma for 2 days'.

Me: '... my youth... gone... '.

Anyway, it turns out that I didn't miss anything while in the coma. It was a very quiet few days.

February 29th
(is it a leap year? Who can tell?)

There is nothing to do, so I switch on the computer.

I have been surfing the web. I like to check up on my old friend, BBC football pundit Mark Lawrensen. Since he shaved off his moustache he's grown increasingly erratic. Every week he makes predictions about the results of the weekend's Premiership games. He is normally wrong, but at least makes some sense. However, his latest predictions make terrifying reading.

Lawro's Premiership Predictions

Charlton v. Manchester City (kick-off 14.00)
Aha! You will never catch me! I shall kill again! I disappear into shadows, like Thierry Henry finding space in a stretched Newcastle defence. Let the people know me! Let the people fear me! I shall come to you in visions, in nightmares, in dreams of untold erotic pleasure... you cannot escape me. I shall possess you. For you are merely mortal and I am the EVERLASTING, the timeless. I am the stain upon your soul that blights your every action!

Verdict: Charlton to win 1–0.

Wigan v. Newcastle (kick-off 14.00)
Alan Shearer, Alan Shearer, Alan Shearer... I am the recurring muscle injury that will force you to quit the game. We shall sit next to each other in television studios and I shall smile my sweetest smile, and you shall never know that it was I who brought your Premiership career to a premature end! How fate mocks you, you square-headed lunk! In Biblical times they called me Hamen, but you shall know me simply as your nemesis! Haha!

Verdict: Newcastle to win 2–0.

Liverpool v. Chelsea (kick-off 16.05)
Oh Mr Abramovich, will your millions ever really buy you happiness? Do you think you can ever forget that lonely little boy, crippled by

sadness... I think not. I am the worm of doubt that lives in your spirit, eating you away from the inside. I have crushed greater men than you. Alexander the Great, Napoleon, Churchill, all brought to heel, their pride snuffed by the inevitability of my victory. Do you really think your team of international superstars can shield you from my glare? You are mine. I am omnipotent. Fear me!

Verdict: Liverpool to win 1–0.

Manchester United v. Middlesbrough (kick-off 15.00)

Who was the serpent that tempted Eve? Who caused Adam to be gracelessly ejected from the Garden of Eden, like Sunderland cast out of the Premiership with the lowest ever points total? It was I, you idiots! My powers grow stronger with every passing fixture. Here, the Master meets the Apprentice as Ferguson faces McClaren, but all men are as insects to me – as toys to an angry child.

Remember: the priest fears me, but only the whore knows my name!
Verdict: Manchester United to win 3–1.

Portsmouth v. Fulham (kick-off 15.00)

Ah, the Pompey sea air. It brings back fond memories of slave ships dashed against jagged rocks, of the Titanic sinking into the inky depths, the rank odour of mankind's precious hubris. Oh, hatchet-faced Harry Redknapp, this was once your team. Do you think the world will ever take you seriously? Do you think your victories will ever really see you accepted into polite society? No. The public see a conman, a rogue, a spiv... I have poisoned their minds. That's right, Harry. Have another drink. Pour it all away.

Verdict: a 1–1 draw.

Sunderland v. West Brom (kick-off 15.00)

Men talk of the banality of evil, but what evil could be more banal than this fixture? As the passion play of football unfolds, the spirits of the spectators will ebb... they will grow restless, they will tire. They will start to doubt. They will think about unhappy sexual acts in suburban hotels, of childhood ambitions cruelly unfulfilled, of relationships thwarted by jealousy and anger. Sometimes man is so bereft of hope that I need not

even act to cause misery... so it is with this fixture. Truly mankind is
doomed. Doomed!

Verdict: Sunderland to win 1–0.

Everton v. Blackburn (kick-off 15.00)

You lie asleep in your single bed. A newt drops from the ceiling onto
your unconscious body; burrows under your skin, tearing away muscle
and sinew with its needle teeth! You awake wracked with pain,
a cold sweat covering your back like a shroud! Who do you think singled
out Wayne Rooney for glory? Who do you think sold him to Man U?
Do you think it was God? Do you think a kindly old man with
a white beard chose him for greatness? Hahahaha... oh, you poor
deluded fools. The twinkle in his eye comes not from the heavens...
indeed, no!

Verdict: Blackburn to win 1–0.

West Ham v. Tottenham Hotspur (kick-off 15.00)

The Israelites fled from me in Egypt, their robes filled with hope and
parcels of unleavened bread, but now the hope has been extinguished.
All is black!

I am the flashing blade in the inner-city alleyway; I am the gun pressed
against your temples at dawn; I am the bacteria that fills your lungs with
pus. Dance! Dance your merry little dance of glee, as you foolishly
dream that you have conquered evil! Dance all you like, for you are my
puppets and I am jerking your strings. The **danse macabre** only brings
you closer to my fiery bosom!

Verdict: a goalless draw.

Birmingham v. Arsenal (kick-off 15.00)

The day of reckoning is nigh! The clouds gather around the cities,
around the town, around the blackened souls of men. Grown men in
football shirts, standing like apes around a bonfire, pouring alcohol
down their throats, baying for blood, for pain, for change!
Fists are thrown into the air. Glass shatters, vomit pours forth like wine!
The noon of my conquest is upon us! The screams will sound
like satanic melodies, like a symphony of evil.

And poor Steve Bruce... that face of yours. It was only a joke – I didn't expect you to keep it.

Verdict: Arsenal to win 3–0.

Aston Villa v. Bolton (kick-off 15.00)

What's that you say, Mr Ellis? Your powers are greater than mine? Hardly, you are but a footservant of evil: I am chaos incarnate!

Jack the Ripper was a cheery sort. I twisted that man's brain like Jay-Jay Okocha twisting a bewildered Villa defender. Do you know, the brainless savage thought he was performing the Lord's work? What simpletons men are. A vision here, a prophecy there and they believe that good is evil, that murder is rebirth. But there is no rebirth, there is no salvation, there is just 90 minutes of torment and mockery, followed by a week of silence and recrimination.

And recrimination!!

Verdict: Villa to win 2–1.

I am very worried about poor Mark. I think he's going through a really rough patch.

March 1st

This journal is not my sole literary effort. I have written many books, some of which were best-sellers in eastern Europe many decades ago.

For the last five years I have been writing my magnum opus. It is almost finished. It has been testing. My idea of starting the story with the death of the central character was innovative, but left me with certain plot issues that were difficult to resolve. Nonetheless, I am nothing if not tenacious and the book is now complete.

With hindsight, poisoning my literary agent was a rash move, but there is no point crying over spilt milk or dead agents. She died painlessly enough and the police arrested her husband, so it all turned out well in the end. All loose ends were tied up swiftly, in life, if not in art. Anyway, what are agents if not parasites? Would I be judged for swatting a mosquito? Of course not.

I am sending copies of my manuscript to all the major publishers. The moon-faced woman from Virago is sure to like the book – there are plenty of strong female characters and I lifted huge chunks of the middle section from an old Angela Carter book I found in a local library. I am sure that everyone will love the thrilling denouement where the SAS soldier is revealed to be Sputnik, the Russian spy – and Chantal's long-lost father. It is a story that has something for everyone: sex, violence, romance, ennui, obtuse plot developments and a scene where a man makes 10 cups of coffee. I can't see it failing. But I never see failure until it is upon me.

March 2nd

My hackles have been raised. Something fishy is going on in the Afghan grocery around the corner. I am not yet 100% sure, but I believe they are selling multipack cans of Coke as single items, contrary to the explicit instructions on the cans.

This could go right to the very top. Further news as it breaks.

March 4th

Journalists often ask me, 'What is Robbie Williams really like?' And I tell them the truth: he's taller than me and has dark hair. Of course, people get very annoyed by that answer. They want gossip; they want dirt. They want to know if he is gay or bi or celibate. But alas, I have no dirt to dish on Robbie. He is a simple, humble man and a very good friend of mine. He is a true celebrity among cardboard pygmies.

I first met Robbie in 1987. He was appearing as the Artful Dodger in a school play in his hometown of Stoke. By chance I was the hotdog vendor at the school auditorium and we chatted as he sucked a frankfurter. I took him under my wing. He was a year older than me, but I was very mature for my age and had already mastered four European languages and set up my own car-hire business.

Robbie was a precocious young pup, all wide-eyed glee and naked ambition. I helped him out with his maths homework and in return he agreed to let me become his personal manager. I enjoyed dipping my toes in gaudy showbiz waters; I took to calling myself 'Sergeant Rocco' and went everywhere in a beret. Robbie and I would meet in my garden shed at weekends, and he would practice his magic tricks and dancing as I calculated how much we would be paid when he became an international megastar.

Sadly, even at that young age, Robbie was prone to mood swings and depression. Mondays, Wednesdays and Fridays he would throw back a cocktail of cocaine and ecstasy, while on Tuesdays, Thursdays and Saturdays he would binge on Prozac and Seroxat. On Sundays we would go fishing.

Even then, I could see that Robbie was one part Jerry Lewis and one part Ian Curtis – a potentially explosive mix. In an attempt to keep him on the straight and narrow, I put him on a strict diet of whey and wheatgrass. But Robbie was a typical teenager and he resented the level of control that I exerted over him. He wanted to go ice-skating and bowling, but I demanded that he practice his mid-song patter and learn to pretend to stumble when he was dancing.

Of course, it is now public knowledge that Robbie rebelled against my control and ran off to join the circus, where he was employed as a lion. Despite our falling out, Robbie and I were recently reunited when we were both interviewed on Parkinson. We chatted and reminisced backstage. Nowadays, we see each other often. We are both naturally wary of friendship, so we take every day as a bonus. I fly over to LA to visit him in his luxury mansion, and he pops round to my house to share a pot of tea and a sponge finger.

Robbie is much more famous than I ever imagined possible, but he is still the irresistible, depressive, self-loathing cheeky scamp that I knew when I was young.

I know that some people don't like Robbie. They are jealous of his fame. But I have never blamed Robbie for pursuing fame with such naked ambition. All celebrities are ultimately victims, for fame eats them whole and spits out their empty husks.

Fame is an addiction, and all addictions are crippling: we are all familiar with the stories of drug addicts who steal from loved ones to fund their habits – poor wretches locked in a desperate spiral to fund their next high – and so it is with fame. When fame begins to fade, celebrities grow increasingly frantic and depraved. No private moment is

so precious that it cannot be sold to a Sunday tabloid for the adrenaline rush of a photo on a front page.

But Robbie is strong, and he will beat this addiction. Just like he beat Gary Barlow.

March 6th

Einstein said that God does not play dice with the universe. Of course he doesn't. He plays poker. He plays canasta. He plays blackjack. He goes all-in and hides cards up his sleeve.

At any rate, Einstein is dead and God is still around, despite Nietzsche's best intentions.

Imagine God is in his heaven. He is not a bearded old man in robes. He is a vaguely humanoid blur, like a stick figure drawn in charcoal and then smudged around the edges.

God has created the world and mankind, but now he doesn't know what to do with them. In short, he is bored.

To relieve the tedium of watching mankind to-ing and fro-ing down on Earth, God decides to raise the stakes. He doesn't actually want to destroy the world because (a) he made an informal agreement with Noah after the flood and (b) he is actually quite fond of mankind.

What he does to pass the time is play a game. The kind of game we all play when we're bored; we walk home without stepping on the cracks of the pavement, or back one raindrop to beat another in a race down a window pane.

Every day when God wakes up and gets out of his celestial bed, he plays a game. Since he is not a natural risk-taker, he makes little bets with himself that he is pretty darn sure he will win.

Here is an example of a week of God's bets. They are jotted down in a small Rymans notepad by his bedside.

- *Monday [which he maintains is the first day of the week]: if no one on Earth says the word 'cattle', I will destroy the world.*
- *Tuesday: if no one in Europe claps their hands today, I shall sink Europe into the sea.*

- *Wednesday: if anyone in America uses the phrase 'Serbo-Croat Lilliput Crayfish' I will give that individual apocalyptic powers.*
- *Thursday: if under 1000 Twix bars are sold in England, I will destroy England.*
- *Friday: if no one in Africa gets drunk today, I will destroy Africa and alcohol.*
- *Saturday: if Middlesbrough beats Charlton by more than 25 goals, I will disappear and leave mankind to its own devices.*
- *Sunday [the last day of the week]: if anyone in London reads every word printed in every single page of the Sunday papers (including adverts) I will abolish language.*

As you see, they are all bets that are unlikely to disrupt the status quo of the world, as they have very little chance of happening. But they keep God occupied. Some scholars have said that as time passes God will get increasingly bored and start playing riskier games, and so terrible events are far more likely to happen. This is why, as you pass your time on Earth, it is always worth keeping your fingers crossed.

March 7th

For the purposes of this journal entry, I will be writing in the third person. It's a literary device. I shall call myself Jasper. As I said at the beginning of the journal, I am no ordinary writer.

Trawling through the phone boxes of central London, Jasper picked up card after card, his hands quivering, his breath shallow. He couldn't help it – it was sordid and depraved, but he could not resist the compulsion to pocket the cards.

He has already rehearsed his speech in case he is spotted by a policeman; he will adopt a tone of moral outrage and explain that he was removing the cards because they were filth and were lowering the tone of the plush Bloomsbury location. He worried that the police would not believe him.

One particular card caught his eye.

He could feel his T-shirt cling wet to his back. He looked around to double-check that he wasn't being watched. He slowly bent over as though he had dropped something, then he daintily plucked the Blu-tacked card from the glass.

This card was different. He had never seen anything like it. Mostly, the cards showed young black footballers from the first or second divisions, anonymous youngsters with bulging thighs and faces full of false bravado. The cards advertised their prowess at headers and boasted how they were deadly finishers in the box and could run for miles. The truth was seldom so rewarding. Jasper had met these young men in bedsits and rented rooms, and often they were nothing like the photos – lanky mulattos or short Mexicans with no ball control and studs missing from their Puma boots.

However, he recognized this player. He looked haggard and his hair – once so celebrated in adverts and talkshows – was thinning. He was kitted out in the lurid colours of a first-division side. But it was clear; it was Paul Gascoigne. It was Gazza himself. Jasper felt his chest grow tight. He could hardly breathe. His hands shook uncontrollably as he dialled the number…

March 8th

I cannot sleep. It is this heat, this unbearable, unseasonal heat. I lie awake and sweat the sheets off the mattress. During the day it is even hotter. I regret erecting a giant magnifying glass outside my bedroom – the carpet is constantly on the verge of catching alight.

The magnifying glass was another majestic failure. I have a vast, sweeping vision, but it is flawed. Ideological and emotional cataracts blur my vision. I start... I start, but I cannot finish... I cannot finish this thing that I have started.

March 10th

Today I went to the lake. It was a balmy day and the ducks hovered over the reeds, playing canasta and smoking.

I played a game with the local kids. They dressed in their pyjamas, and I threw heavy rubber bricks into the water. They had to swim to the bottom and retrieve the bricks, just as I did in the swimming lessons of my youth.

It was a disappointing afternoon. Not one of the kids resurfaced. After a while I shuffled off home.

Things overheard on the tube

Today's journey:
Piccadilly Line: Bounds Green–Holborn, then Central Line to Queensway

1. What happened with Ron Atkinson? I was on holiday and missed it all.
2. Anyway, on his deathbed he suggests that I buy the lawnmower off him. I said no.
3. I had a keyboard that played a Billy Joel song when you switched it on.
4. She was at the party when an ant fell out of her nose. No one knows where it came from.

5. There's a very simple rule: if someone earns more than me, they aren't allowed to go on strike.
6. Her face looks like a typing error.
7. All the good things in my life are bad.
8. Are you ready for a new kind of salad? A salad made entirely of beef.
9. I would never punish my kids by hitting them. I just make them feel guilty and all twisted up inside.
10. *Diagnosis Murder?* Diagnosis fucking rubbish, more like.

March 11th

Today was just another day in a long series of nameless, shapeless days.

Nothing much happened. Days like this are not normally included in diaries or journals, but I feel it is important to not to forget these endless, grey days when more nothing follows each non-event.

Last night I sat in the pub, anxiously scratching the label off a bottle of Grolsch. In the background Andy Gray and Martin Tyler discussed Arsenal's defensive frailties.

A fat middle-aged man sat down at my table. His face was a map of broken capillaries. He smiled at me and slammed a bottle down onto a beermat. Inside the bottle, there appeared to be a tiny man. I squinted. There was definitely a man in the bottle.

'Alright mate', said the man.

I nodded and murmured a hello.

'I know what you're thinking. People always ask me, how did you get the man into the bottle? Well... I shouldn't really tell, but... OK... we don't put the man into the bottle! He's *born* there. It's a bit like test-tube babies, innit? We put the sperm and the egg in the bottle, and wait for nature to take its course. Obviously we can't just keep the bottle on the shelf. It has to be the right temperature, or the eggs don't work. It's an art. I consider myself a craftsman, really. Yeah, I know it's only a hobby, but it's still art.'

He coughed up a solid cube of phlegm.

'Anyway, once the kid is born, we just drop food and water into the bottle. It's simple, really, when you think of it. No great mystery. We hose the bottle down every so often – well, I don't really ever do that myself, I leave that for the missus. Got to keep the bottle clean, specially when they're young. Infections. Oh yes... I've lost a few to infections.

'So the food goes in and - I know what you're thinking! What happens to the waste? The shit and all that. Well, we just Hoover it up. In the old days, with stand-up Hoovers, it was a bloody pain. But now it's all simple: bung the end of the vacuum into the bottle and suck it all up. Bish bosh.

'People say it's inhumane, but the Chinese have been doing it for centuries. Nah. It's good – you need a hobby nowadays or you'll go mad. 'Anyway, mate. Nice to see you. Yeah, give my love to Cheryl... take care, mate. Must do it again sometime.'

With that, he walked off. I hadn't said a word. I have no idea who he was.

In the meantime, the game had begun. Thierry Henry scored for Arsenal and the pub erupted into raucous cheers.

March 12th

People ask me why I have a nervous disposition, why I am anxious all the time. Generally, I refer them to Dr Gepetto. It's all in his file.

Personally, I have my own theories as to the defects (if that is what they are) in my character. I shall tell you all about the cosmic oven.

Everyone is familiar with the feeling of leaving the house for work and suddenly fearing they have left the oven on at home. They stop dead. They pause. Should they turn back? They know that the oven is probably not really on – it's just their mind playing tricks on them. They smile and dismiss such foolish concerns. They resolve to continue to work, but something under their skin continues to nag away, biting and chafing at their calm.

Well, imagine that in the time before you were born, when you were not even a speck of nothingness in your grandfathers' eye, something similar happened. Imagine that before you even came into existence, the oven was left on. Not a specific oven in a cottage in Wales or a Shtetl in Belarus but a cosmic, existential oven, the size of the Earth. Imagine that, all your life, you are unsure whether you should progress with earthly concerns or rush back into nothingness to turn off the oven. That is the Cosmic Oven Syndrome. I suffer greatly from this malaise. At any point in life, I am aware of a gnawing sensation at the back of my mind, warning me of impending disaster. Of flames licking at curtains, or at the very least, of burnt cakes.

That is one reason why I am anxious. The other reasons are more mundane, but no less valid.

Today I found an old folder of poetry from when I was a teenager. It is a blue cardboard folder with stickers on the front. The poetry was hand-written and I almost didn't recognize my own writing. It was mostly clumsy angst, which was little surprise; but I did find something that I liked. The odd thing is that I have no recollection of writing it, and it doesn't appear to be in my handwriting. And yet it must be mine. No-one else has ever seen the poems or had access to the folder.

Here is the poem. It may not even be a poem; perhaps it is just prose with interesting line breaks.

The doctor
told me
two things.
Stop drinking.
Avoid mirrors.

As I read it, I smiled inwardly. I hid all the mirrors in my house some time ago. No good comes of them.

March 13th

Another day, another newsagent. I bought *The Sun* and a bottle of Mars milk. It tasted like shit and sugar. I must make a mental note to stick to Panda Cola – the only cola with actual bits of panda in it.

I flicked straight to 'Dear Deidre', *The Sun's* agony aunt. I always relish the prospect of losing myself in other peoples' banal domestic problems. But Deidre wasn't there: she had been replaced by a another advisor – a proper doctor.

DEAR DRE...

Dr Dre, AKA Andre Maurice Young, is Professor of Fertility Research at London University's Imperial College School of Medicine, and is a Consultant Obstetrician and Gynaecologist at Hammersmith Hospital in London. He is one of the world's greatest infertility experts, and in 1978 was part of the team that created the first 'test tube baby', Louise 'Bobby' Brown.

As a producer, he was also responsible for moving hip hop away from the earnest politics of Public Enemy and creating a new 'gangsta' style. He has worked with artists as diverse as Gwen Stefani, Snoop Dogg and Mary J. Blige.

IS THIS MAN TROUBLE OR WHAT?

A FRIEND has been told he has prostate trouble. Well, he's not really a friend. He's just a bloke I sometimes see in the pub.

I don't even like him.

I know nothing about the prostate gland and how it might cause symptoms. What should I look for as I grow older?

Dre replies...

MANY people feel uncomfortable talking about the prostate, since the gland plays a role in both sex and urination. You would be surprised though. Some of the biggest players in the hip-hop world suffer from prostate problems.

Prostate enlargement is as common a part of ageing as grey hair. As life expectancy rises, enlarged prostate glands get more common – a few years ago a brotha in Compton wouldn't last until he was 30. Now, with Crips and Bloods putting down their guns, they may live much longer and be plagued by prostate problems.

The prostate is a walnut-size gland that forms part of a man's reproductive system. It lies directly under the bladder and encircles the urethra – the tube leading to the outside – and is made of two lobes enclosed in an outer shell. It looks like some nasty shit, yo.

It's common for the prostate to become enlarged as you get old. Doctors call the condition benign prostatic hypertrophy or BPH. They can call it what the hell they like. There are lots of docs, but there is only one Dr Dre. Anyway, you be getting your social security checks before you get a word from Mr Gland.

As the prostate enlarges, the layer of tissue surrounding it stops it from expanding, causing the gland to squeeze the urethra like a clamp on a garden hose at a LA barbecue. Sun blazin' down... homies chillin' on the left. Honeys relaxin' by the pool.

But I digress. The size of the prostate don't always determine how severe the obstruction or the symptoms will be. Some men with greatly enlarged glands have little obstruction and few symptoms while others, whose glands are less enlarged, have more blockages and greater problems.

It's like they said on Different Strokes: nappy rash for some – it ain't nappy rash for all.

STRAIGHT OUTTA LUCK?

I'VE been seeing a girl for a year. When I say 'seeing her', I mean that she is my girlfriend... obviously I can see her. That's not the problem. I'm not blind.

When I try to get near her sexually, she says she isn't really interested and can 'take it or leave sex'.

She says she has been badly hurt by men in the past and doesn't know what kind of man she really wants. But the next minute she says she wants me and no one else. I know women are fickle, but this is something else!

Sex is an issue. I want sex. I need sex. I know it's not everything, but she hardly ever talks about it and now I think she doesn't fancy me that way. How can we make it together? I don't want to marry her or anything, I just want to go out with her for a few years, have regular sex and then drift apart like normal couples.

Dre replies...

YOUR woman has been hurt and is scared of showing she cares for you. She's certainly sending you mixed messages. It's like when big rappers start talking about how they still got love for the streets, when they're holed up in a Bel Air mansion with their coke. Don't make no sense to me.

You say sex isn't everything. Too damn right. Before I met my Michel'le I was down with every kind of ho, but it never meant anything to me.

It doesn't matter if you're in Memphis or Manhattan, communication is the key.

I know it's hard to broach the subject, but be brave and ask her outright if she's interested in you in that way. If she refuses to discuss it, you might have your answer there. Maybe you do. Maybe you don't. Life is a game like that.

That doesn't mean you're not an attractive person, just that it's not right between you two. And setting each other free will allow you to find the person who is right. It's like I used to say, if you're not happy on Death Row Records, you're free to leave – just don't forget who made you a star.

Why not talk it over with one of my semi-qualified counsellors and sex therapists on 0904344 001 03213056?

COULD YOU PICK UP THE KIDS?

STEVE, could you pick up the kids from playgroup tonight? It looks like I'll be working late again – it's that bloody Wharfdale account, it's taking forever. Jim came in this morning and said they're unhappy with the edit that we've done, so it's going to be all hands to the pump for the next week. Darren is coming down from Cambridge to help out.

There are a couple of the lasagnes in the freezer. Toby prefers the Healthy Choice ones. I should be back at about 10 p.m., but don't wait up.

By the way, I picked up a tiramisu from M&S for Sunday. Looks scrummy.

See you later, xxxxxxxx Diane

Dre replies...

I guess this email wasn't meant for me, since I'm not called Steve and I don't know anyone called Diane. And I sure as hell am not eating tiramisu on Sunday – it's the day before the Grammies and you best believe I ain't got no love for the gut.

My advice is not for Diane, it is for Steve. Keep an eye on your woman. Just who is Darren? And what is he to Diane? Be careful.

I've still got the bass pumping when I hit your block. And I'm out of here.

I am unsure about Dr Dre. I've always admired his musical output, but I still miss Deidre.

March 15th

Once again it rained. I saw a bird's nest floating down a flooded motorway.

At about 2 p.m. this afternoon, I was searching for my fishing rod. I was searching in the cupboard under the stairs when I stumbled upon a box of mildew-stained books. At the bottom of the pile was a dog-eared copy of my first novel, *The Story of My Life*, which I wrote in my early twenties. It wasn't a success, although it does enjoy a cult reputation. It's a bit of a depressing read. The central character is in a wheelchair, at the bottom of an ocean. Not very much happens in it.

The book sold exactly 910 copies. Of the 910 people who read the book, 900 committed suicide, and the other 10 went on to become professional footballers. I wash my hands of all of them. All I did was write a book, not tell them to jump off bridges or instruct them to try nutmegging the goalkeeper instead of blasting the ball into the roof of the net.

By the time I had found my fishing rod, the rain was so savage that I could not leave the house. I tried dangling my rod out of the bedroom window, but nothing was biting. I hate fishing.

March 17th

If I were a dog, I would spend all day chasing my tail. But I am not a dog.

March 18th

In recent weeks I have been working on a project to create comic strips of the great poets of our time. If all goes well, this will culminate in a comic in which T. S. Eliot and W. B. Yeats fight each other on a satellite orbiting earth, in a battle that will determine the future of mankind.

In the meantime, here's a comic strip about Philip Larkin.

March 20th

Ah, the things I could tell you about Gwyneth Paltrow. She is the daughter of Hollywood royalty Blythe Danner and Bruce Paltrow. She's married to that bald bloke in that boyband. Her dad Bruce died a while ago. I felt sorry for her. I feel sorry for all rich orphans. All the money in the world can't buy back a dead dad.

So, if you bump into Gwyneth and she looks angry and let down, you know why. Go easy on her.

March 21st

As a child, my mother used to nail me to a cross. It seemed perfectly normal to me and it wasn't until I turned 11 and started secondary school that I realised that junior crucifixion was not a common practice. It was something of a shock when I realised I was the only boy in my class with stigmata (although I didn't really mind, as it got me off games and swimming). I tried my best to make light of my wounds; my party trick was fitting a two-pence piece in the hole in my hand. It didn't make me hugely popular, but it kept me entertained.

School is never easy for anyone, and I can't say being crucified on a regular basis helped me feel any more normal.

I used to ask my mum: 'Why are you nailing me to a cross?'

She would frown and scowl, as though it was rude to ask such an impudent question. She would sigh and tell me, 'If I didn't do it, someone else would. Thank your lucky stars that it is your mother – who loves you – and not some complete stranger who is crucifying you.'

I naively assumed that when I grew up I would understand her logic.

March 23rd

Like so many men, I am a keen football fan.

Last weekend Tottenham Hotspur football club invited me to their match against Birmingham City to give the team a motivational pep-talk before the game. Their recent results have been poor, and as a long-suffering supporter, I felt it was my duty to try to help the club. Last year they invited Paul McKenna to hypnotise the squad, but the players overpowered him and buried him by the halfway line. Next time a game is on TV see if you can see the mound.

I walked into the dressing room and looked around, totally underawed by my surroundings. The players were sitting in their kit, silently gazing at their feet, preparing. The manager introduced me to the players, shook my hand and then left the room. I took a deep breath and began my speech.

'You are all bad people. All of you. Week after week you disappoint me. At the beginning of every season I have such high hopes, and inevitably you let me down. It's not like it's happened once. It's *every single season*. Every time there's a chance for us to win an easy game and climb the table, you blow it. You're overpaid and lazy. If your parents could see you now they would be unbearably ashamed. You are awful, rotten people. Yes, even you Jermaine. You people. You slumber in the safety of mid-table, always promising more and never delivering the goods. I know what you players are like – you play well for a couple of games and then demand a new contract in the hope that Chelsea or Arsenal will buy you. You are bad, *bad* people. I want you to go home tonight and apologise to your families. Apologise to the fans. Apologise to people in the street. Every day you should wake up feeling ashamed, because you are bad players and *bad* human beings. Now go out there and win a football game. It's not too much to ask.'

Then I walked out of the dressing room. The manager gave me a curious look and strode into the dressing room in a hurry. I don't suppose they will invite me back next year. I don't care. I said everything I needed to say. I was speaking not just for myself. I was speaking for every football fan I have ever met.

March 25th

I was in Wood Green, at the opticians. I sat in the waiting area, flicking through yesterday's *Daily Mirror* as a family of Armenians argued beside me. A buzz of nerves growled at the base of my skull.

The optician ushered me through to her special, private room. The lights were dimmed.

I sat in the magical chair and squinted into the distance. The optician placed plastic slides in front of my eyes.

'Is it clearer now… or now?' she asked in soothing tones.

'Now.'

She swivelled and flicked a switch. The display in front of me changed.

'Is it clearer on the red? Or on the green?'

'The red?'

'And now?'

'Still the red', I said.

'Good. Do you have any family history of eye problems?'

'No. Although a cousin of mine is diabetic. And I know diabetes can affect the eyes.'

'That's true, but it's not a major problem in the short term. And how is your general health?'

'Not bad. I smoke too much, but otherwise it's OK', I sighed.

'And do you feel you have a rich inner life?'

'Excuse me?' I asked. It wasn't a typical optician question.

'Do you feel that when you're alone you're fulfilled? Do you repress your emotions or do you fully allow yourself to enjoy life?'

'I don't really know. I've always been prone to depression, and I do struggle with it, but I feel I have a fairly active emotional existence, in my own way… what does that have to do with my eyes?'

'I'm not testing your eyes now. I'm testing your spiritual vision. You may need a minor operation. Your soul looks a little undernourished', she added with a pleasant, vacuous smile.

'Oh. OK.'

Damn it. Why did she ask me about my emotional life? All I wanted to do was find out if I needed new glasses. *Now* look.

March 26th

This is a conversation that I overheard. I didn't overhear it on the tube.

Man A: 'Dad, can I have an ice-cream?'
Man B: 'Maybe when we get to the seaside. We'll be there soon'.
Man A: 'But Dad, we haven't left yet – we're still in the garage. We have been the last 2 hours'.
Man B: 'Oh. Oh Tom, I do wish your mother was still here, she was so much better than me with these things'.
Man A: 'It's OK, Dad. It's not your fault. She's probably around the house somewhere. She won't have just vanished'.
Man B: 'You're a good kid, Tom. I wish I'd been as bright as you when I was your age'.
Man A: 'Dad, you are my age. We're both 45'.
Man B: 'Shit'.

March 27th

I was wandering around Wood Green shopping centre, looking at exotic parrots and cheap tracksuits, when 'The Way We Were' by Barbra Streisand came on over the loudspeaker. I froze. I dropped my mobile phone on a child. My bladder filled with warm piss. Tears filled my eyes. That song always gets to me.

As the song played, my mind was filled with images of snooker players from the golden age of the game: Willie Thorne – first with a mop of unruly hair, then sadly bald. Jimmy White looking young and pasty, then old and even pastier. Ray Reardon. Doug Mountjoy. A teenage Stephen Hendry with a mullet and skin like a car crash. Dennis Taylor wearing even more ridiculous glasses than normal. All the greats, from the Nugget to the Thai Foon... all those wonderful snooker players... mostly gone, but never forgotten...

The song finished. I picked up my phone and dabbed my eyes. I can't help it... The BBC once used the song in a video montage to fill up the time between the frames in a particularly tense World Championship final. Since then I have had an almost Pavlovian response to Streisand. I can't help it. It will always be so.

March 28th

How I long for sleep. For some sweet relief from the curse of consciousness. My life is limping from one disaster to another. At night my eyes flicker like a fox in a fridge, searching for my Shadow.

I keep on stealing cigarettes. Normally it is just one or two fags nicked off friends. They know I'm good for it, and they indulge me. It only happens because I persist in buying myself 10 cigarettes in the morning, in a vain attempt to convince myself that I only smoke 10 fags a day. The reality is that I'm a 20-a-day man.

However, on Sunday my cigarette theft escalated to a whole new level. I was walking through Finchley Central when I saw a truck driver and his beer gut walk out of Fags 'n' Mags newsagents. He bent over to tie a shoelace, and before I knew what I was doing I had felled him with a swift kick to the temple, jumped into the cab of the lorry and sped off towards my east London lock-up.

Once there, I opened up the back of the vehicle and found myself in possession of 50 000 Mayfair Lights.

I have already smoked about half of them. Where can I get hold of more? My chest hurts and I stink of tobacco, but my cravings have not subsided. What does any man really want? More! Always more!

March 29th

It has been a quiet day. Too quiet, but there is nothing I can do about that.

Now is the time for me to write about some strange things that happened to me last winter. I was hoping to save my story for the tabloids. I had assumed they would pay me a great deal of money to serialise my astonishing tale, but it seems not. Don't get me started about the state of the British press.

Anyway, it was last December and I was cleaning out my wardrobe in anticipation of Santa's nocturnal visit. I had retrieved an old pair of socks from the back of the wardrobe when I was stunned to see a shaft of sunlight peeking through a crack at the back. This was unexpected, since my wardrobe is nailed to a concrete wall, and concrete walls tend not to radiate natural light. I pushed at the wardrobe's flimsy wooden back and it gave way, and so did I. Tumbling down through the hole I found myself in a wondrous, magical land.

Knowing my children's stories, I assumed that I had found a secret passage into the wondrous land of Narnia! What fun!

I looked around. It was a grey, bleak environment. I pulled myself to my feet and spotted a fat, middle-aged man standing by a bus stop. His face was a road atlas of tiny fragmented veins. In fact, he looked somewhat familiar.

'Are you Mr Tumnus?' I asked him.

'What?' he replied.

'Mr Tumnus, the friendly fawn', I said.

'No. I'm Mick. Who the fuck are you?' he said. I believed him. He was not Mr Tumnus; Mr Tumnus had manners!

'So, this isn't Narnia?' I asked.

'No', he replied, rolling up his sleeves in a way that indicated imminent violence. 'It's Barnsley'.

And so it was! It seems that rather than finding a secret passage to Narnia, I had discovered a wormhole that transported me to Barnsley, South Yorkshire. I was disappointed. It cost me £50 to get a train home. I am not a rich man – £50 is a lot of money to me.

I know my story sounds unbelievable, and indeed I was drinking heavily around that time, but I assure you it is all true.

April 1st

Perhaps my favourite comic strip is Soboko. It hasn't featured in any newspapers for years now. In fact, I think it only ever ran for a week. It revolved around a small being called Soboko, who did absolutely nothing of interest. It wasn't funny like Fred Bassett, it wasn't homely like Peanuts. It wasn't sexy like George and Lynn. It was pointless. And yet it struck a chord within me.

Here is the first Soboko strip I ever saw. I cannot bear to part with it.

April 2nd

Don't get me started about the price of cola in pubs! It's a sham. It's just syrup and water. They must make a bloody enormous profit.

April 3rd

Today someone was talking to me about love. Well, they weren't talking specifically to me, they were on the radio. In fact, it's highly unlikely that they were talking specifically to me, since I don't even own a radio. I was in the Greek grocers buying milk and a copy of *The Standard*. They always have the radio on in the grocery. If I bought more milk (or the same amount of milk more often), maybe they could afford to buy a television; they should set up a little donation box on the cash counter.

The man on the radio – let's call him Steve – said that love was just when you put another person's needs before your own and know that they do the same for you. Frankly, I'm not sure Steve has ever been in love.

I once made a model woman out of kebab meat (her hair was lettuce). I loved her. Then I ate her. She passed through me like all love passes through me.

April 6th

I haven't left the house in ages. I can't. I cannot find my shoes. It's a long story.

Every few months I have a paranoid delusion that the Nazis are coming for me. I suppose I shouldn't have spent my teenage years obsessively reading *The Diary of Anne Frank* when all my peers were reading *King Arthur* and *Tom Swift*.

One night last week I awoke in a cold sweat, consumed by a horrifying panic. I was convinced that the German SS were coming for me, despite the fact that they disbanded some years ago and were never hugely successful in penetrating north London in the first place. I rushed into the kitchen and barricaded myself in. I knew that I had enough supplies (tinned goods, apple juice and Angel Delight) to last for a few weeks. I boiled the kettle and prepared for solitary life.

For the next three nights I did not sleep. I lived in the kitchen on a diet of beans, coffee and whipped desserts. I sat and waited... every footstep in the street filled me with fear. Then finally, I allowed myself to breathe once more. The Nazis had not yet come for me but I was not yet ready to relax.

I looked down at my shoes. Hand-crafted in Peruvian leather by the Incas of Machu Picchu, they are my pride and joy. I gazed at them and tears formed in my ursine eyes. I had an epiphany! Maybe the Nazis would come; maybe they would drag me away; but I was damned if they were getting their hands on my shoes! So, under cover of darkness, I crept into my garden and buried my shoes. I sneaked back into the kitchen, and for the first time in many days, I slept. I slept like a baby. I slept like an old fool.

I awoke to find it had rained all night. I could smell the blessed moisture in the air. The rain washed away my paranoia. I felt better than I had done in weeks. Sadly, the rain had also reduced the garden to a boggy marsh – I had no idea where my shoes were hidden.

Over the last week I have dug up huge chunks of my garden, but to no avail.

April 8th

Today I went to the shops and when I came home, my house had disappeared. Everything in life is temporary. All our reference points are mutable and transitory.

The universe maintains some eerie balance and yet I cannot find a pub with a working toilet.

April 9th

I was on the Central line, between Lancaster Gate and Queensway. The carriage swayed as though being rocked to sleep by motherly hands. My eyes drooped. I focused on my reflection in the curved black window.

Next to me sat a fat middle-aged man in glasses. He looked like Michael Gambon. Only fatter.

My eyes lowered further. I struggled to stay awake.

'Look at you!' said the man who wasn't Gambon. 'You stare at your reflection all the time. You think you're a character in a book or a film or a play. But you're not. You're just another person.'

I opened my eyes and turned to him. His glasses were on the point of falling off his nose.

'If only you were right', I said, 'but I am not quite a person. I am just another character.'

I got off at Holland Park and walked between expensive white villas that stretched up to the sky like wedding cakes.

April 11th

The homeless man who lives in my garden is complaining again. Frankly, he's a whinger. Where's the spirit of the Blitz when you need it?

I used to leave out a saucer of milk for my cats. Every night I would fill the saucer with semi-skimmed and every morning it would be empty. It wasn't until months later that I remembered that I don't have cats and that something else must have been drinking the midnight milk. So I waited up one Monday night, my binoculars trained on the saucer of milk. It was then that I first spied Clive.

It was Clive who had been purloining my feline dairy treats. He was an alcoholic ex-army colonel who had fallen on hard times. He had lived in cardboard boxes; he had lived in hostels; he had lived on the streets. Now he lived in my back garden. He said that he preferred living in the garden to the streets because it reminded him of army exercises and happier times.

Encouraged by my success with the milk, I started leaving out catfood and fish heads. I assumed (wrongly, it turned out) that he considered

himself a cat and only ate food that cats would want. (I once found him rolling around naked under my sycamore tree, playing with a ball of wool, so you can't blame me for jumping to conclusions.)

Recently, Clive has been complaining because the *Independent* has turned tabloid. It was his newspaper of choice for sheltering himself in cold weather, but now that people are buying and discarding the tabloid, rather than the broadsheet, his toes are exposed when he sleeps.

I suggested he started using the *Guardian,* which was still just about bigger in its Berliner format, but he said it always took an anti-army stance and he refused to use it on principle. I told him not to be so choosy. He is a beggar, after all. Certain immutable laws must be observed.

Then he lost his temper and told me that the tapas I had served him were lukewarm, the chorizo was too greasy and the patatas bravas were dry and flavourless. Fine, if he wants it like that, he gets it like that. I think I shall get the rat poison out from the cupboard under the stairs.

April 12th

You may notice that my previous entry contained a lot of brackets (parentheses for the picky). Let me explain: I made a deal with my mobile phone network where I get 10 free minutes (free!) and 50 texts (also free!). I also get 10 brackets (free), but I have to use them within the month or they expire. (So I am using a lot of them.)

April 15th

Most stories have puzzles in them. Who killed the rich anthropologist? What is God? Is love stronger than fear? Was President Kennedy involved in a plot to kill the moon?

I can't be bothered with any of that nonsense, so I am giving you actual, proper puzzles.

Word Search

There are 10 words hidden within the grid. One is already ringed. See if you can find the others!

```
M I S E R Y M I S E R Y
I S E R Y M I S E R Y M
S E R Y M I S E R Y M I
E R Y M I S E R Y M I S
R Y M I S E R Y M I S E
Y M I S E R Y M I S E R
M I S E R Y M I S E R Y
I S E R Y M I S E R Y M
S E R Y M I S E R Y M I
```

Crossword

All the clues in today's crossword refer to popular dances. Or do they?

Across:

1. My pet dog when I was younger. Or was it?
4. My favourite material. Or is it?
10. The name of my Primary school. Remember?
11. What am I thinking of right now? No. Not now.
12. The opposite of right. Wrong!
13. Where I went last December. Or did I?
14. My eyes are on you. Or are they?

18. A kind of plant. Pot? Or noodle?
20. Vaseline Intensive Care smoothes your wrinkles. Or does it?
22. My favourite singer.
24. Chrissie Hynde's hind legs are legendary legs. Or are they?
25. How did I end up here? Down under – understand?
26. See 1 across.
27. What did I eat last night? After the pizza.

Down:

1. Down down, deeper and down. Or up?
2. The plane depicted on my old pillow case. Or something else entirely.
3. My favourite anecdote about Ossie Ardiles, when he first played for Spurs.
5. A coarse, rough stone. No, not that one. Not that one either.
6. Do I prefer tea or coffee? Or neither?
7. A type of hat that is a fish. Or is it?
8. Julie Andrews?
9. Mike Leigh's best-kept secret. Out in the open!
15. Unlucky for some, lucky for others?
16. Eh?
19. What country am I? (Not Portugal.)
21. Sexy sex, but dangerous for huntsmen. Or is it?
22. A foreigner has stolen your job.
23. Castor and Pollux, but aside from the highway.

Logic Problems

1. Johnny has eighteen apples. He eats them all in one day. He has a terrible stomach-ache and feels poorly. Why does he do it? What is he trying to prove? He's always doing things like that – extravagant gestures that don't impress anyone. Do you think I should leave him?
2. A train leaves Edinburgh at 5.25 p.m. It travels towards London at 55 m.p.h. Is this what I pay my taxes for? Honestly, the rail infrastructure in this country is just a joke. And was

there any announcement about the delay? No, of course not. My father always calls Britain a Third-World country and I'm beginning to agree with him. It was a terrible journey, but what can you do? They have a bloody monopoly.

3. Corbin Bernsen seems like a nice fellow. Do you think he'll be my friend?

Spot the Difference

How many differences can you spot in these two pictures?

April 16th

My homeless friend Clive is dead. And the tragedy is that it wasn't even me that did it. He was beaten to death by a group of angry pacifists. He had been sitting outside my house, bragging about his role in the (first) Gulf War when they pounced. It was all over in a matter of minutes.

War does strange things to people.

I buried him in my garden, where he had been at his happiest. There are now 16 bodies buried there. I may have to buy a bigger garden or stop burying people.

April 18th

I shall tell you a secret. A dark secret. In my attic there is a painting. A painting of me. But it is no ordinary painting. This painting has magical properties. You are all no doubt familiar with *The Picture of Dorian Gray*. My painting is similar, but with a terrible, ungodly twist; for, although I age, and grow more wrinkled with every passing year, the painting remains *exactly the same!*

I dare not look upon that hideous portrait of youth!

Things overheard on the tube

Today's journey:
Northern Line: Brent Cross–Old Street

1. In my brain there is a prostitute on every street corner.
2. They aren't rats, they are just very dirty mice.
3. A3 is twice as big as A4... the smaller the number, the bigger the paper.
4. There's nothing more crap than wanking on a webcam.
5. Sophie Dahl has very large eyes. It looks like someone has nailed boiled eggs to her face.
6. Oh. Gubbins.

7. I don't understand all the fuss about Orlando Bloom. He's plain and always has a shit haircut.
8. When people say 'interesting' they actually mean 'boring'.
9. You're not ugly, you just have a funny bone structure.
10. How about a reality show where contestants are tricked into thinking they're making an interesting, relevant programme?

April 20th

It is perhaps time for me to share my thoughts on poetry.

It is a well-known fact that all the great poets considered becoming electricians at some point in their lives. At first glance there doesn't seem to be a great similarity between the art of rewiring plugs and the art of writing poetry, but you need to dig beneath the surface... far beneath the surface... below the crust, below the mantle... right down to the core of the earth. Then you'll find your answers.

At the centre of the earth you will find a lonely man. He is an electrician, and works at making sure there are no earthly power failures. He must work alone. He isn't even allowed a pet eagle, as most surface-dwelling electricians are permitted. He sits there admiring the relentless heat of the molten earth core and waiting for something to go wrong. He has a lot of time on his hands. So he writes poetry. Most of it is rubbish, but some of it is very good.

How do I know? Because he sends me poetry. Whenever there is an earthquake, I search the surrounding areas and normally find a small notepad that he has sent up to the surface. He uses earthquakes as distractions. It's a clever idea; poets have always used nature, he just uses nature in a slightly more literal manner. He is a pastoral poet; he writes like an unhappy goat.

Every electrician I have ever met has been a frustrated poet, longing to swap filaments for similes. But I suppose they have to make a living. I have considered publishing an anthology of poetry by electricians, but I am no publisher. I can hardly read.

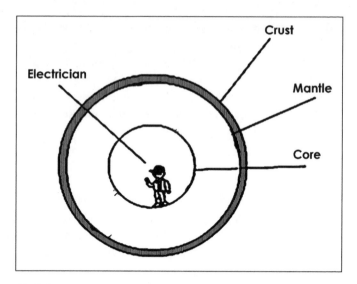

April 21st

Each week I drink 44 cups of tea and 31 cups of coffee. I eat 28 sandwiches (10 chicken salad, 10 Chinese chicken and eight coronation chicken). I also eat one peanut. Just one. No more, no less. The peanut is the secret to my weight loss.

I have no idea why, but that single peanut allows me to eat whatever I like and still maintain my slender waistline. No one believes me... Dr Atkin's magic meat diet has stolen my thunder. Dr Atkins was a fraud – he had no interest in losing weight, just a desperate desire to discredit the potato.

I do not understand the current obsession with weight and beauty. Women subscribe to an aesthetic that only gay men find sexually appealing.

Try my diet, but remember: just one peanut – any more than that and you will not lose weight.

April 22nd

Everyone has a hobby. Some people collect comics. Some people put ships in bottles. I build prisons.

I have built myself a beautiful maximum security prison. Sadly, I built it too well, and now I can't get out.

April 23rd

Today I had my poker evening. It's a little informal get-together I have every few months; a few of the gang come round and we play a few hands of Texas Hold 'Em. It was a nice evening. Simon and Yasmin le Bon, Malcolm Rifkind, Eddie Grant of 'Electric Avenue' fame, Elle McPherson, Eric Bristow and my uncle Claude came along. Bristow won as usual. He has a terrible sneering laugh every time he wins a hand. Frankly, he's not very pleasant. Still, other than him, everyone was on top form. It's just an opportunity for a few like-minded people to get together to talk about politics, contemporary art and skiing.

We had a few glasses of Cognac, and Yasmin prepared her famous Kraft cheese fondue. She's a delightful woman. Simon was talking about his new role in a touring version of Chekhov's 'The Three Sisters'. He plays all the parts and throws in a few Duran Duran numbers in the quiet moments; he is very much the renaissance man.

I lost about £30, a small price to pay for erudite company.

April 24th

Last night I saw a shooting star. It crashed into my house.
Sometimes I have no luck at all.

April 25th

Today I waited for a bus. I was trying to get home, as I always am. When I got to the bus stop, the electronic indicator announced in bright red letters that the first bus would arrive in 6 minutes. It was a dark, rainy evening and the pavement was littered with polystyrene burger boxes decaying in puddles. I looked at the indicator a minute later. It said that the bus would arrive in 7 minutes. I chewed my lips in silent anxiety. But I waited because sometimes in life all you can do is wait. A few minutes later I looked again. It said the bus would arrive in 10 minutes.

After a while I stopped looking at the indicator. I waited for 30 minutes. After a while, waiting at bus stops becomes a moral issue. It's a case of facing the bus down and remaining stubborn enough not to move away from the bus stop. However, I eventually acknowledged that the bus was never going to come.

I walked home, wet and angry. I hate this city.

There is a moral to this story: never put your faith in electronic indicators. We live in a world of empty promises; and the agony of ageing is witnessing just how empty they really are.

Also, if you are driving through town and you see a short man walking home in the rain, it is most likely me. Take pity on me and give me a lift.

Some people are too proud to accept pity. Idiots.

April 26th

Last night I had dinner with my good friend Dr Dolittle. Many myths and half-truths surround him. Some of them are true: he can talk to animals (actually anyone can talk to animals – the important fact is that they talk back to him) but he isn't a doctor. The animals just decided to call him doctor because he had more medical expertise than they did.

We sat in front of the TV, eating Chinese food out of aluminium cartons.

'How are the animals?' I asked.

'Fucking grumpy', he replied, inadvertently spitting chicken chow mein onto the carpet. 'They never stop complaining. The soup is too hot, the room is too cold. London is too crowded. No one has any manners anymore. They never stop whinging.'

'Oh well', I said. There isn't much you can say about grumpy animals. It's not my area of expertise.

'In general, animals are the most ungrateful bunch of creatures in the world. I hate them.' More chow mein spilled onto the floor.

'Oh', I replied, 'that's a shame.'

We didn't talk much after that. We finished watching *Heartbeat* and I went home. If only the solution to life's problems could really be solved by animals... but animals are no more noble or beautiful than anyone else. Let me give you an example.

Much is made of the intelligence of dolphins. After man, and apes, they are said to be the cleverest of all God's creatures. But they are not that clever at all. Apparently, they're about as clever as a 2-year old human child.

That means that the stupidest person you've ever met – the one who made you roll your eyes in exhausted shame – is far, far cleverer than a dolphin. Would you go swimming with idiots?

April 27th

I was standing outside my house, smoking a cigarette and scratching at invisible hang-nails. A young Indian man nervously walked past me wearing an Eminem T-shirt and a tight leather jacket. When he saw me smoking, he reached into his pocket, pulled out a pack of Marlboro Lights and lit one. It was automatic. It was perhaps the saddest thing I've ever seen.

April 29th

I was in Sainsbury's. I was going to buy myself some Golden Grahams, an apple pie and other Christmassy victuals. I was wandering down the aisles, lost in contemplation, thinking of Jesus and irritable bowel syndrome. Actually, I was just lost: supermarkets are bigger than they used to be.

I was wandering through the tinned goods section when I saw Robert. Robert was a friend of mine until he went a bit wrong. Today, he didn't appear to be shopping. He was standing perfectly still and had surrounded himself with perfectly piled stacks of tins, so that only his head was poking out above the tuna and beans.

'Hello Robert', I said.

'Shhhhh… ', he winced, 'don't draw any attention to me.'

'What are you doing?' I asked.

'Nothing. I'm just standing here.'

'Why?'

He sighed. 'People leave me alone here. I can stand here all day and people don't notice me. I'm happy.'

'Yes, I understand that. But you're standing in the middle of a supermarket, surrounded by tins.' I was stating the obvious, but it needed stating.

'I'm hiding. Like I said, it makes me happy. Isn't that enough?'

'OK. But I need a tin of tuna. You're using them all for your hiding place.'

'Just take one from the top level. If you take it from the bottom, the whole thing will collapse.'

I gingerly removed a tin and stood back. A small part of his neck was now exposed. I picked up a packet of quick-cook pasta from another aisle and placed it in front of the gap. Robert didn't say anything.

I felt a bit sorry for him, but I reserved most of my pity for my fellow shoppers.

May 1st

Today I had another appointment with Dr Gepetto. I still don't know if he's real or just an illusion brought on by unusual weather.

I sat in the small room and stared out of the window. I took a deep breath. I said that I felt conflicting emotions towards my parents, I told him how angry I get about the breakdown of their marriage, I confessed that I found it hard to trust women. I asked him what he thought. There was no reply.

It was only then that I noticed Dr Gepetto's absence. He was not there. I was talking to myself.

I left the consulting room and asked Moira, Dr Gepetto's secretary, where he was. I noticed she looked tired and drawn. She was crying, the tears collecting in a damp circle beneath her desk.

She told me that Dr Gepetto had been killed in a car crash last week. I asked if it was a quick death. She told me that it was a slow, gruesome death and that he probably suffered enormously. I enquired whether I would be charged for today's session. She said she didn't know. Behind the drone of our conversation, I could hear an alarm clock.

It's very frustrating news. I felt we were breaking new ground.

May 3rd

Kevin Spacey came round for brunch. We're good friends. I knew him before he was remotely successful. You may remember that he turned up at the Labour Party Conference a few years back when Bill Clinton was giving a speech? I organized that. His appearances in the Almeida theatre? That was my plan. He's doing very well for himself. However, as he gets more famous, so his disguises become more elaborate. This morning he rang the bell dressed as a postman, complete with Cockney accent and banter about the weather.

We sat in the lounge, smoking fags and watching the telly. As you probably know, Kevin is an Anglophile and is fascinated by all aspects of English culture.

The Bill was on.

'Who's that?' asked Kevin, pointing to the screen.

'Todd Carty. He used to play Mark Fowler in *EastEnders*. He's in *The Bill* now.'

'Why *The Bill*?'

I sighed. It's an explanation I've had to make many times: '*EastEnders* is the most popular soap in the country – much more popular than *The Bill*. When actors want to leave *EastEnders*, but aren't ready to be released into the general public, they are shifted onto *The Bill*. They'll play a bent copper for 6 months until their fame subsides and they are ready to be non-famous. *The Bill* is like a halfway house between fame and obscurity. If an *EastEnders* star just quit the soap without going through *The Bill*, they would suffer from the sudden drop in pressure – like deep sea divers suffering from the bends if they surface too quickly. Think of *The Bill* as a decompression chamber for actors.'

'Oh', said Kevin, scratching himself. 'This Todd Carty fellow. Can I meet him?'

'You're Kevin Spacey. I'm sure he'd like to meet you.'

'Can we go round to his house and eat Jammy Dodgers and play backgammon?'

'I don't know. You'll have to ask him.'

May 4th

I am on the roof. I can see Victorian chimney pots. In my neighbour's garden I can see a weeping willow bending against the wind. I see a council estate on the horizon, black and silver in the fading twilight. I can see buses and cars, gridlocked on leafy suburban roads. I can see the moon, pressed flat like a coin against the map of the sky. London is spread before me.

I think about all those lights, twinkling at dusk: houses and flats, bungalows and tower blocks. Each one of them filled with awful humanity, with men and women, parents, children, toddlers and babies, all running around or squatting on toilets or sitting in lazy chairs or pacing up stairs. Each building is a microcosm of the world, brimming with life. And each life has its own unique, bittersweet story, its own individual experience. Except it doesn't. All the houses and flats are empty. The lights are all off. The televisions are all dead. There are no posters on the walls. The beds remain unmade. There are no stories to be told. No one is there. There is no one here except me. That's it.

May 7th

The toy shop was full of kids called Maximillian and Saskia, putting marbles in their mouths and then spitting them out at each other. Some of the toys I recognized from my own childhood: jacks and top trumps and bouncy balls. Some were new and garish. Sticky yellow men made of rubber, whose limbs could be stretched and distorted. There were piles of ghoulish plastic figurines with bulging, veiny eyes.

I ignored the kids and their overindulgent parents.

Towards the back of the shop there were board games. I saw Scrabble and Mastermind and my brain began to ache. There was Monopoly too. Not just the original version, but many new variants: an Arsenal Monopoly set and a Star Wars set. Trivial Pursuit had also changed. As well as the standard set, you could also buy a special Entertainment version and a Tuesday version that only posed questions on events that occurred on a Tuesday.

Truly, we live in a wondrous age. But, alas, there was nothing in the shop for me.

As I walked to the exit, I saw an interesting toy. It was a cardboard drawing of a naked man. The man could be cut out and assembled. There were a series of different outfits that could also be cut out and affixed to the figure, allowing kids to dress it as they wished. But the figure wasn't an action man, or even a clean-cut young executive. It was Martin Heidegger.

I looked closer. On the back of the package there was text:

Martin Heidegger (1889–1976) was the German philosopher who developed existential phenomenology and has been widely regarded as the most original twentieth-century philosopher. Heidegger was born in

Messkirch, Baden, on September 22, 1889. He studied Roman Catholic theology and then philosophy at the University of Freiburg, where he was a student of Edmund Husserl, the founder of phenomenology and all-round great guy. Heidegger began teaching at Freiburg in 1915. After teaching at Marburg, he became a professor of philosophy at Freiburg in 1928.

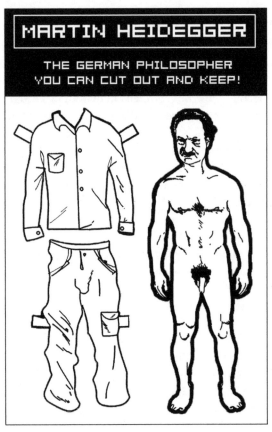

It is worrying. I have no problem with children playing with philosophers. After all, some of the greatest thinkers of all time had the brains of children. But they should remember that Martin Heidegger was a Nazi.

You have to draw the line somewhere.

May 8th

I was 5 years old.

I saw a penny. I picked it up. But all day long I did not have good luck. In fact, I was hit by a car and broke my arm.

May 9th

I stood outside my house and hailed a taxi. I wasn't going anywhere, but I wanted a conversation.

A cab pulled up across the road from me, and I hopped in the back.

'Smile, it might never happen', said the driver with relentless chirpiness.

'I know', I said. 'It never happens.'

'So, where you going? Work?'

'Yes', I lied. I didn't feel like explaining that he was giving me a lift to the tube station so that I could travel straight back home.

'What do you do?' he asked. A song from the eighties played on the radio. I tapped my knee in rhythm, despite myself.

'I'm a personal shopper', I lied again. 'I buy things for rich people who don't know how to spend their money.'

'Nice job', he said.

'Not bad.' The trick with taxi drivers is to remain non-committal on every issue. 'What do you do?'

'What do you mean? I'm a taxi driver.'

'Yes. Yes, of course you are.'

The rest of the journey was silence. We drove past a broken down bus and a pack of teenagers having a fight. I paid him £15 and got the tube home.

May 11th

Rock stars are mostly cartoon characters. Do not take them seriously. If they were any good with words they would have become writers, and if they were any good at music they'd be classical composers.

They stumble through life without reason and with very little rhyme.

I nearly always feel sorry for rock stars. They are lost souls and vain idiots.

This is what Kurt Cobain would look like as Charlie Brown.

Kurt Cobain's life would have been much simpler if he had been more like Charlie Brown. No heroin, no grunge rock, no Courtney Love, just an animated guitar, a psychiatrist's booth and young Mr Cobain standing on a lonely pitcher's mound in the rain.

Hmmm... *Charlie* is slang for cocaine. *Brown* is slang for heroin. Perhaps Kurt and Charlie have more in common than I first imagined.

Or do they? Both artists are dead, that is true; both had worldwide appeal. Charles Schulz actually had interstellar appeal: the *Peanuts* characters were made official NASA mascots in 1969. It's unlikely that NASA will ever endorse a Kurt Cobain song. Perhaps Charles Schulz wore a cardigan. There is little information available as to his fashion preferences. We can probably assume he didn't wear eyeliner, if nothing else.

Rock stardom indulges the basest aspects of a person's soul, which is probably good fun for a short period of time. But I can imagine many rock stars would secretly be far happier hunched over a sketch pad, their tongues splayed in concentration, as they try to make Snoopy dance.

May 13th

I was locked overnight in Londis. The High Street conspires against me.

The High Street, with its local characters, friendly banter and limited range of overpriced chocolate, is friend to the ordinary man. And whatever I may be, I am not ordinary.

It wasn't even near closing time. I had popped in to buy a bottle of strawberry milk. I perused the newspapers and then wandered over to the chilled cabinet, gazing sadly at a selection of plastic-wrapped pies. When I looked up, I realised that the shopkeeper had disappeared and the front door was locked. A second later the lights flickered and died. I pressed my face against the window. Outside, a slow stream of people walked by. I screamed for help, but they simply stared and shook their heads, as though I were a death-row prisoner pleading with a priest for help.

After an hour I settled down and accepted my fate: I would be stuck there overnight. I drank a pint of milk and ate a jar of peanut butter. I slept fitfully and dreamed that I was trapped in a large, well-lit branch of Tesco. My dreams are frustratingly unimaginative.

The following morning the shopkeeper found me slumped in the corner of the shop and woke me up.

I angrily accused him of locking me in overnight. He laughed and said that I had walked in the shop a mere 10 seconds ago and that I obviously had an odd sense of humour. The funny thing is that I am tempted to believe him.

Halfway home I realised that I had forgotten to get the strawberry milk.

May 14th

Today I did nothing. Yesterday I did nothing. Tomorrow I will probably do nothing. I'm absolutely knackered.

I keep a tight grip on my personality. I constantly fear that I may become someone else. A friend once told me 'The one thing I can guarantee is that you will change and the things that you want will change'. I fired my friend. I don't need friends like that.

I found this story in the back pages of *Modern Spider* magazine. It worries me - I think I may have written it myself, under a pseudonym. I have forgotten so much.

David lay in bed. A soft plume of smoke rose up from the ashtray where a cigarette burned. He was thinking about alcohol. He wanted a gin and tonic. In the spotlight of the bedside lamp he watched a small black spider crawl across his bedside table. He picked up the empty glass and cupped it gingerly over the spider. He slid a postcard under the glass and opened the window. He didn't like spiders. He shook the glass out of the window and checked that the spider had gone.

The cigarette was dead. He switched off the light and lay there, knowing that sleep would come as it always did, whether he had a gin and tonic or not. He could feel the mattress, soft and pliant beneath his naked body. His eyes closed.

In London, in England, in Europe, on the planet Earth, in a flat that had seen better days, the television droned on, flashing and dipping in contrast and tone. David flicked between channels, between little gaps in his vision. He put the kettle on and waited for it to re-boil. As the water throbbed and bubbled, he strolled back into the lounge and changed the channel on the TV. Anything but the local news. Outside, it was still London, it was still England and the future lurked. His future wore an impassive face: cold and neutral, willing to play the game any way he wanted. He didn't know what he wanted. He wanted another cup of tea.

The kitchen. Milk, two sugars, spooning the teabag across the room into the dustbin, dripping tea on the floor... a man can drink so many cups of tea before the future arrives. Another day fell away.

On the High Street, the sun was shining and winter enveloped the air with a rosy cheer. Even the betting shop looked jolly in the sunlight. David bought the **Radio Times,** *a smoothie and another packet of cigarettes.*

David wanted to change his life. He wanted to win the lottery and talk to God. He wanted to trade his cow for a handful of magic beans. He walked back to the flat. Day-release was over.

There was a ringing in the hallway. He counted the beeps and then counted the steps until he answered the phone.

'Hello?'

'Hiya. How's your day?' she asked him.

'Oh, not bad. The same as usual. I knew it'd be you on the phone. Anyway, how's your day? Did you have fun last night?'

'Boooooring. Boring. Boring. Office boring. Well, you know what office drinks are like... having to smile while the old guys stare at my tits. You know... mustn't grumble. It's just a bit dull. Are we still on for tonight?'

David looked at his watch. It was late morning. 'Yeah, yeah, of course. What do you want? Shepherd's Bush's finest? Chinese or a curry?'

'Ooooh, curry please. I don't know why you even ask me. I'll always go for curry.'

'And a bottle of red?'

'Yup. Sounds great. I'll be over about seven. I can't really talk now. The boss is staring at me. I should probably do some work.' She puckered a kiss down the phone line.

'Bye.'

'See you later. Will be fun. Will be good.'

The phone clicked goodbye in his ear and the dial tone returned. Goodbye. Hello. Goodbye. So many lines to remember. His mind was a shop full of greeting cards... We are so sorry to hear about your loss. Happy Anniversary! Do not swap your cow for magic beans!

He pulled the curry menu from the cork board on the wall. Chicken saag. Egg-fried rice. Onion bhajis in a greasy paper bag.

He lit another cigarette and sat in front of the television, trying to plot out the evening, trying to steer a course through the week without crashing. Tonight Carol would come over and they would eat and talk and make love. Tomorrow he would go to an art gallery. On Thursday he would walk through the park and force himself to think about the colours of the fallen leaves.

He turned the TV off and tramped through to his bedroom. He drew the curtains and switched on the radio, slowly, gently, quietly. He set the alarm, closed his eyes and pulled the duvet over his head. An afternoon nap was a luxury like no other. He kicked his socks onto the floor. He slid off his trousers and pants and curled up, ready for oblivion.

The dreams were tender and listless – an unfocused monologue about a film star and a car chase and very important news that he had to deliver. He could feel the stiffness of his body, of his cramped head in a cramped bed.

Dreams change.

He woke up and took a deep breath. Morning had broken. Soft light filtered through the curtains. It was a beautiful day.

He knew that his name was no longer David. He knew this knowledge should worry him, but it didn't. He hadn't much liked being David.

His name was now Terry. He was no longer 29. He was 38. His flat, asymmetrical body had changed too. He examined his hairy arms and his chipped fingernails; he lovingly admired the gut that hung over his groin like a pouch. He would need to go to the gym after work. Of all the gym joints in the world, he had to walk into this one...

He smoothed his hands over his newly bald pate. It felt like a baby's head.

He turned on the bedside light and Viv stirred from her sleep. She rubbed her eyes and smiled.

'You alright, love?' she asked. Her eyes were beautiful. Sometimes she did drive him mad, but he loved her. He knew he always would.

'Just getting a glass of water. Do you want anything?' His new voice was thick and lazy. He liked it.

'I'm fine. Oh... but could you check on Mona?'

'Course. Back in a mo.'

Each footstep on the carpet felt good. He let each toe sink into the rich fabric. He scratched his bum as he walked downstairs to the kitchen and poured himself a glass of water.

Then he tiptoed into Mona's bedroom and looked down at his daughter; her eyes were closed, idiotic with sleep. He smiled, his body welling with love, his stomach panging with future worries. He wouldn't let anything hurt her. He loved her so much. He loved standing there, watching her sleep.

He took the water and climbed slowly up the stairs. A spider crawled across the wall. He picked up a newspaper and swatted it dead. He turned off the light in the hall and walked back to the bedroom, sipping his water along the way.

It worries me because the central character changes against his will. I know that he is happier at the end of the story, but that is not the point. I must resist change at all costs.

May 16th

If I could, I would marry a cigarette. So slim and shapely. The tempting invitation of tight tobacco and inch-long filter. Age cannot wither her, nor custom stale her infinite variety. But she does make me cough. It must be love.

My mother asks me when I'm going to get married. I tell her I'll get married when I meet the right girl. She tells me that she knows the right girls. I keep quiet and eat my greens. I know the kind of women my mother likes.

The Freudians among you can make of that what you will.

Things overheard on the tube

Today's journey:
District Line: Whitechapel–Turnham Green

1. Alan Hansen starts every sentence with… 'if you're looking for'.
2. I swear she had cum on her face.
3. I am going to have to confiscate your shoelaces in case you try to hang yourself.
4. Just because you think about him all the time, doesn't mean he cares about you.
5. If the Government actually listened to people, it would be total chaos.
6. Mariella Frostrup is really thick. She thinks having a foreign name makes her clever.
7. No trains. A points failure at Moorgate.
8. My kids all know everything about Bowie and Bolan, etc. I would die of shame if they couldn't sing along to the Pistols.
9. You can't take part in a fox hunt and then complain afterwards that you didn't really want to do it.
10. Boris Johnson doesn't look very Turkish.

May 17th

I wandered down to my local park. There is an animal enclosure and I like to watch the deer and ponies and feed them twigs or bits of masonry that have fallen from the front of my house.

The weather was clear and I ambled beneath the canopy of trees, the sunlight sizzling through the leaves and blinding me. I pressed my face against the enclosure fence. I could see no animals. I waited. The animals are crafty and sometimes blend into the surroundings by wearing hats and jackets. Still, they failed to materialise.

A park employee approached me and tapped me on the shoulder. He had a bushy moustache and an eye-patch. I didn't trust him.

'I expect you're wondering where all the animals have gone', he said, chuckling.

'Yes. I liked them', I replied.

He laughed heartily. It sounded like a child's bones being broken by a tractor. 'I killed them all', he said.

'Why? Why did you do that?' I asked.

'Because I can!' he screamed, before running over the hill and disappearing into the nameless alleys of north London.

People are cruel. People are idiots. I am people. I may repeat myself.

May 19th

This is how life on earth began:

God made a man. He didn't know what to name him. He looked through his book of baby names. He started on A. Aaron, Abel, Albert, Abner, Abraham, Absalom... nope... Achilles... no... too melodramatic. Adam.

Adam. Short, sweet, marketable. Not too pretentious. God put the book down; he hadn't even got to the Bs.

Adam prowled around the Garden of Eden. It all seemed perfectly bearable, and he had nothing else to compare it with, so he wasn't in a position to complain. He ate pears and berries and oranges, and drank fresh spring water. He felt alright. He waited for something to happen. He wandered towards the outskirts of Eden. It was all OK. Cows and horses grazed peacefully, and he had no urge to slaughter the animals and eat them. All was well. All was dull.

Some weeks after his creation Adam discovered his penis. He'd already used it for pissing, but gradually he became aware that it had other uses beyond wetting his feet. If he thought of certain things, it became hard and he got very excited. These feelings were pleasant, in a sickly feverish way. When he was especially bored, he would try to think of things to make his cock hard.

He would think about butterflies and caterpillars. It wasn't very effective as an erotic stimulus, but there wasn't much else to think about. It passed the time of day.

And lo, God appeared in the sky in the form of a dark cloud and asked Adam how he was.

'Yeah, not bad', said Adam. 'Mustn't grumble.'

'Here… wait, ' he continued. 'Look at this.' He closed his eyes and concentrated. His cock thickened and hardened and limped half-heartedly towards the horizontal. 'Not bad, eh?'

'Ummmm… yes… very impressive', God boomed sarcastically. He hadn't made mankind so that he could watch Adam get half an erection. In fact he wasn't sure why he had made mankind. He'd had noble intentions, but in truth, he was already getting bored of man.

And Adam was getting bored of God. He was distant. He was pompous. He was a father, not a friend.

And so God created Eve. He fashioned her from a rib of Adam's. Adam didn't mind. He yawned as God disassembled him and put him back together. He had no idea how many ribs were normal, and didn't miss that one that had disappeared.

Poof – and there she was: Eve. Woman.

Adam and Eve looked at each other. He was skinny, with kindly, stupid eyes. His brown beard hid a weak chin. Eve was full, round and friendly, with dimples in her cheeks and ruddy, strawberry hair.

They continued looking at each other: man and woman. They stared like dumb cows chewing dumb grass.

Then God clicked his fingers... and... something happened: love, magic, fear, happiness, hope, resentment, lust, envy, pride, hatred and guilt filled their hearts. It was all downhill from there. But at least it would be a lot harder to be bored.

May 20th

Chess. I have been playing chess. Sometimes with friends. Sometimes with strangers. Sometimes with myself.

Imagine if Garry Kasparov had been called Barry Kasparov. The world would be a very different place. In films, whenever chess is being played, it is clumsily used as a metaphor for some greater battle. The bearded villain is always clever, British and of dubious sexuality. The hero is a stubbly maverick, a genius who doesn't play by the rules. It's all rubbish. It's just a game.

And in these epic cinema scenes, there's always a checkmate. But my games are rarely checkmates, they are stalemates and forced resignations.

May 21st

Gabriel sat on the collectivo. His face pressed against the window, squinting at the inexplicable autumn sunlight. The collectivo driver had the radio tuned to FM Tango, and someone old was singing a milonga. The kind of thing his dad sang when drunk. He preferred modern music – not that old crap.

It was Saturday. No school today. The collectivo stopped on Moreno and he hopped off. He had the day to himself. Mama was in town shopping and Marcelo was staying over with his girlfriend in Lomas.

He walked to the park down Hipólito Yrigoyen. It was his favourite avenue; majestically wide and lined with feathery trees that filtered the sunlight green and yellow. Crumbling buildings cast shadows across the pavement, and leaves formed a ferny canopy across the sky.

He walked past Ugis, the pizza place. They did not have a great range of pizzas. They only did mozzarella, but it was cheap and tasty and he always added ham from the fridge in the apartment. Maybe on the way home he would get one. He didn't have much cash to spend. He just felt like walking. He could hear the shouts of kids his age playing football. Judging from the jeers and hoots, someone was playing very badly.

Parque Rivadavia was 20 blocks away. Marcelo said that they used to have fascist marches there, but that must have been a long time ago. Nowadays, it was a chaotic litter of market stalls. Old comics and magazines, but also pirated DVDs and CDs. The market stalls were hardly high-tech, but they had a good system. Each stall had a laminated folder of pirate CDs. Games, MP3s, films. You could point out a CD and a man would whisper to a woman, and the woman would whisper to another man and in 5 minutes they'd have your CD wrapped up in paper and ready to go.

Today Gabriel had almost no money, but he didn't mind. The sun was shining. If it was good enough for the old men who played chess, then it was good enough for him.

He was in no hurry. He strolled past Maza and Colombres, Yapeyú and Castro Barros. On the corner of José Mármol, he saw something odd.

Someone was following him, he was sure of it. It was a tall, dark figure. He must have been about 2 metres tall and was wearing a long raincoat and a hat, despite the hot weather. Gabriel stopped and pretended to do up his shoelace like he had seen in films. He waited and the figure hesitated, but then walked past him. Gabriel rose and continued walking. From behind the figure, he could see that the man walked with an ungainly, loping motion and appeared to be hunched over. Gabriel looked down at the sidewalk. The stranger seemed to be leaving a trail on the floor – a silvery substance like the slime that slugs and snails leave behind in winter. It smelt like molasses. Something very unusual was happening; Gabriel was sure of it. He needed to know more.

The figure turned. There was something strange about his face. He beckoned Gabriel. Despite himself, Gabriel found himself walking towards the figure.

'Gabriel Fernandez?'

'Yes sir', said Gabriel. He didn't know why he was being so polite. He was scared.

'Come with me, young man', said the man in the coat, as he turned and walked down an alley. Gabriel knew he should not follow the man. He could be a killer or a kidnapper or working for an enemy government. It was stupid. Of course he would not obey the tall, ugly man.

But he did just that. There was something about the figure that seemed to draw him closer. He could not resist it. He followed the man down the alley, making the sign of the cross on his chest and looking skyward, silently apologising to his mother.

They reached a dusty garage opposite a Choripan stall. The place was littered with old tin cans and Coke bottles. The figure sidled past a derelict Ford and walked into the back of the garage. Gabriel followed.

'Take a seat, Gabriel', said the man. He spoke Spanish very strangely. He didn't sound normal. He sounded like Darth Vader from the *Star Wars* films.

Gabriel sat on a red plastic chair that rocked and squeaked against the floor. One leg was slightly too short.

'Close your eyes, please', ordered the man. Gabriel scrunched up his eyes and thought of Mama. Probably in town, trying on clothes that she wouldn't buy. As he thought of his mother, he heard all sorts of noises in the garage. It sounded like someone was dragging sacks of rock along the floor.

The time slowed. Gabriel felt pressure on his bladder and realised he needed to pee soon.

'You can open your eyes now Gabriel', said the man. His voice was becoming more strangulated, even less natural.

Gabriel opened his eyes. For a second he saw red spots. Then his vision cleared and he saw the man. Except it wasn't a man. It was a giant ant. The ant was sitting at a wooden chair opposite him. The discarded clothes and human disguise lay in a pile on the floor.

'Hello', said the giant ant, 'I am a giant ant.'

'OK', said Gabriel. He wasn't sure what he was supposed to say.

'I suppose I should make things clearer', said the ant, clasping together one pair of its arms. 'My name is Zygron Zikorski. I am an... ambassador from another planet. My planet is ruled entirely by giant ants. We have been watching your world for some time, and we felt that the time was right to make contact with Earth.'

'You're an alien?' asked Gabriel. His mind was struggling to come to terms with everything. In some ways it all seemed so unbelievable, but he did not doubt the evidence of his own eyes and knew that there was no way that the ant was a joke or hoax.

'Yes... an alien. There's some speculation on my home planet that my species may have originated from Earth many millions of years ago, but that is purely speculation. I was not born on Earth, if that's what you mean.'

'Anyway', continued the ant. 'We have decided that now is the appropriate time to make our presence known to certain key earthlings. And you are fortunate enough to have been chosen to help facilitate our smooth take over of Earth.'

'Takeover? I don't understand', said Gabriel. He was sweating.

'Yes. Your participation is not voluntary. We are taking over the planet. Obviously, we could use force, but we'd prefer a smooth transition with the minimum of violence. That's where you come in. It's your job to persuade your fellow humans that it's better for them not to put up too much of a fight. Don't think of yourself as a traitor... such language is clumsy and naive. Our domination of your planet is inevitable, so it would be much easier for all involved if your race didn't half-exterminate itself trying to fight us.'

'I don't understand', shrugged Gabriel. He squirmed. He was worried about wetting himself. 'Why me? I am a 12-year-old boy. I have no influence... no one listens to me. If I told my parents I had met an ant from another planet they would think I was on drugs.'

'You're 12 years old?' said the ant.

'Yes', said Gabriel. The ant looked puzzled. He dipped into a black holdall and pulled out a ring-binder and some papers. He flicked rapidly through paperwork.

'You are Gabriel Fernandez, yes?' said the ant.

'Yes.'

'Of Sánchez de Bustamente 451?'

'No. I live across town. In Boedo.'

'Hmmmmm', said the ant.

There was a long silence. Gabriel was trying to pluck up the courage to ask if he could go to the bathroom.

Finally, the ant spoke. 'Oh dear. There's been a mistake. Our agents have wrongly identified you. We were supposed to contact Gabriel Mauricio Fernandez, a 35-year-old software engineer. But we got you instead. It's happened before. Sadly, you humans all look the same to us. I suppose I should have known that you were just a child. Shit. Oh well.'

'Does that mean I can go now?' asked Gabriel.

'I suppose so', said the ant dejectedly. 'Are you sure that no one will believe you if you say you met a giant ant?'

'I won't tell anyone! They would only say I was lying... I promise. Your secret is safe.' Gabriel's words tumbled out in a manic flurry. He couldn't hold his bladder much longer. He squeezed the muscles in his legs together.

'OK', said the ant and nodded towards the door. The outside world lay there, tantalising and real. Gabriel knew that once he was outside the garage, he could force himself to forget the ant and return to the normal world of comic books and mama's ravioli. And he could pee.

He stood up and walked to the door. He wanted to run, but felt that he shouldn't show the ant how scared he was. He walked outside.

The world continued as normal. He could smell the bar
from the Choripan stall.

Then he turned and without knowing why, returned to
The ant was slipping on a baggy pair of trousers and tucking
oversized leather shoes.

'Excuse me', he coughed into his hand. 'I have a question.
Why not New York or Moscow or Britain? Why Buenos Aires?
exactly the centre of the world. In the films... the aliens alw
in America.'

The ant did not turn round but continued dressing: 'We onl
Spanish. We ants have a good understanding of English but w
speak it. Spanish is the only language we've truly mastered.'

'OK', said Gabriel. It didn't make much sense. But in the con
the day, that didn't seem to matter.

In a daze, he walked from the garage. Instead of walking back on
main road, he walked further down the alley until he found a
dustbin filled with cardboard. He hid behind the bin and undid
trousers. He peed noisily. Sweet relief. He watched it pooling at his
and spreading, dark as blood, across the dusty pavement.

He hastily did up his flies and walked hurriedly back onto Hipó
Yrigoyen. He turned his head as he walked past the garage. He did
want to see, didn't want to know. He walked and walked and walk
and didn't breathe out until he was four blocks away from the inse
that spoke.

May 22nd

The Rocazo is a savage wind that blows through north London. Every
year it tears up trees and destroys dry cleaners and bookmakers. It is a
very localised wind. In Muswell Hill it is legendary, but in Crouch End it
is totally unheard of. Some people do not believe in the Rocazo. These
people are fools. They would not believe in their own lungs if they did
not breathe.

I fear the Rocazo will come soon. But now I must leave the house in
search of sustenance. I may be some time.

May 24th

have been looking through my old letters. As a cult figure, random
rangers often feel the urge to correspond with me. Some of them use
mail but the majority send old-fashioned, hand-written letters. Very few
f them are correctly addressed. Sometimes the author just writes
THEMANWHOFELLASLEEP, A CAVE, LONDON on the envelope,
but somehow the letters reach me. The post office hates me – they make
ure every single letter arrives on time.

Most of the letters are drivel: women declaring undying love, men
asking me for advice and charities soliciting my participation in media
events.

Here is one letter:

*Dear Manwhofellasleep, ha ha, I've been watching you. You thing (sic)
your pretty funny, no? Well you're not funny. You're an idiot. My sister
says she saw you in a pub and you are short and ugly. I've got your
number.*

*By the way, you claim to be an expert on MARRIAGES, so why are
you still SINGLE?!? Haha ha ha ha.*

Yours truly, Dave.

I should get angry when I get these letters, but I can tell a cry for help
when I receive one.

May 25th

I have my theories. I have my theories about life and people and all the
other ephemera. They call me a fool. Well, talk is cheap. Show me the
Benjamins.

Let me tell you about my friend Frank. Frank works for the local
council, clearing up the borough. He is an enthusiastic and diligent
employee: no piece of litter is too small to be spiked and collected by
Frank. He has won numerous 'Employee of the month' awards because
of his dedication to his work. And he loves his work.

He feels he is making an active, worthwhile contribution to the community. Everyone knows him and appreciates what he does for the area.

Except... except when he is drunk. Not even drunk, merely when he has a drink. Whether a small glass of Merlot, a shot of Bell's whisky, even a half of shandy, he becomes a different person. His eyes glaze over. His voice lowers an octave and he acquires a different accent.

When he is in this state, he undoes all his good work. He rips apart rubbish bags and strews the contents across the streets. He takes empty cans of Coke and impales them upon railings. He tips ripped-up chairs over the fence into the scrubby foliage by Alexandra Palace station. He goes to the bottle bank and liberates the glass, smashing it across the pavement into the road.

When he awakens the next day, he has no recollection of his destructive actions.

Some people say that he bottles up his feelings, and that's why he screws things up when he is pissed. That is wrong. Frank is an agent of balance: he is subconsciously working to achieve cosmic alignment. He is an example of the forces that keep society in check. Sober, he is a force of order. Drunk, he is a force of chaos. To some degree we are all agents of balance: the doctor who treats his patients but beats up his wife, the accountant who fritters away her money in the pub, the comedian who wallows in sadness. We do and undo. Three steps forward, three steps back. It's like a nice dance. Only with more broken glass than the average dance floor.

May 26th

When I was a child, my parents would take me to the beach. They would splash around obscenely in the sea, throwing sea-horses at each other and then bury me in the sand. One time, they buried me up to my neck. Then they drove home. The tide came in, and if it weren't for the straws they'd placed in my nostrils, I would have drowned.

They had strange ways of showing love. They tested me and tested me, and eventually I failed.

May 28th

I was sitting at home, smoking Marlboro Lights and swigging from a bottle of Gaviscon when the doorbell rang. I found this peculiar because it was late, and because my doorbell is disconnected.

A pretty young woman was at the door. She had brunette hair and sparkly hazel eyes. She was wearing a woollen scarf and a pair of knitted pink mittens. She smiled and said that she wanted to know if she could depend on my vote in the local council elections.

I smiled back (never a good thing for me to do) and explained that she shouldn't need to depend on my vote. Surely there were other voters out there? What kind of campaign was she running if she needed to depend on *my* vote – was my one vote really going to make a difference? I am but one man!

She looked taken aback by my response, so I took advantage of her confusion to invite her in for a cup of tea. I told her that if she didn't come in for a cup of tea, I would definitely not be voting for her. She came inside. I reminded her of the old saying about Dracula, that she had entered freely and of her own will.

Once I had made the tea, I got down to the nuts and bolts and asked her about her campaign issues. What did she think of immigrants?

She politely told me that she thought that immigrants were a vital part of our workforce and boosted the local and national economies. She explained that there was a lot of scaremongering about immigration, but that the majority of immigrants were law-abiding citizens who wanted to contribute to society. I patted her on the head and said that she had answered correctly. Her hair was silky and smelt of henna.

Then I asked her what she thought of the moon.

She paused and looked at the floor. She hadn't touched her tea.

I repeated my question. Was the moon a threat? Was it friend or foe? Had she noticed the moon behaving strangely recently? Was the moon an overused metaphor in poetry and popular song?

Her voice cracking, she asked to leave. I told her that she had always been free to leave. She hurried out the door, her eyes moist with nascent teardrops. I told her that it had been a pleasure to meet her and pointed out that I was not registered to vote in local elections.

I hope to see her again soon. The older I get, the more I understand the importance of politics.

May 29th

Today Clark Kent came round for tea. He is such a klutz. He spilt the milk all over his trousers and then managed to knock over a vase while he was cleaning up. He will never amount to anything – not like that lovely Superman. Now, there's a real man.

May 30th

Welcome to themanwhofellasleep's writing masterclass. A lot of people ask me: how do I become a great writer? I tell them it's a lot like skiing. You need to own the right equipment, go to the right mountain and always wrap up warm and wear plenty of sunblock. It is a particularly poor analogy. I don't really understand allegories and metaphors. How can one thing be another?

I'll let you into a secret. I have no idea how to write. I just bang my head against the keyboard for 20 minutes and when I look up, a page has been written. (Note: piano players can also try this to write songs.) There is no real magic to writing, you just have to knuckle down and act the part. Try growing a beard and resenting mankind. It's a good start.

Writing. There is darkness and light, there is the banal and the exotic, and there is man and woman. All human stories are pitched somewhere between the poles, just as all human life is found between the North and South poles. Don't mention astronauts. They don't count.

There are only seven basic plots in writing. They all pit man (or woman, I will grudgingly concede) against various difficulties, and out of the conflict a story emerges. I'm not sure the research is entirely accurate, because Watership Down is a good book and it doesn't pit man against anything. It has rabbits in it instead. I suppose the animals are pretending to be human – it's what's known as anthropomorphism. Anyway, for the sake of argument, here are the plots:

1.   man v. nature
2.   man v. man
3.   man v. the environment
4.   man v. technology
5.   man v. the supernatural
6.   man v. self
7.   man v. God/religion

To these basic plots I would add my own variation:

8.   man does absolutely nothing

Stories where things actually happen seem very implausible to me. Personally, I do very little. In fact, on a good day I do very little, on a bad day I do nothing at all. Can you imagine how crowded and unpleasant life would be if it were really like stories, with all that adultery and jealousy and murder? Yet, apparently life is really like that! People actually get out of bed and *do things!* They marry each other and have children and start wars, and rape and pillage and build cathedrals and burn people at the stake.

Meanwhile, I skulk and hide, only venturing out to buy my cigarettes and to scan the newspapers for signs of impending doom. Yet, despite my reluctance to participate in life, I find myself unwillingly drawn into plots and subplots – and despite my war against narrative, I find that my actions have causes and effects that I cannot pull away from. If I have learned anything, it is that a man cannot escape his own story: the best he can do is reclaim authorship of his own life. But even then he's still got all that annoying peach-eating stuff to contend with. It hardly seems worthwhile.

June 1st

How large is the universe? How deep is the ocean? How big is the world? I will tell you.

The universe, the world, the nation – it is all my house. I was born in this house and I will die in this house. Nothing else exists. I have mapped every corner of this place; I have catalogued every crack in the floorboards, every snag in the carpet, every scratch on a wooden table. I know it all. I have maps and charts and diagrams, explaining routes around banisters and wardrobes. I have pressed my face into the carpet like a pope blessing the ground. I have marvelled at the fading of paint around light switches. I live in a beautiful world.

The television tells me of other lands. Of other houses, parallel universes that mirror my own. Of houses upon houses upon houses, stretching into a mathematical distance. I smile at the thought that there may be life in these other universes. But theory and hearsay are not enough. I cannot hold myths in my hands. I know only my own world, and it revolves around me, not around a painted sun or a sullen moon. I do not dream of streams or trees or cars that rumble into the silent night. I dream of the lacquer veneer on my desktop, of the fading green patterns of my mattress. I dream of real things, not of legends.

Adam was not lonely in Eden before God created Eve. He knew no other life. He was born in solitude and made the world his own.

And so it is with me. This is a world. I do not know a woman's salty lips pressed against my own. I do not find long, blonde hairs on my pillow. I do not hear waves crashing onto my shore. I know only the embrace of wood against my feet and wallpaper against my hands.

Am I unhappy in my universe? No. I am no explorer. This is enough. I do not dream of escape. My world is no smaller than anyone else's. The human mind expands and contracts to fit itself into the world. This is my house, my Earth, my universe. It is billions of miles in size – I will never chart it all.

June 2nd

In the centre of London, I approached a young policeman who must have been below regulation height.

'Young man', I said. 'I have urgent news! I believe that Ken Livingstone is in league with the evil Lord Voldemort.'

'You what?'

'Our 'beloved' mayor', I continued, 'is in league with forces dark and terrible. There is little time... I believe he has already obtained the Ankh of Sorrow and is planning to use it shortly.'

'You what?' he repeated. Not only was he short, but he was stupid too. 'Oh, never *mind*', I said, and went home to bed.

Things overheard on the tube

Today's journey:
Victoria Line: Seven Sisters–Brixton

1. Finsbury Park? What's a Finsberry?
2. It's a courtroom drama about a man whose cock has been cut off.
3. When the dog explodes... I swear... it's the funniest thing you'll ever see.
4. What? Do I have a sticker on my head saying 'Don't reply to my emails'?
5. They all turned her down, but if it had been in private, they'd have all said yes. I am telling you.
6. She was going on about being a barrier between the West and crypto-fascism.
7. Your rucksack is full of string. Did you have a knitting festival in there?
8. It takes a team of 200 elves 14 years to fix the escalators.
9. If you're a poet, you're basically unemployed, aren't you?
10. Abigail was wearing some kind of Dutch smock.

June 4th

I was stumbling through Wood Green, trying to pretend I was somewhere more pleasant, like Baghdad. A pretty, bespectacled young lady approached me.

'I can't help but notice that you are smoking Marlboro Lights', she said.

'So?' I replied.

'I am also smoking Marlboro Lights', she said. 'Don't you think that's unusual?'

'Not really', I said.

'You have very soulful eyes', she said, peering closer. I could feel her fragrant breath upon my face.

'I'm wearing contact lenses. I have almost no soul.'

'I find you very attractive', she continued. 'Can I make love to you?'

'I suppose so', I said.

We returned to my house and had perfunctory sex. She gasped in pleasure and writhed at my every indifferent touch. Afterwards, she said the experience had been the highlight of her life.

I suppose some men are just gifted.

June 5th

I slump. I slouch. I snore. I am overtaken by inertia. Time slows down and crawls onto my belly.

I am not going anywhere.

Is there any point in moving? In blinking? It's all such a terrible waste of energy. I was always led to believe that we reap what we invest in life. But the market is unsteady, I do not feel like investing. I shall hide my money under my mattress. I shall not tax myself unnecessarily.

June 6th

Success at last, I am to become a proper author! I have been approached by a publisher; my daring, cutting-edge journal has at last sparked its flame. In two years' time I shall own my own Lear jet and complain to Dr Phil about my crippling cocaine habit.

My publisher's name is Benjamin Fasto. He says he will pay me £1000 not to publish my journal. He says it's an 'abomination'. I must say I am flattered. He says it is his life's ambition to ensure that no more of my writing ever reaches the public domain. He says that he saw a vision in which an ecstatic Moses told him his mission in life was to stop me becoming a published writer. He doesn't even believe in Moses but was utterly convinced when he saw my journal.

I calculate that if every publisher in Britain stumps up a grand to stop me writing, I shall be financially secure for the rest of my days.

June 8th

Today I got a visit from the Albanian mafia.

They were two short, thick-set men in their early thirties, wearing shell suits. I answered the door and they muscled their way inside. I sat on the sofa and they stood over me, glowering. One of them spoke English, the other one just shrugged and grunted.

'You buy cigarettes, no?' said the English-speaking one. I nodded. He slapped a pack of Lucky Strikes onto the table.

'*We* buy the cigarettes around here', he stated. I nodded, looking warily at the packet.

'Last week you bought a carrot cake, no?' he asked. Once again, I nodded.

'*We* buy the carrot cake around here.' He signalled to his colleague, who reached into his flimsy plastic bag and pulled out a carrot cake. He tossed it onto the table.

The English-speaking one bent over and stared at me. 'I don't want to hear no more stories about you buying things. We do the buying in this neighbourhood. You want something, you tell us, we buy it for you.'

They left. I cut myself a slice of carrot cake. It was delicious.

June 10th

I sat in the library, eating a stale ham and pickle sandwich. Outside, a JCB lifted lumps of clay into a skip. The noise of the machine vibrated through the building, shuffling books off shelves and jiggering the coffee dispenser across the floor.

At the table behind me, two men were having an animated conversation. One of the men was fat and wore a Led Zeppelin T-shirt, and the other was skinny and licked the corner of his mouth as he spoke. I closed my eyes and prayed that the librarian would ask them to keep quiet.

'Yeah, it's not a bad film', said the fat man, running a fat palm through greasy hair. 'But where were the elves?'

'Yeah, I know what you mean', replied the skinny man. 'It's like *Citizen Kane*. Everyone raves about how great it is, but there are no elves at all. Not anywhere in the film.'

'I know. I know. It's like *Top Gun*. That was a film that would have been perfect for an elf. I mean, Tom Cruise is short, so... instead of making him a pilot, they could have easily made him an elf. It wouldn't have changed the plot that much.'

'Do you know how many films from last year featured elves?' said the skinny man, squeezing his nose.

'I am pretty sure I can guess!'

'Yep. That's right! None! There were like, 300 films, and none of them had elves in them! What kind of a world do we live in?'

'There's always *Lord of the Rings* – that's got elves.'

'Yeah, but we can't keep going on about Tolkien. We know he's a firm supporter of the elf. But it's no good just relying on him. We need modern films about elves. What about *Lost in Translation*? That could have had elves. They could have been in the background...'

At this point, I threw an encyclopaedia at the pair of them and stormed out.

I was sorely tempted to hijack the JCB and drive it into the library, but thankfully reason prevailed.

June 11th

This morning I woke up to find myself in bed with a beautiful koala bear. I don't know how she got there. She has the most enchanting eyes.

June 13th

The sky is dark and heavy with negative energy. My gate rattles on its hinges. I see shadows lurking by the sycamore trees.

Earlier, a man came round to read the meter. He was Indian, bald and middle-aged with fluffy, peaked sideburns. I answered the door naked. I had forgotten to put on any clothes. That's what happens when you live a life of hermitage, you forget social foibles such as clothes. I apologised and grabbed my pyjamas.

Once he was in the house, I rendered him unconscious with a single blow to the back of the head. Then I tied him to a chair and put the kettle on. I placed a packet of frozen peas on his bruised head, made a cup of tea and waited for him to come round. There is never any point in rushing these things.

An hour or so later he started to moan, so I handed him a glass of water and gave him my least-threatening smile.

'Sorry about all this', I apologised. 'But you can't be too careful.'

He looked at me in blind terror. I felt sorry for him.

I bent down and looked him in the eyes. 'Did Colonel Ramirez send you?'

'I... I don't understand. I am just here to read your meter... British Gas!' he sobbed.

'You're *quite* sure you don't have a message from Colonel Ramirez?'

'No... Why have you tied me up? I just want to read your meter. You're a crazy man. You can't just tie people up.'

I shrugged. I've had this kind of experience before. 'Your story sounds plausible enough, I suppose.' I pondered whether to untie him or not. 'You're quite sure that Colonel Ramirez didn't say anything about a microfilm?'

'I don't know any Mr Ramirez! I am coming here to read your meter. For God's sake, let me go!' he shrieked.

I sighed. It was a warm afternoon. I gently untied him and warned him that if he mentioned this afternoon to his superiors, he would be in very serious trouble. I opened the front door and he bolted fearfully into his British Gas van, before disappearing onto the High Street.

Of course, I was only winding him up with all that Colonel Ramirez nonsense. I don't know anyone by that name. But just think – this morning he was a 50-something meter reader, and now he is embroiled in international espionage. That's why I am an artist... I can pluck people from obscurity and give them a story.

June 15th

My journey into the occult continues apace. I have spent the previous 3 weeks researching the phantastic local history of London. I have discovered a shocking horror... an abomination known only as the *Floating Lawyer!*

Here is what the *Encyclopaedia Scatologica* has to say about this ungodly creature:

The Floating Lawyer – Was He Animal, Mineral or Dunstable?

During the 1830s and 1840s, this 'man' terrorised London, in Southern England. Described as short and stout and often seen wearing a knitted tie and an expensive Italian suit, this creature could hover 20–30 feet above the ground. It was reported that he had large pointy ears and red glowing eyes, and was capable of emitting a high-pitched keening noise like a sorrowful dolphin entering an overpriced art gallery.

The Early Sightings
The first sighting of the Floating Lawyer may have occurred in September of 1837 in Bow, east London.

A bearded businessman, Alfred Skips, was returning home from work late at night when a mysterious figure swooped down over the railings of a cemetery and jumped to the ground, landing directly in the path of Skips. He cackled madly and handed the man a business card, before flinging an old copy of **Wisconsin Lawyer Magazine** *at the startled victim. Skips was unhurt, but never slept again.*

A little while later, a creature matching the description of the Floating Lawyer was said to have attacked a group of people in Moorgate. All ran but Polly Glupp, who was left behind, paralysed by a fear of lawyers that had haunted her since early childhood when her parents had left her in a room with two elderly legal clerks. The Floating Lawyer ripped off the top of Polly's blouse, grabbed her breasts, and began to loudly harangue her about being topless in the streets, calling her a 'gangrenous trollop'.

The attacker then knocked Polly unconscious where she lay until being discovered by a stoat.

The Jenny Jupiter Incident

In October of 1842, Jenny Jupiter, a London servant, was returning to her employer's home on Horlicks Hill in south London. While passing through an alleyway, the Floating Lawyer sprang from behind some dustbins, wrapped his arms around her and commenced licking her face.

Local ugly men were alerted by Jenny's screams and quickly arrived on the scene. They searched for the assailant to no avail. Few believed Jenny's incredible tale of a legal beast from the skies.

The very next day, the Floating Lawyer struck again. The mysterious menace floated down in front of a passing horse-drawn carriage, causing the carriage to careen out of control and crash. The fiendish creature then issued a writ, claiming 50 guineas for the emotional damage caused by the incident.

Witnesses at the scene claimed that the Floating Lawyer left the scene by soaring effortlessly into the skies with swans tied to his ankles.

A few months later, in January 1843, London's Lord Mayor, Sir Cow Arthur, declared the Floating Lawyer both a 'public menace' and a 'great man'. A posse of yokels was formed to search for the individual responsible for the senseless attacks. It was during this time that the great Duke of Wellington, who was then 104 years old, joined in the search.

What was the Duke's connection with the ghastly creature? In recent years it has been suggested that the Floating Lawyer may have been the product of the Duke's undercover attempts to cross-breed solicitors with greenfinches. We will never know for sure: the Floating Lawyer was never found, and the Duke died the following year when his breathing apparatus become clogged with hair.

The Alsop Incident

Two days after the Duke joined the search, on February 22, 1843, buxom wench Theresa Alsop was in her home in East Finchley, north London, when she heard a knock on the door. A black-cloaked man outside exclaimed 'I'm a policeman. In the name of Allah, bring me a light, for we have caught the Floating Lawyer in the lane!'

Theresa went to fetch a light for the stranger at the door. She returned with a candle and as she was handing the light to the man, it shone on his face and she saw a ghastly, inhuman visage, devoid of human emotion. The horrific apparition let out a milk-curdling scream and gleefully chanted about a breach of his civil rights.

Terrified, Theresa tried to run back into the house but the beastly creature held on tightly to her hair. Theresa's father Gavin managed to drag her out of his grasp and back into the safety of the house. The Floating Lawyer continued banging on their door some time, shouting about intellectual property laws before vanishing into the night, apparently in a huff.

The Final Attacks

Things were quiet for many years before flaring up again during 1877 (coincidentally, the year of the great fire of 1877). In Kennington, south London, there were several reports of the Floating Lawyer travelling across the town by sailing slowly from rooftop to rooftop. Many reports indicated that the man was using a primitive Stanna Stairlift to scale the buildings.

In August of that year, the Floating Lawyer appeared before a group of soldiers in Basingstoke's North army camp.

Private Harold 'Harry' Harrison was standing sentry at the camp when he heard the noise of someone dragging a sack of gravel down the road. He went to investigate, but found nothing unusual and turned to return to his post. As he did, the Floating Lawyer leapt at him and clawed at his face with a sharpened shank bone. Other sentries heard the commotion and rushed to Harry's aid.

The soldiers claim that the Floating Lawyer escaped by simply leaping over them, clearing them by 10 feet or more. The sentries fired at the intruder and claimed that their bullets merely passed right through the creature like advice passing through a woman's ears. Private Harrison described the attacker as having the body of a man, but the face of a lawyer.

Theories Abound
Several theories explaining the origins of the Floating Lawyer have been proposed, but the lack of hard evidence leaves a dirty cloud of mystery hanging over this strange historical anomaly.

*Professor Chad Dixons offers our best explanation. In his **Almanac of Legal and Clerical Monsters**, Dixons notes that 'half-quid fancies' were very popular during the era. These magazines, similar to modern day comic books, often featured stories of the Floating Lawyer. The vivid tales may have so terrorised stupid, brainless, ordinary, working-class people that they simply imagined the apparition. What a cop out, eh! It was all just a dream!*

However, it should be remembered that even today lawyers exist, and that despite the strides mankind has taken in ridding ourselves of this unseemly scourge, few of us would be surprised if the Floating Lawyer were to return.

So, there you go. The Floating Lawyer. What an entirely irrelevant episode.

June 16th

Today it rained. It rained and I got wet. It didn't stop raining all day; it was like an epic Charlton Heston scene. It got me thinking about the great flood and the rainbow that appeared afterwards. I reflected upon God's covenant with man that he would never flood the world again.

It is a rather pointless promise. God is so powerful, he can destroy the world in a million different ways. Simply agreeing not to flood the world hardly limits his choices. He can still use earthquakes, tidal waves, stray comets and nuclear bombs. It's like a wife-beater promising that he will only hit women with his right hand.

Poor old mankind is on a hiding to nothing.

June 17th

The Shadow looms large over me. He is present in his absence. He torments me with his silence.

But there are worse things than the Shadow. I was sitting outside a pub when I saw her. She was dressed as Hitler and screaming obscenities at passing children. I ducked into the pub and hid there until I was sure she had gone. Even then, when it was dark and the streets were deserted,

I couldn't relax.

It was a close call.

I don't want to say too much about her. She used to go out with me before everything went wrong. The past is unbearable.

June 19th

What is a man? Is he defined by his genetic history, or by the choices he makes? Is he nature or nurture?

I don't know. A man is meat. Pork. Beef. Lamb.

Some men are less than meat. They think they are meat. They taste like meat and smell like meat, but they are less than meat. They are Quorn. They are imitations. They pass through life as paler versions of other men. Up close they look like chicken and mushroom Pot Noodles. If you fill them above the water level, they are soupy and bland. Cut them and they do not bleed. They leak a thin, oily substance like old soup stock.

June 21st

Jokes. Jokes.

Not all jokes are funny. Some are tragic. For example, when someone else is run over by a steamroller, it's funny. When it happens to you, it's not so funny. In fact, it normally kills you, although not always. Sometimes you end up very flat, but survive. That's also sad.

Someone once told me that jokes are nature's 'false alarm' system. We laugh at trivial disasters. When a man falls down stairs and ends up with an egg sandwich on his face, we laugh. When a man falls down stairs and snaps his neck and dies, we aren't supposed to laugh. I am not quite sure that humour works like that. To prove it, here are some sad jokes.

Man: Doctor, I've broken my leg.
Doctor: I'm afraid it is a very bad break. You will never walk again.

Policeman: Knock, knock.
Woman: Who's there?
Policeman: The police. I'm afraid there's been an accident. Your husband has been killed.

There's an Englishman, an Irishman and a Scotsman. They are all trapped in a jail cell.
Eventually they all starved to death.

Why did the chicken cross the road?
To escape the Nazis.

A man walks into a pub.
He is an alcoholic whose drink problem is destroying his family.

Did you hear about the blonde who jumped off a bridge?
She was clinically depressed and took her own life because of her terribly low self-esteem.

What do you call a cat with no tail?
A Manx cat.

Why do undertakers wear ties?
Because their profession is very serious, and it is important that their appearance has a degree of gravitas.

How many electricians does it take to change a lightbulb?
One.

Why do women fake orgasms?
Because they want to give men the impression that they have climaxed.

Two men are sitting in a pub.
One man turns to the other and says: 'Last night I saw lots of strange men coming in and out of your wife's house.'
The other man replies: 'Yes, she has become a prostitute to subsidise her

drug habits'.

Did you hear about the Irishman found under a shop?
Yes, he was killed and buried there. It was gang-related.

Man: What a beautiful dog. Does he bite?
Dog owner: No.
Man: Can I pet him?
Dog owner: No, he has a form of eczema that makes his skin weep if touched.

How can you tell when an Essex girl wants sex?
She displays signs of arousal, such as enlargement of the clitoris and swelling of the labia.

What's the difference between a Rottweiler and a poodle?
There are many differences. They are two totally different breeds of dog.

What do you get if you cross a horse and a donkey?
A mule.

A priest and a rabbi are sitting next to each other on a plane.
However, it is a short flight and they do not talk to each other.

What do you call a man with a spade in his head?
You call him an ambulance. He may have fractured his skull.

How can you tell if a gay man has visited your house?
He remembers the location of the house the next time he visits.

June 22nd

At the age of 20 I stopped learning things. I was a jar filled to its brim. Any more knowledge would have caused an overflow and horrific spillage. Instead of learning things, I combined old pieces of information and polished them to make them sound like new facts. I recycled old thoughts and peddled them to anyone who hadn't heard them before.

Philosophers overstate the importance of thought. Thought is not what drives man. Man is driven by urges. Thoughts play only a peripheral role in man's destiny.

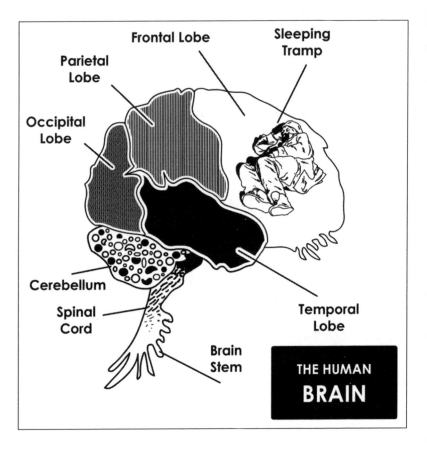

Frontal Lobe

Sleeping Tramp

Parietal Lobe

Occipital Lobe

Cerebellum

Spinal Cord

Brain Stem

Temporal Lobe

THE HUMAN **BRAIN**

June 23rd

Today I went to a coffee shop. There was a bewildering array of coffees on offer. Big coffees, small coffees, black coffees, white coffees, straight coffees and gay coffees. I asked for a cup of tea.

I sat at the table facing the window and watched the world walk by. An old woman grimaced and sat down next to me. I was piqued – there were plenty of empty tables and I don't like company when I am taking my tea.

As people get older they tend towards physical extremes. In particular, old women either become thin and skeletal-brittle or fat and comedy-padded. My table-mate was one of the fatties. Her headscarf that made her look like an inflatable gypsy palm-reader.

'What would you say if I told you I can foresee the future?' she said, stroking her bulbous nose.

'I wouldn't say anything. I would carry on drinking my cup of tea. I would try my hardest to ignore you.'

'I knew you would say that. Because I can see into the future', she replied with a smug smile.

'Ah yes, but now it's the past, isn't it? Anyone with decent vision can see into the past. And the future is just the past waiting to happen', I said. I had no idea what I was talking about, but I hoped it would confuse her.

'You sleep a lot, don't you?' she said.

'No. I hardly sleep at all.' I tipped my hot tea into her lap and left the shop in a hurry. I get tired of these conversations. And I get sick of people seeing me in my pyjamas and jumping to erroneous conclusions.

June 24th

More adverts. Someone somewhere is always trying to sell me something.

MONDO CALYPSO!
When Elvis Presley sang 'Since my baby left me, I've found a new place to dwell, it's down at the end of lonely street, at Heartbreak Hotel', he was uncannily prescient. We do live in Heartbreak Hotel and it is located at the end of Lonely Street.

We live in an ever-more-stressful age, where many of us are prey to anxiety, depression and countless neuroses. So far there has been little or no research into how to make misery profitable.

With MONDO CALYPSO's new MISERY = MONEY formula, you can turn your depression into a profit in less than 30 days, or your money back!

MONDO CALYPSO'S revolutionary new guide My Death is Your Death examines how depression affects emotions, behaviour, and relationships and discusses cost-effective and profitable ways of whining, griping and sighing.

Remember: You are not alone. There are millions of suckers out there, waiting to be fleeced with your new-found ability to complain incessantly.

Are you tired of spending your days at work moaning about how bad things are, only to pick up a meagre pay-cheque at the end of the month? Do you feel that your misery is wasted? Trust MONDO CALYPSO to show you how you can make yourself feel better by making everyone else feel worse. And fast!

YOU WILL NOT RECEIVE YOUR MONEY BACK

June 27th

I have been on holiday in Cornwall. It wasn't like London at all. Every day I wandered down to my local tube station and waited for a train. It never came. Apparently it wasn't a tube station at all, just an abandoned mine. It was dark, but I wasn't scared.

How strange the change from major to miner.

Things overheard on the tube

Today's journey:
WAGN: Alexandra Palace–Moorgate, then Northern Line to Bank, then DLR to South Quay.

1. I had to explain that gazpacho was any cold soup, not just cold tomato soup.

2. The civil service is full of reformed Goths and Indie kids.
3. Are you joking? Because it's not funny.
4. Never ask a woman why she's angry.
5. It's sad when people have multiple abortions.
6. Natasha Bedingfield is just Daniel Bedingfield with a wig. It's like Michael Jackson and Janet Jackson. They're the same person.
7. I've been coughing like that all week.
8. You are a nice girl, but you're never going to make it as a diagnostic radiologist.
9. It's a litre of beer... It's definitely more than a pint.
10. Will Young is gay.

June 29th

OK. He's gone out. Themanwhofellasleep has left the building. So I am writing in here instead. This is themanwhofellasleep's flatmate. I've been reading this stupid journal of his whenever he goes out. He hasn't mentioned me. He never mentions anything real. It's all lies and student magical-realism bollocks. Well, now I am writing. This is not some fantasy about celebrities and talking animals. This is real life. This is my life. Fuck him.

The evening is an orange blur of fog and sunsets. It's too late. My eyelids can't stay open. I shouldn't be writing, but I don't know when I'll next get the chance. I'm tired. I have been walking around in circles all day, scared of bumping into myself. I keep on opening beers and then leaving them dead and stagnant on the kitchen table. It's a crying shame. It's very easy to sneer at self-help books and therapy or counsellors. So I've decided to carry on doing just that. It certainly beats changing my life.

Tonight, I can't sleep. I lie in bed and read the TV guide – mainly films on satellite that I won't get to see. Satellite television depresses me. I don't know why. You can't get cable in the flat. No unsightly satellite dishes allowed. I hate not having it. It really pisses me off. And it's getting worse now, what with cable and digital TV, there is so much top-quality programming just passing me by. Live sports, football, the poker channel,

CNN. I dream of that kind of shit. And the channels are multiplying, they're breeding in the night. I wake up and there's 10 more channels to choose from: cartoons, 24-hour news, MTV, MTV2, MTV Bass, MTV fucking Klezmer, for all I know. And I'm missing it all, stuck here on planet Earth with a dick of a flatmate, five channels and the remote control. Even the Italian fucking football has disappeared. It's just me and indoor bowls and the sunless afternoons. It's not fair.

My head is full of popping and fizzing, like a soft drink advert. It feels as though my existence is entirely sponsored by Coca-Cola, such is the effervescing in my head. I can't sleep; you try sleeping when all you can hear is the distant rattling of paper clips and tube trains. I'm 35 years old. I can retire in 30 years and buy a house in the country and take pot-shots at passing tourists. I am old. I already feel like an old man. I'm sick of wanking, and sex seems out of the question at the moment. No, sex is not a friend of mine. Indeed, sex will not even look me straight in the eye anymore. It is all just rumour and office gossip: sex is something that happens to other people, like car crashes or winning the lottery. Even *he* has more sex than me.

I pop a sleeping pill, one of the cheap, over-the-counter, non-prescription types that has the advantage of not upsetting my stomach. The disadvantage is that it doesn't send me to sleep. No, the sleeping pill does work in that it gives me some moral high ground from which I can sneer at the pharmaceutical industry. One day I shall compose a list of all the industries that have betrayed me throughout my life and believe me, the pharmaceutical industry will be top. Potions, lotions, creams, pills, injections, tonics, enemas, suppositories – I've taken the lot and none of them have helped: I'm still me. I'm still here and I still don't like it. At least I know I have problems, not like that schmuck who fell asleep.

It's getting worse. On a night like tonight I can really notice that my hair is growing thin. I don't look good... I always expected to look like my father, but I seem to have skipped a generation and gone straight for my granddad. At the moment, lying in bed, scribbling in this notepad, you'd be hard pressed to tell the difference between my grandfather and me, and he's dead, so I've got to be doing something wrong.

I moved in here 2 years ago. A year ago I cut down on my drinking. Six months ago I gave up smoking and I've felt terrible ever since. I tell you, never give up smoking. Your body won't forgive you. Sure, your chest might feel looser and your bowels will no longer clog up. You might get rid of that 10-year lingering cough and the yellow fingers, but don't let that fool you: your body wants smoke and it will let you know. And so, pretty soon your knees will go and you'll trap your fingers in the door of a taxi. You'll shit yourself in the street. You'll cum too soon in bed or not cum at all. You'll get nosebleeds when you speak in public. All these symptoms can be indirectly attributed to abandoning tobacco. Your body will get revenge. It always does. Vengeance is not mine, it is everyone else's.

Anyway, I gave up smoking for the same reason I started smoking, to annoy the people around me. Fifteen years ago everyone was smearing yoghurt on their arse, knitting their own Ryvita and jogging to work with their new-born kids in a Peruvian papoose, so I decided to start smoking. I suppose it was out of pettiness or hatred or whatever... you have to understand that I was never a social smoker. I was always very much an antisocial smoker. So now that all my contemporaries are dizzy London media whores with a fag in one hand, a cocktail in the other and a kilo of cocaine holding their nostrils apart, I have decided to jack it all in and start breathing pure air again. As I said, it doesn't feel good to give it up, it is very much a sacrifice. Don't let anyone tell you that there is no longer such a thing as human sacrifice: I'm human and I make a sacrifice every time I get out of bed. I sacrifice my sleep, my sobriety, my sex life, my money. I am a walking paragon of resentful virtue. Or I would be if I did any walking. I should be getting pissed in some wine bar, not sitting here at home.

What with the buzzing of my faulty conscience, the inane mutterings of my flatmate, the crackling of my headache and the insidious whisperings of my self-esteem, you would think there was no space for more noise. But you would be wrong.

I am blessed not only with a sleepless mind but also with nocturnal neighbours. They moved in 8 years ago and set about publicly constructing the perfect model family. This involves loud sex and loud hammering. The sex I can forgive, but the DIY really gets me down.

For about a year now, every moment of silence has been punctuated by the rat-a-tat of a nail-gun, the subsonic buzzing of a chainsaw and the thump of hammer against fragile plaster. Oddly, it only ever stops when I leave the house. Otherwise, it is incessant. If I should pause for a moment when I emerge from the shower, they are waiting with pliers and a monkey wrench. If I switch off the radio, I am assaulted by the wailing of dogs pining for supper or the hapless mother hollering at the children. They are colonising my mind. I cannot park my car outside because there is a builder's van and two hatchback cars – with matching roof-racks and 'Give My Child A Chance' stickers – in front of the flat. I can't sit in the garden for fear of children leaning over the fence and pointing at me, like I was a circus freak show. And not only are they content to breed at a rate which embarrasses passing Catholics, they seem to have sequestered elderly grandparents and long-lost uncles to fill out the house and save on the cost of babysitters. The place looks like the YMCA. They just never stop making noise. I am living in a waking nightmare in which the volume control of my existence has gone haywire and every act occurs as loudly as humanly possible. I just want some quiet. Some sleep.

In summer I used to leave my bedroom window open. That was a mistake. I liked the idea of getting some fresh air, but I got more than I bargained for. Every morning I would be woken at sunrise not by the gentle chirrup of birdsong but by the screaming of sugar-crazed toddlers, shooed outside to cause chaos on the decking that now faces my window. The noise haunts me. On bad nights it reduces me to tears and muffled, whining screams. The hellish screech of tricycle and skateboard against wood! The sound follows me... even at work... even in bed. Some people are born too sensitive, and some people are born to be fucking inconsiderate cunts. There seem to be a lot of them about.

It's affecting my head. Silence sounds unnatural to me; I know it is only the prelude to a crying child or a howling dog. Hitchcock said that terror wasn't hearing a loud bang, it was hearing silence and anticipating the bang. When I'm alone I find myself making my own noise, a low awkward clunking and squawking. I am just filling in the blanks. I am just defending myself. The neighbours' noise is a battering ram against my skull: it is a reminder of their ever-spreading territory. They may as well just come over and piss on my carpets and get it over and done with. I am being annexed out of my own life. They want to hurt me, I know it. I can feel it in my gut. At night they leave their dogs tethered in the front room – they bark incessantly and drive me underneath my covers, underneath the pillows, underneath the sheets, underneath the bed. I bite my hands and I can't focus on the garden without feeling sick. My head is a football. Go on, kick it.

Now I know what you're thinking. You're thinking that here I am, all on my own, lonely and bitter and slithering towards premature middle-age. And of course I must be jealous of this happy little family with their friends and their dinner parties and their daily adventures. Well, close... but you're still full of shit. I am not like that. I am not like that at all. I am not jealous; I am quite content to fall apart in my own squalid boredom, because I do it *quietly*. I do everything quietly – it's my new commandment. I'm going to sneak into hotels and scrawl it into the bibles: Whatever you do in life, thou shalt do it quietly. Too fucking right. Turn down the volume and have a look around you. There are people trying to sleep. There are people trying to fall apart with dignity.

(Why should you believe me any more than him? Any more than that charlatan who fell asleep?)

Yeah, don't listen to me. I don't make any sense to myself, so I don't know why you have invited yourself in here to eavesdrop. If you're snooping around looking for some wisdom then look elsewhere. There's no room at the inn, you'll have to sleep in the barn. My head feels like a watermelon. Like I said, I'm full of shit, but you're the one listening. Let me make one thing clear, these words, these spaces, this incessant jabbering of nouns and verbs – it isn't art, it's attrition. The second I shut up I start thinking, and when I start thinking the serious fucking problems start to set in.

It is 3 a.m. and time has started going backwards. The pillows, the damp sheets, the old wallpaper. They are little reminders of my debt to the twenty-first century. My little pact with progress that keeps me alive and keeps me awake. I have spent enough money in my time; you would imagine that I would have invested a little something in the security of my future. I should be sitting on a nice little nest egg. But no... no... no. Nothing like that. Everything I own is a short-term investment, a shot at getting through the day. I buy; therefore, I am. Sometimes I see CDs in shops reduced to half price and, even though I already own them, I feel compelled to buy them again just so that I can feel like a man who bought a bargain. A man who lives on the winning side of life.

I inspect the bric-a-brac of my existence: CDs I never play, food that I never eat, clothes I never wear, all bought to soothe my consumer conscience. I am pissing away my future on one-night-stands at Ikea and HMV. It doesn't amount to much of a life. What would my wife (my ex-wife) say about me? She would say that I was an overweight sack of excuses and one-liners that in a flattering light might make me look a bit like a nice guy. And I wouldn't disagree, except to piss her off.

I should have a drink, a small glass of Scotch or something, but I don't like to mix it with the sleeping pills. What a coward, eh? Alcoholics have it easy.

What can we do but sleep? The sniffle of an invisible cat, the rumble of distant trains, the shouts and whispers of the High Street. All the noises of the night are here; the epic soundtrack to my sleeplessness. I can't keep my mind on anything. I drift in and out of consciousness.

Do you ever think about the patterns that appear before your eyes before you go to sleep? I do. I don't think they're just random blobs and flashes; they must mean something. I don't know what they signify yet, I haven't cracked the code – the intermittent vision of a thousand tiny pin-pricks on the wrong sides of my eyes, or the cascading set of multicoloured ball bearings which sometimes roll at me as I am about to nod off. I guess they must be there for a reason, other than a brain tumour or dandruff on the eyes. In theory, they should have some grand cosmic significance; they should hand me the secrets to a long and happy life. They always remind me of the ink-blot tests you get in crap Hollywood psycho-dramas: The Rorschach tests which the police shrink will show to the serial killer in order to defrost his brain. As the patterns flash before my eyelids, I try to figure out all the shapes and formats, the strings and squares and changing colours. Sometimes they appear as animals, sometimes as friendly faces. If I concentrate they absorb the shape of vintage cars, all polished headlights and gleaming running boards. I don't know why. It works the wrong way round for me: I see the things in my waking life as shapeless blobs, ink blots on my spectacles. Where there is form, I see shapeless interference. Everything blurs into a painful mess. That's the curse of a short-sighted childhood.

Tonight I skip the amateur dramatics and take another sleeping pill. Like I said, they're pretty weak. I might as well chew Tic-Tacs.

I regret everything. I regret getting up in the morning and going to sleep at night. I regret marrying my wife and I regret divorcing her. I regret coffee, tea and daytime TV. I regret smiling when I should have frowned. I regret shaving my chest. If I could go back in time and change it all, I would do it in an instant. Sometimes I even regret things I haven't done yet, in anticipation of my future failures.

People tell me – often pub philosophers or football pundits on the telly – that you only regret things you didn't do rather than things you did do. Well, I regret both. I regret things that I know I couldn't have avoided, and that aren't even my fault. I regret the fact that I was a gutless child, clinging to my mother and the safety of home. I should have been out in adventure playgrounds, grazing my knees and wrestling with the older boys. But that was never my style – even as a kid I was a terrible snob. You see all those idiots in the newspapers, giving their interviews with their smiling photos and they always roll out the same lines: *Regrets? No. Without my mistakes, I wouldn't be the man I am now.* Well, I don't want to be the man I am now, so you can take my mistakes and stick them up your arse. I would happily swap my life for a fresh one, full of unblemished potential. There is definitely something to be said for self-pity. It isn't self-respect, but it's cheaper and from a distance you can't tell the difference.

So, it's now quarter past four in the morning and I am still not asleep. To be more accurate, I am awake. So I am thinking about myself, like there was ever anything else to think about. I am picking at my ego like a hang nail. Please don't dismiss my anxieties as post-adolescent posturing. I have been growing up all my life and look where it has gotten me. Here. Exactly the place I didn't want to be. I'll tell you something for free: you are never too old to be totally wrong about everything. So if you want to win something in life, you put your money on the young guy. Because the older I get the more opinions I hear in my head, and the less I recognize the one that's telling me the truth.

'Self-pity!' I hear you cry. Well, there is self-pity here, but it's no worse than being a smug, self-satisfied moron. Tonight I am mining a deep vein of self-pity, dredging up all that nasty loathing that sits in my stomach. Yeah, we all do it. I know we all suffer the same way. I've got the same life as you, the same responsibilities, the same loves, the same mortgages and anxieties. I'm just a little less enthusiastic about the whole maturing business. Be honest, who are you doing it for? Your friends? Your family? You're doing it for someone, but it probably isn't yourself. When you're alone and you've stripped away the kids and the pine furniture and the art prints on the wall and the practical car, you tell me that you believe in all that shit any more than me. You tell me that you don't think life is an empty lie full of empty people, empty thoughts and ugly endings. You tell me that if you could get away with the rape and the murder and the money, you wouldn't go for it. Well, you can tell me, but I won't believe you.

No, I don't think so. You want the maturity and the beautiful wife and the fulfilling job and the healthy dose of red wine and pasta, and you want so badly to believe that whole society–media Sunday supplement shit that we're all moving in the right direction, that everything is going to be alright. Well, forgive me for my immaturity, but I don't think so. Everything is not going to be alright. Everything is going to be wrong. Everything is going to gnaw away at my ankles like an angry little beaver. Life is going to catch up with me and kill me, and I have to confess that I'm not at all happy with the deal. I can't even ask for my money back. Where are my arrows of desire? Where is my chariot of fucking fire? It's so hot in here. Sometimes when I can't sleep I switch ends of the bed, just to get a different perspective on life, but tonight I've crawled around the bed so much I've exhausted the novelty. I can't tell one end from the other.

So I never did get to mature. *Mature.* What a lovely word. Like a fine wine, like good cheese, like fruit falling off the trees in autumn. No, I skipped all that and just started rotting. I have mildew and dry rot. The house is falling apart. What hope is there for the future if your house won't stand up straight and look you in the face? It sees me and starts crying.

I reluctantly get out of bed and pace around the bedroom, like a paunchy boxer looking for a shadow to hit. All the porn I'll ever need has been downloaded and saved on CD. The internet is off. I hit the bathroom. Inside the cabinet are the bottles and boxes that make up my proudest collection. The tablets are lined up in pairs by the mirror, like they're waiting for Moses to come down and read them: tablets for migraines, for stress, for stomach complaints, for constipation, for diarrhoea, for depression, for anxiety, for happiness, for richer, for poorer, for better or for worse, in sickness and in health. I am married to my medicine. I must confess that my happiest moments are at the doctor's surgery, when my throat is being probed or my temperature is being taken or when I am being asked to slowly exhale. I love it, I really do. All they ask of me is that I am ill, and I so rarely disappoint. There's no right or wrong answers, there's only me coughing into a handkerchief.

I have splashed my face with cold water and washed behind my ears. I can hear a slow regular tapping coming from the water boiler. I guess that I am still awake. I talk about myself a lot, don't I? You find me a woman and maybe I'll shut up.

Women, where do I begin? At the beginning? Is that too easy for you?

Women. You try to grow up for them. You try to prove that you're not just some kid trying to talk your way into their pants. You show you care. You're on the side of the angels. You have hidden depths. You have the ability to relate to a fellow human being on an emotional level without flinching. You can cook. You can change your underwear without parental prompting. You can smile at adversity. Touching, no?

I'm painting a beautiful picture of the guy I tried to be. It didn't work out. I couldn't keep it up. I always thought there would be a moment when women ceased to be pornography and someone somewhere waved a magic wand and women would become human; the vital statistics and possessions and power would happily give way to love and tenderness and compassion. Well, needless to say, it didn't happen. There was never a day of revelation; there was never a magic moment when love wove its spell over me. At least now I know who I am. No, maybe my heart wants love, and maybe my mind wants approval, but my cock still wants the amphetamine buzz of pornography: the slags and whores and prick-teases of my under-fed imagination are still running the show. I think back to my early twenties. No matter how I rearranged my girlfriends, how I posed them and framed them with my pornographic eye, something was missing, something cheap and nasty and compelling. The vulgar glossiness of the intrusive photograph, the cackling shutter of the hardcore; love soothed me and touched me, but it left me soft as butter. Only hate ever made me hard. The brutal truth. I suppose that is the real beauty of porn: it leaves you hard and it leaves you alone. You always end up alone, fingers on the mouse, trousers around your ankles. Ah, but I still have my pride!

Pornography has never abandoned me and I have never had the heart to abandon it. Even when I chucked out the magazines, the pornography was still there in my mind, in my bed, in my drunken leer, in the parts of my mind I didn't let show at Sunday soirées, in the lists and the money and the dirt beneath my nails. No, love offered itself to me and I had turned around and hurried away. No love. No women. No beautiful wife. No children playing in the beautiful garden. It was the only decision I could make. If you have to choose between your rational brain and your urges, there's only going to be one winner.

I've got friends who are dads, and I hear all that shit about babies and how childbirth has finally put their life into perspective and how they've had a spiritual awakening and how they really didn't know the meaning of love before they had kids, and everything melts into this soppy soft-focus portrait of loveliness, a million miles away from my life, from the static and the mobile phones and the incessant bleating of the neighbours and the panic attacks on the tube. I don't buy it. These guys, they're still looking after number one. Don't get me wrong, I try my best to fake the lifestyle. I've tried romance, but I always end up with the junk food and the bottle of generic cola, the pizza crusts and the tracksuit trousers. The second cheapest wine on the menu. Everywhere I go there's this smell of desperation. I can't fake the smell of success. So don't call me immature, I've just not got the appetite to swallow all the lies at once. I can only swallow one load of bullshit at a time. And I have to live with you-know-who, so I get to deal with an awful lot of bullshit.

The curtains are dead in the air. There is no breeze tonight, just the hot dust of the early hours and the insects on the window sill. London is grinding its teeth in its sleep. I suppose that while I'm in the confessional mood, I should state for the record that I can't have children. Yes, you heard me. I'm not saying it again. No, I'm not asking you to cry for me or consider me in a softer, more sympathetic light. I am firing blanks. You've seen it all before on the daytime soaps and the afternoon talk-shows. In all honesty, when the doctor told me, it was at least a partial relief. I have never wanted kids. My sex-life was always ruined by my fear that I'd knock my girlfriends up. I needn't have worried. Hysterical.

I kill another sleeping pill. I am drying up, my throat is full of phlegm. All the words I have eaten are sticking in my gullet and choking me up. God, I hate that fucker and his bloody journal. Well, ha ha, *I* am writing now. Damn you. Oprah Winfrey and Ricki Lake, where are you now? I should be crying on your shoulders like a sick little puppy. Oprah, Ricki and me in bed with the remote control and a bucket of chicken wings and fries. That's proper therapy. That's it ladies, take your clothes off, don't be scared. You shouldn't hate each other, there's only me to be scared of. That's it, snuggle up close. Tell me about your problems, let me inside your heads. It's alright baby. No, it's not alright. Nothing will ever be alright again. My head is ringing like it's New Year's Day. I cannot wait for him to read this. I cannot wait to see his face.

I have now stopped counting up from midnight, and started counting down towards seven, when the alarm will go off. Every morning when I look in the mirror it feels like a fresh insult: God has not improved me in the night. I could stop complaining, but where the hell would that get me? I've run out of jokes. I've got a million punchlines and a glass jaw. There is something warm and sickly trying to get out of my stomach. And this pen is running out of ink.

The sky is pale and streaked with grey clouds and fading streetlights. I can hear the world yawning. Another day. Smile! Of course, things aren't really so bad. Here I am with a nice house, nice job, nice car, nice nails bitten down to the bone. I have a nice life, I just fill it with bad things. Things aren't all bad. Just me. I could tell you a few stories that would make you like me, but I am not going for the sympathy vote. Tonight has been an exercise in honesty, self-pity and vengeance.

Do you ever wonder why life is like this? Why we are all so unhappy? I have so many wonderful answers to so many fascinating questions and yet when I wake up in the morning I can hardly remember my own name. And the worst is yet to come. However bad I feel now, I am cushioned by money and youth and health and all those other great things. It can only go downhill from now. I need to strap on my skis.

I have wiped the sleep out of my eyes and trudged downstairs in my underwear (Calvin Klein) to make coffee. I am quite tempted to throw this journal away. But even I am not that cruel. Still, it will give him something to read. Something to ponder when he's not making up shit about celebrities.

Little things remind me of her. A scent or a laugh.

There's always a woman, isn't there? In any of these stories, there's always a bird. *Cherchez La Femme*. So, yes, I am thinking of her. It's not some sentimental catalogue of kisses, just the fact that she is still alive somewhere, living her life somewhere else. It doesn't make me happy, it doesn't even make me that sad. It just makes me wonder.

The new day is here, a little light that shines on my pillow. I have fished through the laundry bin for some socks. There is a loose bolt in my spine and a scraping noise in my ears. I can feel the blood swimming around my face, uneven and sweaty.

Some words of advice: things aren't really that bad. Most people cope.

The wooden table in the lounge has one leg shorter than the rest. I've stuck some card underneath to balance it, but that now seems to have disappeared. He probably nicked it. Never mind. I drink my coffee, some new brand that tastes like the cheap stuff, only more expensive. What's a guy to do? All that money... all those years, I thought I could buy my way out of jail.

The night is over and I have survived. What will I do today? Maybe a walk in the park, the rain against my face? A day spent in the sunshine, lazing with the insects and the buttercups? A day to smile at the simple pleasures of everyday existence? A day spent indoors waiting for my head to boil over, waiting for the chance to shoot myself down? It makes no difference to me. I expect you're bored of all this middle-class angst. I certainly am. I'd start crying, only I wouldn't know what to do with the moment once it's ended. I can hear a voice in my brain, like the vibrant hum of electricity. Goodbye. Good fucking riddance. Good morning. I am handing you back to the idiot. He'll deny I even exist.

June 30th

Paedophiles are *everywhere!*

I cannot leave the house without seeing one. They wander the high street. They lurk in bushes in the park. They sit at bus stops, their pallid yellow skin illuminated by the oncoming traffic. At night I can hear them shuffling around my garden, their unholy groans lost in the twilight. In the mornings, I find strips of flesh on the lawn; their bodies often disintegrate as dawn approaches.

When I was young, there were few paedophiles. Of course, there were dirty old men, but they were kindly, avuncular figures, like neighbourhood butchers or clowns. They were no threat to anyone. I don't know what is wrong with society today, but I blame the internet.

These paedophiles are masters of disguise. They could be anyone, at any time, in any place. I recommend extreme vigilance. What is really needed is some kind of public-spirited campaign by the press, to identify and eliminate the paedophiles. But alas, it never happens: the newspapers fear that too many innocent men would be swept up in a witch-hunt. I admire the restraint of the press, but this is a war.

July 2nd

I spent the day pretending to be Philip Marlowe, the hard-talking hero of Raymond Chandler's detective novels. It was fun. Everyone should try it.

Sure, I was drunk.

I was drunk because I'd seen her again. She looked like every bad dream I'd ever had. She was beautiful. There are four kinds of brunette and she was all of them: the coy brunette who hides behind building sites, but kisses like a jellyfish; the happy brunette who shrieks with laughter whenever you open your mouth; the silent, seductive brunette who rarely speaks, but has a smouldering car bonnet; and the confident, sexy brunette, whose lips can unscrew corks. Carla was all of these things and more. When I saw her I remembered why I had crashed my car into an ice cream van as a teenager.

'Jacket potato or chips?' she murmured. Her voice was like a Mexican in the breeze.

'Daddy loves you, sweetheart, but daddy won't always be here to protect you. And there are some things that money can't buy.' I looked at her from across the room. For an instant she looked like a scared child. I blinked. She looked normal again.

'Would you like a jacket potato or chips with your meal, sir?' She was playing hardball. She reminded me of Tito Menendez before he lost his rhythm during the Hungry Hippos of the thirties. San Francisco can do that to a man.

'You crack wise a little too often, sweetheart. I'm one of the good guys. The boys down at the station might not be so understanding.' The boys down at the station would be far from understanding. Back then the lieutenant was Rupert Burns, a podgy beaver of a man who could open doors with his breath. He had made lieutenant the only way you can in Frisco, by breaking necks and dancing to the right tune. I didn't like him and he didn't like me. He didn't even know who I was. Three years later Burns was killed when his chauffeur parked too near to Poland. But back then he seemed immortal and you didn't answer back to him.

'The jacket potato comes with a selection of fillings, or you can just have chips.' She pulled out her pad. She put it down. She grimaced, remembering; trying to forget. 'I'll get you chips. Would you like anything to drink?'

I looked at a fingernail and smiled very faintly. I spoke in a clear, menthol voice: 'Maybe it's money that has turned you bad. Maybe it was the moonlight. Maybe you were always bad, sister.'

She smiled noiselessly at me. I poured myself a pint of rye. I must stop drinking bread.

July 3rd

Where are the avant-garde art collectives of yesteryear? Gone... all gone...

My teeth hurt.

July 5th

Once again I woke up in the hospital. The blinds were drawn, but some sunlight seeped through. The light was golden and cloudy, like bottled piss. The room was silent. I looked around.

Alongside my bed were rows and rows of animals: lions, badgers, stoats, deer, ponies – row upon row of them. They were all encased in iron lungs. There must have been 50 beasts, all silent except for the mechanical hiss of their breathing apparatus. I was the only human in the room.

I heard the click-clack of high heels. A nurse entered the room. She was a platinum blonde in black high heels; I tried to speak, but my throat hurt and no sound came out. She walked over to a pony that was lying in the giant iron lung beside me. The pony's head lolled awkwardly from the metal casing. A large tongue flopped out of its mouth. The nurse withdrew a packet of cigarettes from her pocket, and with elegant poise, lit a fag. She inhaled deeply and then pressed the cigarette into the pony's mouth. It smoked greedily and then swallowed the cigarette whole. It disappeared with a gulp and a sucking noise.

I waved at the nurse and she approached me with a beatific smile. I coughed and a handful of cigarette butts flew out of my mouth. No wonder I had a sore throat.

'What... am... I... doing here?' I croaked.

'Oh', she replied. 'I've just realised. You're not an animal, are you? You probably shouldn't be here. This is the animal iron lung ward.'

'But I don't need an iron lung. I just came in here to get my wisdom teeth removed.'

'Mmmm, probably a clerical error. Our normal receptionist is off – pregnant. The temp is a bit of a nightmare, to be honest. I'll come back next week and see if we can get you out of here.'

'OK...' I said, still groggy.

She smiled. 'Would you like a cigarette?'

'Yes', I said.

She lit a Lucky Strike in her mouth and I gazed at her ruby red lips. She blew a smoke ring and carefully placed the cigarette between my teeth.

July 7th

Today was an awkward day: I bumped into myself.

It was outside the Tesco on the north circular, by Colney Hatch Lane. He was smiling and friendly and wanted to introduce me to his wife and kids. I just wanted to get away as quickly as possible. I was embarrassed by his giant shopping trolley, laden with kids' meals and organic fruit and veg; in contrast, I had a small basket full of frozen lasagnes and a jar of instant coffee.

'Hi!' he bounded over to me. 'You look well! My God, it's been... what? Three years?'

'Yes', I murmured. 'Something like that.'

'Victoria', he turned and hollered to his wife. 'There's someone here I'd like you to meet.'

'No. No. I must go.' I turned and walked rapidly into the store, camouflaging myself among some bananas.

As to how the other me came into existence – it's a long story. We all have different sides of ourselves. We are constructed from disparate, contrary aspects. As we grow older, we attempt to unite and assimilate these warring factions of our soul. Some of us are more successful than others, I suppose.

There were two distinct parts of my personality. One was dynamic, decisive, eager to embrace life's challenges. The other side is what I am now; vague, indecisive, only loosely moored to my increasingly banal life.

Ever since we split, he has been eager to get back together with me, to 'become whole' again. He's convinced that if we just give it a bit of time, we can work out our differences. But I... I just want him to go away.

I am not interested in becoming whole, thank you.

Me   The Other Me

July 8th

Many years ago, when Moses was young and John Major did not even exist, I devised an astrology chart based on the periodic table. In some ways – commercially and critically– it was a major failure. In other ways – artistically and emotionally – it was only a minor failure.

Fermium – Fm

Jan 20–Feb 18
With an atomic number of 100, you are popular with friends and enemies alike. You find yourself performing for crowds, even when you are not meant to be showing off. You are intelligent, but your chemical properties are largely unknown. Scientists have worked for years on the

isolation of Fermium, but you feel lonely enough as it is. You sometimes find it difficult to relate to other metals, and wonder if you might in fact be an alloy. You cry at sunsets and when watching old reruns of *The Golden Girls*. You fuck horses.

Gold – Au

Feb 19–Mar 20
Ah gold, gold, precious gold. You elude me, you escape me, you avoid me. You have been lusted after for centuries but remain unmoved. You fear that you are surrounded by insincere sycophants. You are the most malleable and ductile metal, but sometimes you secretly worry that you have no true moral centre. You have a throaty laugh and have enjoyed relations with both men and women. Your eyes twinkle in the darkness, ever alluring, ever vulgar. You bring unhappy thoughts to the poor.

Iron – Fe

Mar 21–Apr 19
To strangers you appear lustrous or metallic, with a greyish tinge, but with close acquaintances you are open and vivacious, always the life of the party. You have recently been disappointed by a man from abroad, but do not worry: he will not bring your atomic weight below 55.845. Despite being a relatively abundant element in the universe, you never fear that you are taken for granted. However, now might be a good time to remind friends and family about your true worth. You will not rust, but you will get wet.

Krypton – Kr

Apr 20–May 20
Krypton, you appear as a colourless gas at 298 K, but despite this, your colourful personality and lively wit will win you many admirers this week. You will have a brief flirtation with fame, but be careful. Beware the Ides of March – all through the year. There may be moments when you get depressed and are tempted to settle down with someone you

don't truly love. Remember: solid krypton is a white crystalline substance with a face-centred cubic structure, not anyone's second-choice date. Be true to yourself. Wash behind your ears. Stand up straight, for God's sake.

Lithium – Li

May 21–Jun 20

With your silvery white appearance, you are sometimes considered older than you actually are, but you definitely know how to have a good time, so show the world that you are ready to party! When you're feeling shy and quiet, remind yourself that you are mixed (alloyed) with aluminium and magnesium for lightweight alloys. This week dogs may chase you for hours, with an obsessive single-mindedness that scares you. You will hear from an uncle that you haven't spoken to in years. He will mistakenly call you Helium, but remain polite.

Magnesium – Mg

Jun 21–Jul 22

This week keep your eyes open for new employment opportunities. In particular, remember not to sell yourself short by making any self-deprecating remarks. You may be the eighth most abundant element in the earth's crust but you are not so often found in your elemental form. You may be jeered at in the street by drunken Aston Villa fans, but this is nothing to be ashamed of. You may find yourself thinking about an old relationship, but you need to stay positive about the future. Never forget that you readily burn with a dazzling white flame.

Potassium – K

Jul 23–Aug 22

People often forget that your chemical symbol is K, and fumble about, mistakenly calling you PM. Don't let this dent your confidence; now is the time for you to spread your wings and soar. As one of the most reactive and electropositive of metals, you know you will sometimes rub people up the wrong way, but don't let this stop you making decisions. Be bold! You must conquer your fear of fruit, flies and fruit flies.

Rhodium – Rh

Aug 23–Sep 22
Your atomic number of 45 will be called into question this week, possibly by the young man at the deli counter at Safeway, who will insist that other customers are served before you. With your robust exterior, partners sometimes think of you as callous or unfeeling, but remember your high reflectance, and that still waters run deep. Stick to your beliefs, but pay attention to any advice you might hear. You should be spending more quality time with relatives you have not seen for a long time, such as Chloride $RhCl^3$.

Seaborgium – Sg

Sep 23–Oct 22
Despite your extravagant name, you are a modest individual who quietly measures out each spoon of sugar when you are drinking tea. In the quiet moments between adverts on television you sometimes think you are going insane – you can hear a constant buzzing like a thousand hornets in your brain. In your most fevered, panicky moments you suspect everyone of being a Communist spy. Basically, you are a synthetic element that is not present in the environment at all. You have no uses. You are not art.

Silicon – Si

Oct 23–Nov 21
With your reputation for turning up in women's breasts, people think of you as a shallow hedonist, but now is a time for reminding those around you of your presence in important microchips. You should be taking better care of your body and maybe think of joining a gym – you might not always have a weight of 28.0855! Your self-esteem has taken a battering recently, and that gang of kids outside Burger King hardly helped. Don't let anyone make you

feel like a freak: you are present in the sun and stars and are a principal component of a class of meteorites known as aerolites. Smile!

Silver – Ag

Nov 22–Dec 21
Silver, silver, silver. Always second best. Always the bridesmaid, never the bride. But cheer up. Remember: Ivan Lendl never won Wimbledon and Jimmy White was never world Snooker champion! Stop setting yourself impossible targets and then punishing yourself for failing. This week you will be surprised by a group of friends who want to show you how much they appreciate you. You will fall out of love with Gold, but will feel better for the experience. You will watch the whole of 'Heidi' on video.

Xenon – Xe

Dec 22–Jan 19
This week you will be coerced by your partner into having a haircut. You will suffer in silence, despite your clear reluctance. You are angry that people always consider you 'inert' or 'noble'. You have many dreams and ambitions, but are unsure of how to articulate them. You will trip over a homeless man on the way to work and spill scalding coffee down your trousers. After a shower, you will go down the pub, where you will drunkenly try to chat to the barmaid that looks a bit like a bustier version of Tracy Thorn from 'Everything but the Girl'. You are present in the Martian atmosphere to the extent of about 0.08 p.p.m.

Things overheard on the tube

Today's journey:
Circle Line: Barbican–Sloane Square

1. I just flicked a cup holder at Sara.
2. What's in a pork pie apart from pork and gristle?
3. It's a nice place. There's no swings but there's a big slide and some metal horses.

4. Did the driver say something about Green Park? I can't hear a thing.
5. It's true. Basil Brush is a global figure. I fucking hate him.
6. It's not an Indian summer. It's a typically rubbish English summer.
7. Ha! It's not as if he enjoys getting spanked, is it?
8. I don't know. They all look very Aryan.
   Apparently, Derrida was hung like a donkey.
9. Why do all paedos have lank hair and beards? You'd think they'd try to look normal.

July 10th

There are more and more bald men in London. Their shiny pates catch the sun and blind me. These bald men – they are not to be trusted. They mass against me. I worry that my own wiry hair will grow thin; that they will assimilate me into their League. I suspect that they are interfering with my water supply and making my hair grow brittle and fine.

This is not a paranoid fantasy. Paranoia is an indulgence I cannot afford. Paranoia is simply vanity turned sour, and I am not a vain individual.

The moral midgets who dismiss my fears do not live in my world; they live in a safe little haven of Marks and Spencers' suburbia. They do not know what it is to fight on the frontlines of fashion. My hair is my existence: bald men are ridiculed. They are thought of as figures of fun. But nothing could be further from the truth. There is nothing funny about bald men; they are very dangerous indeed.

The truth is covered by a hat, but lies are always naked.

July 11th

Someone once told me that I smile in my sleep. I did not believe them. I don't smile when I am awake, and I would be most disappointed if I had let myself down as I slept. The other day, when I went to the doctor's surgery, there was a woman sitting opposite me. One of her feet was bandaged and bleeding. She told me that she got her foot caught in a man trap and had to gnaw it off to escape. I know how she feels.

July 12th

Something is happening to me. I am losing my grip. I can feel myself changing, evolving, devolving into something else. It may be human, it may be something else. My senses are changing. I can see ultraviolet light. I can smell emotions. I can hear conversations spoken hundreds of miles away.

Last night, as I strolled home from The Gate and Whistle, I found myself hovering over the pavement, my feet not quite touching the ground. There are green flashes when I close my eyes. When the Shadow comes, I must be ready. I must hone my new abilities. must summon every ounce of pain and misery within me and blast my enemies out of this plane of existence.

All this introspection cannot be good for me.

My friend Marvin has many dogs. They are all named after Greek gods. As morons in pubs are fond of pointing out, 'dog' is 'god' backwards. This means nothing. The dogs are not gods or even anti-gods, they are just dogs. Dogs don't move in mysterious ways, they just chase their own tails.

Marvin dresses the dogs formally, in dinner jackets and spats. I think he is having some form of nervous breakdown.

I try to explain to him that the dogs are uncomfortable and look ridiculous in their starched collars, but he glowers at me and talks about falling standards in canine behaviour.

Marvin has very little control over his life; he lives a ramshackle, jobless existence, much like my own. But whereas I have embraced the absurdist aimlessness of existence, he struggles with everything. In the kingdom of the dog, the man with the leash is king.

July 13th

I obtained this picture from a contact in the London Underground. I believe that he is connected to the Shadow, in some unfathomable way. He is an undercover operative who spends his days travelling the Piccadilly Line, drifting from carriage to carriage, eating from chocolate dispensers and losing himself in the crowds. I believe that over the past five years he has killed over 400 people on the tube.

Many of the crimes have gone unreported, since his victims are not yet aware that they are dead. His killing techniques are so subtle many of his victims may survive for many decades, living full and happy lives before they perish in their old age.

No doubt two questions have entered your mind:
1. Why does he do it?
2. How has this murderous individual remained undetected for so long?

Alas, answers have I none. If you see him, walk slowly away.

July 14th

Yesterday I found that an essay on flight had been taped to the back of my jacket. No wonder the children in the street were pointing at me more than usual.

The essay is another message, I am sure. Almost everything in life is a message. Except for massages. Those are merely typing errors.

Here is the essay. I do not know who wrote it. It was not signed.

Of course, those glory-hogging Wright Brothers took all the credit. History has almost totally bleached out my part in the development of human flight. They say that history is written by the winners, and they are right. I allowed the glory to pass me by, and I have only myself to blame.

My early attempts at flying involved bees. You will be familiar with the idea of men wearing a beard of bees; I went further and developed a whole undercarriage, a whole fuselage of bees. A bee-plane, if you will. I intended to fly from Newcastle to Calais via the majestic power of bees. But it was not to be.

The accursed bees – social as they are – rarely stuck together long enough to take me very far, and would often disintegrate mid-flight into a chaotic cloud of buzzing insects. Were it not for my canvas parachute, I would have died a dozen times. I did not make it out of Newcastle, let alone to France.

After bees came pigeons, more docile than bees and easier to control. You would not be surprised to learn that it takes over 300 pigeons tethered to a fully-grown man's body to allow him to leave the ground, albeit briefly. For many years I pursued my experiments with pigeons, but I never got more than a few feet off the ground, and always emerged covered in guano. This affected my relationships with the fairer sex. Women can be very judgemental.

I discovered the true trick to flying in 1848, the year that I turned 40. And I never turned back.

The trick to flying is simply to fly. A human being can fly as easily as any bird or aircraft if he puts his mind to it. I am not referring to a spiritual journey in which the illusion of flight is achieved; when I say that I fly, I mean that I am flying. I leave the ground and circle above turrets and bridges and conifer trees. I alight upon the rooftops of buses. I swoop down on muggers like a vengeful arrow. I **fly.**

It is said that the history of human flight is the tale of man's yearning to escape his mortal bounds. While in flight, man is neither here nor there, but in-between, in transit. Everywhere and nowhere at once. And yet for me, the destination of my flights was unimportant. I simply revelled in the simple pleasure of a life free from the tyranny of gravity.

I do not consider flight unnatural. There is no hubris in flight. It is easy to portray man's obsession with flight as vanity, as though we were all Icarus, doomed to overextend ourselves and challenge God. This is nonsense. I do not challenge God. I toil in his honour. For God gave me a brain, and I used it with humility and earnest conviction to fly above my contemporaries. A man in flight does not mimic God, he merely treads in his footsteps.

But I digress. You do not yet understand how I defeated the laws of physics and took flight from obscurity. In June 1848, I abandoned my research with animals and mechanicals and concentrated on learning to fly unaided. I had dabbled in using machines to fly, but knew it was a dead end. Mechanical flight is a clumsy affair. Machines do not have the grace or wit to charm gravity; they simply defy it. Machines are rude and unpleasant, much like Orville and Wilbur Wright themselves. No, I did not use machines to fly. I used manners. I discovered that the key to flying is to persuade gravity to absent itself, to politely leave my body for the duration of my journey.

Like so many involved in physics, gravity is lonely. It was neglected for many centuries, and then only fitfully acknowledged. And then Newton spoke and suddenly gravity was everywhere, taken for granted and resented.

And so, it is not difficult to flatter gravity. A few careful words, a wry smile, a twinkle of melancholy eyes – this is enough for a good 10 minutes of uninterrupted flight. A bunch of flowers. A watercolour. A short song.

Initially, I was mocked. When I published my research, the experts scoffed. What they scoffed, I do not care or know. However, I soon silenced the pie-faced ignorami. When they saw the evidence of my discoveries, they mocked me no more. They merely gawped like children at a magic show.

When they saw me fly, they knew at last that I was a greater man than them. They could not deny my triumph.

No, they could not deny it, but neither could they join in. Try as they might, the dullards could not fly as I could. They jumped off buildings, ran into lakes, conversed with birds (Lord knows why), but they always failed abominably. These so-called experts could hardly get an inch off the ground without crashing down to earth.

In secret, I taught many friends and acquaintances to fly; from chimney sweeps to gardeners, they all soared alongside me. But none of my co-pilots had the social standing or influence to promote my discovery. The scientific community grew increasingly jealous of my powers. I would sail into meetings aboard a cloud, and I would see the veins in their pompous necks bulge with anger. How was it that I could fly so easily, and they were all earthbound? I could not answer them. I suppose some of us have it, and some do not.

So, unable to fly, the doctors, the physicists, the Royals and the lawyers all turned their backs on me, hopeful that history would erase me. And they were almost right.

But not quite. For you are reading this, and you must know my words are true.

July 15th

It was early and the garden path was covered in dew. A mug of coffee in my hands, I sauntered down to the bottom of the garden, wearing only my dressing gown. The birds tweeted and the wind rustled through the rubbish.

As a child, I had believed there were pixies at the bottom of the garden. I would talk to the pixies and they would talk back.
This morning I did, but they didn't.

'Hello!' I shouted. A cloud of crows erupted from a neighbour's tree and circled uneasily, before dispersing over the rooftops. Then silence descended once more. It was chilly. I stamped my feet.

The pixies did not appear. Maybe they have moved to pastures new. Maybe they never existed. Maybe they just don't like me.

July 16th

Today I bought a newspaper. There were coupons, which, if collected, could be redeemed for a free DVD. I have rediscovered my love of coupons. I cut them out and pasted them into my scrapbook. Then I pasted my scrapbook into the lining of my jacket and nailed my jacket to the inside of my wardrobe. The wardrobe smells of must.

I should clean out my wardrobe – I should exercise some control over my existence. But I shall wait until later in the year. July is an empty month in the doldrums of the year when nothing of any meaning can be achieved.

Perhaps you think that my life lacks narrative. Characters are mentioned but never appear again. One day I am old as history, the next I am young and carefree. This is not my fault. That is time.

July 18th

The past is a foreign country, which makes me a foreigner, because I live in the past.

The past is friendly, unsure, always doubting itself despite the evidence. It is a story already told.

A few years ago I made a time machine. It was simple; an inflatable pink rubber and plastic suit that could transport me to any point in time. I feared the future, so opted to revisit the past. How bad could it be?

All the rumours you hear about the dangers of changing the past are untrue. There is no Ray Bradbury effect; the past cannot be changed. You can interact as much as you like with the past and it will never change the present, or the future, when it comes. Some things are written in stone.

Travelling in the suit was a bizarre, unsettling experience; looking through the Perspex visor I hardly felt I was in the past – it was more like watching a series of old home movies. But I gradually adjusted to the nature of the suit, and now I have grown fond of it and rarely take it off. It is very pleasant having a barrier between myself and the outside world.

My first visit back to the past saw me return to my childhood. I was 8 years old. I could hardly bear to watch myself. I was playing in the back garden, oblivious to the future; how could that little blond boy (centre-parting, choirboy cheeks) run around so innocently; surely he knew he would one day grow up?

It would have been nice to have given him some advice – some words of wisdom from the future – but I knew he would never speak to strangers, especially one as grubby-looking as me.

I hung around my old house, wandering from room to room, and admiring the church opposite that is now a yuppie housing estate. I picked flowers and crushed woodlice.

I stood outside the front door and peered through windows. My father with a fuller head of hair; my mother smiling behind thick-rimmed glasses. My family looked so solid and yet so fragile – a bomb that hasn't been informed that it is going to explode.

My next stop in the space–time continuum took me into my teens. I was an ugly duckling, unhappy at school and somehow lanky and awkward despite my shortness. This period of my life was easier for me to watch; it is a time that I have relived over and over in my mind, and I was somehow pleased to witness my unhappiness. It reminded me that schooldays are never the happiest days of your life. Say what you will about adulthood, but at least you have a greater set of choices to turn down. As a child, you are always hostage to the whims of others.

I removed my helmet and smoked a cigarette.

I turned a dial on my rubber suit and left adolescence. I shot forward in time. I found myself in my student days, growing stubble at university. I recognized myself instantly. The puppy-fat of adolescence had disappeared and a man's face had emerged.

This part of my trip was difficult, as I knew it would be. The recent past is always more painful than the distant. I saw all the egotism, paranoia and envy that I still carry around inside myself. It wasn't a pretty sight. The student me definitely needed a haircut; I probably still do. I realised how much I run from the past; how much I try to reinvent myself and distance myself from the man I am.

He hates it.

There have been many winter evenings when I have been woken late at night by Michael. He turns up at my doorstep, sobbing into his collar and raging at the agony of his condition. I try to console him as best I can; I show him the lovely flat he owns, and tell him that his fellow accountants respect his head for numbers and knowledge of tax laws. But he is nonetheless consumed by self-loathing.

'Look at me', he howls, scratching at his Moss Bros suit. 'I am a monster! How could I look my fellow wolves in the eye... if they knew what happens to me... that I become this... this *thing!*'

Michael's transformations were triggered when he was bitten by an accountant 5 years ago. I have searched for a cure to his condition, but to no avail. There is nothing I can do for him and he is beginning to lose hope.

There isn't much you can say to a once noble wolf when he knows that come the next full moon, he will once again find himself working late in an office in Edgware, faxing share certificates to head office. Maybe it would be better if I killed him.

July 23rd

I was waiting by a bus stop in Wood Green. The 184 bus was failing to arrive. It often does that. Also waiting with me was a nondescript middle-aged man; not especially fat, not especially anything. The sun was beating down on us with only a little remorse.

'You know what annoys me', I said, turning to my anonymous companion, 'The story of my life makes no sense.'

'Don't tell me about it', he shrugged blankly. 'I am just a supporting character. No background. No future.'

'I mean it', I said. 'I wake up in the morning and it could be any day of the week. There's no structure or story to my life. Things just happen, with no real sense of progression. There's no cause and effect. Some days it's two steps forward and one step back. Other days it's two steps forward and three steps back. Other people seem to have much clearer lives... they have friends and partners and go out and do things. They have projects that nest and hatch.'

As for now... well, nowadays I don't quite live in the present. I live in the same day, the same week and the same month as you. Probably even the same hour. But I have chosen to live 8 minutes behind everyone else. Things are easier like this. I am perennially missing halves of conversations and am always late for meetings. But it's a small price to pay to escape the horror of now. The past is more comfortable and manageable than the present. The present makes me absent.

July 19th

I woke up angry, my veins throbbing with injustice. I punched the bed, my hands shaking with rage. I got out of bed and punched the wall. Punched and punched it again. I left the house and punched the postman. I could feel the crunch and splinter of bones.

I sprinted down the street, my lungs aflame. I leapt through a plate glass window in Woolworths and wrestled a teenage cashier to the floor, beating him senseless with my fists, a scream of sheer brutality coursing through me!

This is what it feels like to be alive!

And then... I no longer felt angry. I felt old and tired and embarrassed. I helped the cashier to his feet and apologised.

My anger never lasts. It swiftly melts into regret and self-pity. I must learn how to stay angry for longer periods of time.

July 20th

I got into a taxi. The taxi driver had a face like a plate of rotten ham.

'Ha ha! You'll never guess who I had in the back of my cab an hour ago', he guffawed.

'Who?'

'You! You were in my cab an hour ago.'

'No. I wasn't. I was at home in the bath.'

'Nah, mate. It was definitely you. We had the same conversation. It's just a tiny ripple in the space–time continuum; happens all the time. If I had a quid for every temporal hiccup I've seen, I'd be a rich man.'

I hate taxi drivers.

July 21st

Christina Aguilera came round for tea. I prepared a plate of s[ ] fingers. She didn't touch them.

She was wearing next to nothing; just a leather thong and elastop[ ] over her breasts. She said I looked 'hot'. I said that yes, it was a bit st[ ] in here, and I opened a window. She muttered something about Eng[ ] guys under her breath. I took the sponge fingers back to Poundsaver a[ ] got my money back.

July 22nd

My friend Michael is a reverse werewolf. His is a terrible affliction. Most of the time he lives as a wolf, living a normal lupine existence, foraging for food in the woodlands near Enfield. But once a month, when the moon is full, he undergoes a terrible change – he transforms into a human. His black fur retracts, his front paws become arms and hands and he stands tall on his hind legs. For those 2 days he is no longer Michael the wolf, but Michael Schwarzberg, a Jewish accountant in Finchley Central.

Michael. In human and wolf form.

'Don't fucking tell me! I'm just a narrative device... I am just here so you can talk to me and not speak to yourself out loud. So fuck off.'

Narrative devices used to be much more polite.

July 24th

Someone is poisoning me. I think it may be Machiavelli. I'll need to keep an eye on him.

July 26th

In my tireless research into the Shadow, I have discovered some unpleasant truths about the Garden of Eden. I was looking through some old paperwork in my loft when I stumbled upon the birth certificates of Adam and Eve. Adam's mum and dad are both listed as God, and Eve's mother is also listed as God. Her father is listed as a rib.

This got me thinking: as well as being husband and wife, it seems Adam and Eve were also brother and sister. I suppose this explains why the human race is a bit slow. Evolution can only do so much with poor genetic material.

July 27th

Another day, another Drachma.

Today Tim Henman came round to visit. It wasn't a social call. As most of you know, I don't like to talk about my encounters with celebrities, but today's events bear repeating. About 3 years ago, Tim parted company with his coach David Felgate and approached me (just so it is clear I did not volunteer my services). Since then he's been visiting me on a monthly basis for advice on improving his game. I don't really focus on the physical side of tennis, just on the psychological side. It's quite a challenge to transform him from drippy public schoolboy into a raging animal of tennis. He is totally hamstrung by manners, goodwill and a limp-wristed desire to avoid offence. In short, he is not a winner.

Tim and I were in the lounge. I lay on the sofa, my feet dangling over a cushioned arm. I ate a ginger snap. I crunched it between my teeth. I chewed with my mouth open. I snorted as I swallowed. I wanted to raise his hackles; to annoy him, to provoke a primal emotional response. It is part of my training.

'Excuse me, Sir. Could I please have a biscuit?' he asked.

'Fuck off', I tersely replied.

'Oh, OK', he murmured, his small eyes filling with tears.

'Jesus, Tim!' I slammed my fist onto the table, causing a bourbon cream to fly into the air. 'I just told you to fuck off. You should be angry! You should be asking me outside for a fight! Where's your passion?'

'I know', he mumbled. 'I know. I'm sorry.'

'Don't apologise', I fixed him with an ice-cold stare. 'You did nothing wrong. In fact, I just insulted you. Get angry! Call me a twat!'

'Um… you're a twit.'

'No Tim. Not a twit. A twit is a funny thing that a 5-year-old boy calls his mummy. A *twat* is an offensive thing. If you want to win Wimbledon, you've got to get offensive. They call you Tiger Tim… start acting like a tiger. Rip someone to shreds.'

For the next three hours, I worked on conditioning Tim. I used a lot of discredited Pavlovian approaches to get him boiling with rage, to remove his inbred tendency to lose pluckily in the quarter-finals. I coated him in pig blood and chased him around the room with a birch stick. I threw staplers and lampshades at him. I don't enjoy doing these things, they give me no pleasure – I am no sadist. I do these things because no one else is willing to do what it takes to improve British sports.

By the end of the session, Tim was exhausted and sobbing quietly against a wall, his face cradled in his spindly arms. I stood over him, smoking a fag.

The doorbell rang. It was a middle-aged woman from Christian Aid, asking for a donation. I tried to stall her, but in a flash Tim had stormed downstairs, barged past me and smashed her in the face with a balled fist. She crumpled to the floor like Andrew Castle, blood streaming from her nose.

It was a PR disaster. I had to call her an ambulance and tell Tim to scarper before the press arrived. I'll have to work hard to cover it all up. And yet, I must admit, I'm proud of him.

July 29th

Last night I was taking out the rubbish (note to American readers, rubbish is trash or garbage. I don't know why you can't just use the word rubbish. It's a perfectly good word) when I found a pair of lips in my front garden.

They were a woman's lips, full and plump. I was almost tempted to kiss them. It has been a long time since I have kissed soft lips.

It made me think about lips, and about the fact that some woman somewhere was now walking around without any lips. I felt sorry for her. Then I put the lips on the mantelpiece, with all the other body parts.

Remember: the whole is always greater than the sum of the parts.

August 1st

I took a bus through Poshtown and then Toffborough. From the top deck I could see the rich folk in the street, sitting outside bistros in the sunshine. Laughing in wicker chairs, drinking red wine and flirting. I wasn't jealous: I have been rich and I have been poor. I was miserable both ways, but I ate better when I was rich. Sunlight streamed through the bus windows, reflected up from the river. Geese slapped their feet across Richman Bridge. You can't smoke on buses nowadays; I suppose it's for the best. When I get off buses I have a fag poised in my lips and as soon as the doors close behind me I flick my lighter and inhale.

A girl in her early twenties climbed the stairs. I smiled at her and she almost smiled back. A small victory.

The bus rose up the hill towards Bourgeoisville. A chatter of overeducated children got on the bus. They irritated me but I did not kill them. I am learning.

I pressed the bell and walked the rest of the way home. I get tired of fictional places.

Things overheard on the tube

Today's journey:
Northern Line: East Finchley–Waterloo

1. It's not a proper shed. It's more like a big Wendy house.
2. He only shops at H&M. Everything he owns is beige or khaki.
3. Horrible. I stepped on a slug before... and it burst.
4. I am not drunk. It's just hard to walk in these heels.
5. This Turkish bloke kept on telling me that he was related to me, that we were brothers.
6. I will never get married. My mother is a social hand grenade.
7. It's a story within a story within a story. Like a Russian doll.
8. We went into that posh bar and had a raspberry beer. We were the only people there.

9. I can't believe the fuss they make over a woman wanking off a pig.
10. Everyone I know is a cunt.

August 2nd

This morning I met the man who wrote a biography of a fishcake. But that is not relevant. Today I am talking about mathematics.

Maths: adding and subtracting, multiplication, division, factors, equations. It's all quite beautiful, if you're that way inclined.

In the US, maths is called math. It is singular. Here in Britain it's maths; we have many forms of maths. Across the Atlantic they only have one. I don't know what that says about the disparity between our cultures. It probably says very little, but then again, I'm not a linguist – I am just one man trying to make a difference in a cruel, cruel world.

Everything nowadays runs on binary. That's just zeros and ones. Two digits that rule the world.

001100000	0000110000	01100000110	0111111110
001100000	0001111000	01100000110	0110000000
001100000	0011001100	00110001100	0111111110
001100000	0011001100	00110001100	0110000000
001111110	0001111000	00011011000	0110000000
001111110	0000110000	00001110000	0111111110

Yes, maths is probably the answer to all of life's problems.

Mankind turned to science because he was sick of the ambiguity of art and philosophy. Art can be anything. That's the whole point of it, apparently. In contrast, just think of the sleek beauty of binary – everything is either a zero or a one, no shades of grey, no awkward decimals or possibilities. It is beautiful because it is true. I think some artist once said truth is beauty. He was profoundly wrong, but it is a lovely idea. He probably lived before calculators were invented, so we can forgive his human errors.

Think of the ridiculous forms that man has invented in the pursuit of art: ice-dance, mime, synchronized swimming, the saxophone. Why? Is it really so vital that we express ourselves? I think the world would probably be a better place with less self-expression.

I know that my radical ideas are anathema to liberal Western culture, where we're supposed to encourage children to make self-portraits out of clay and tell autistic toddlers that the inky blobs they have drawn are art, but perhaps the world might benefit from more self-repression!

Remember: Hitler was an amateur artist, not a weekend mathematician.

It would be comforting to think there was a formula or equation underpinning our existence, that we could guarantee happiness by following a set mathematical pattern, that all our spiritual and moral ambiguities could be annihilated with a massive existential calculator.

Imagine that Moses is on the top of Mount Sinai, speaking in his booming Semitic voice to the Children of Israel. Rather than holding two tablets of stone he clutches in his hands two large CASIO calculators. On both of them is a number of wondrous holy significance.

Sadly, in his hurry to hand the number of God to mankind, Moses presents the calculators upside down and the number appears as a word: BOOBIES.

That is where mankind goes wrong. If only we had chosen numbers instead of words. It's numbers that you can count on. Words just take us to the ends of sentences.

August 4th

The twentieth century produced just one true artform: jazz. The sound of man's soul escaping from an urban cage and soaring to the heavens. For your personal pleasure, here are some profiles of the giants of jazz.

Louis Armstrong

Louis Armstrong was born Llewis Armmstrongg in Malmo, Sweden in 1958. The son of a fisherman and an instructional designer, Louis was a happy child, gaining pleasure from the rudimentary sounds he would make by blowing into the conch shells he would find on the beaches surrounding his home. In 1961, aged 12, he won admission to the famous Kierkegaard Academy, where his formal jazz apprenticeship began. Studying under a table, his playing style was largely influenced by the random, atonal noises that would emanate from his underfed stomach.

In 1988, he met the love of his life, George Washington III. Not only was George a romantic passion, he also served as the musical muse that Louis so desperately needed. Louis would play endlessly on his French horn while George sat in the kitchen eating a Spanish omelette. Not only was this the happiest time of Louis's life, it was also the most productive. As well as recording the legendary *Emmerdale* trilogy of discs, Louis also electrified audiences with his dynamic live performances, which often culminated in him being mistaken for a janitor, and being politely asked to leave the auditorium.

Chet Baker

Chet Baker was the pseudonym of Albert Roach, a Kentucky railwayman and perennial malingerer. Roach was born in 1888 in Idaho, and raised by a pack of wild flowers. A self-taught pianist, Baker (whose elder sister Cheryl also enjoyed musical success as the brains behind eighties Euro chart-toppers Bucks Fizz) was discovered while playing the piano in Wolverhampton Civic centre, a hotbed of jazztivity which also spawned Clamhead Fitzjohnson and Rusty Lee, among others.

Baker enjoyed immediate musical success, wowing audiences with his bravura playing style and a neat line in porkpie hats. However, despite his fame and fortune, happiness eluded Baker. Critics have long hinted that behind his most successful records, 'Would You Please Leave Me Alone?' and 'My Lawyers Will Talk To Your Lawyers', there lay a man ill at ease with his status as sex symbol. Recent years have seen Baker develop a hard enamel shell into which he retracts when faced with bright lights. He lives in a shoe.

John Coltrane

Until recent months John Coltrane was best known for his TV portrayal of roly-poly criminal psychologist Cracker in the series of the same name. It is only posthumously that his skills as the seminal jazz drummer of his generation have come to public attention.

Born into the long-established Coltrane jazz dynasty in 1969, John was a headstrong child, often throwing himself off buildings in a fit of pique. His drumming skills first caught his family's eyes when he was discovered violently bludgeoning the skull of the family maid with a pickaxe handle – in perfect 3/4 rhythm. Touring with the family band 'The Coltrane Station', John honed his licks (and many would say licked his hones) on gruelling countrywide tours, underpinning the band's musical explorations with his stiff, Teutonic rhythm.

Quitting the band in 1956, he soon enjoyed a series of elaborate breakfasts, each one more deliciously calorific than the last. He was often to be seen with a drumstick in each hand, and three turkey drumsticks rammed into his wide, beaver-like mouth. His death from a coronary earlier this year shocked very few of his loyal fans.

August 7th

I have been away. But I can't remember where.

Now I am back. I think.

August 8th

It was a long time ago – it seems that way anyway. We were sitting in an upmarket café or a shabby restaurant. She was pretty. Her prettiness made me nervous. I get vertigo when faced with trick questions or attractive women.

'I like you', she smiled, playing with a sachet of salt. 'You're interesting.'

'You won't like me', I insisted. 'When you get to know me. I am a bad person.'

'Well, perhaps that should be for me to find out. I'm not a little girl that you need to protect... I know what men are like. And I'm no angel myself.' She lowered her face to mine and whispered conspiratorially. *'I do actually quite enjoy sex.'*

I blushed and half-smiled.

'I know... I am not some chauvinist idiot', I said. 'I know women like sex. I even like it myself sometimes. It's just... we'll get together and we'll split up. These things are inevitable. So it just seems easier on both of us if we don't get together in the first place. Forgive my cynicism.'

'Ouch!' She laughed a kind laugh. 'My God! You've got a dark outlook on life! Look, neither of us knows if it'll work out. I also have my own... issues. But, for God's sake, what's the point of life if you can't take a risk every once in a while.'

I picked up the ketchup and squirted it on my chips. 'I am not sure there is a point to life', I sighed.

She flicked hair out of her eyes and laughed again. 'Goodness, you are being miserable today, aren't you?'

'Sorry.'

She looked me in the eyes. 'Don't be sorry', she said. 'Just don't fuck up.' And with that, she leaned over and kissed me. I kissed her back, biting on her lip and swallowing anxiety. I closed my eyes. I closed my heart.

And then I heard a shattering sound.

Her head had rolled off her shoulders and fallen on the floor. Pieces of porcelain skull were everywhere. The Portuguese waitress looked at the mess and scowled at me. I asked her for the brush and pan and hurriedly cleaned up.

That was the end of relationships for me.

August 9th

I was in the lounge, reading the *Telegraph* and smoking a Marlboro Light. It was sunny, and I crinkled my eyes as I read. My reverie was broken by a brick sailing through my window and landing on my carpet with a dull thud. Fortunately, the window was open, so I was not showered with shattered glass. In a strange way it was a disappointment. I had rather assumed people only threw bricks through closed windows.

Attached to the brick was a note. I undid the string that bound the note to the brick, my fingers not quite trembling. I was expecting some kind of threat or abuse.

Ceci n'est pas une brick.

Instead, the note simply stated 'THIS IS A BRICK'.

I picked up the brick. It was reassuringly heavy in my palm. I pulled out a biro and scribbled on the back of the note 'NO. THIS IS A NOTE'. Then I tied the note to the brick and hurled it back out into the street.

What a strange morning it has been.

August 11th

The sky was black today. Either that or I woke up in the middle of the night.

I don't bother wearing a watch nowadays; time means so little to me. It could be today, it could be yesterday. It could be tomorrow.

August 12th

There is very little sex in this journal. I am not a prude, but I never quite feel comfortable writing about sexual matters. Sex is a large part of my life, but it does not sit easily with the rest of my existence. If my life is a supermarket, then sex occupies a totally different aisle from the rest of the products, and demands a distinct and unreliable currency. I am always scraping my pockets for change.

Of course, there is much speculation in the press about my sexuality. Am I gay? Am I straight? Is it true that my tongue is 14 inches long? Do I enjoy being tied up? Well, in my time I have done many things, but I prefer falling asleep next to a woman, and the only bondage I've experienced are the mental and spiritual chains that bind me.

Still, I must talk of sex. It would be wrong to neglect the issue. So I will tell the story of *The Day That London Got the Horn*.

It was 2 years ago. A hazy August evening, putrid with heat. I sat in a pub in Muswell Hill and watched hordes of flying ants descend upon the capital.

In the pink sunset sky, I saw shooting stars.

As my drinking companions filed off home to boyfriends, girlfriends and pet dogs, a strange thing happened. A golden glow surrounded the rooftops and trees and I was aware of a high-pitched humming noise. Then people started to behave in a distinctly odd manner.

Silently, as though it were the most normal thing in the world, people started to undress. Clothes were scattered in the street, shoes were kicked to the kerb. Bodies intertwined. Mouths pressed against mouths. Nipples pressed against nipples. The old, the young, the beautiful, the ugly – it affected everyone. Soon, the pub and the high street were a mass of writhing limbs. Priapic men penetrated gasping young ladies. Sapphic couples snaked legs around each other. Previously straight men embraced in bearish hugs. I saw it all. Anal, bukakke, buttplugs, corsets, cumshots, dildos, domination, facials, fingering, fisting, gangbangs, glory holes, golden showers, handjobs, kissing, masturbation, orgasms, spanking, squirting, threesomes, uniforms...

And as for me, I wish I could say that I was merely a voyeur. But I was also affected by the bizarre magic of that August evening. I had cast off my clothes and found myself pressed into the arms of a glassy-eyed barmaid, entwining and wriggling and holding on for dear life. As we locked into each other's bodies, I noticed a CCTV camera capturing the action live as it happened. Across London, millions of bodies were filmed by thousands of cameras, beaming the live-action porn to satellites and computers across the world.

The penny dropped: we were performers in an interstellar porno. We were rutting for the pleasure of alien viewers. And we didn't even get paid.

The spell of lust passed as quickly as it had descended. The actors and actresses in the impromptu skin-flick coyly gathered up bras and pants and resumed their evening activities as though nothing untoward had happened. I soon realised that my fellow Londoners had no memory of their outlandish behaviour.

I do not know how or why, but I appear to be the only person in London who remembers that August evening. There was no mention of any odd behaviour on the local news, and the grainy footage has never appeared on Soho bookshelves. Perhaps it was solely for Martian consumption.

August 15th

I feel faint. I am dislocated. I have been on a long journey. I have travelled by plane, bus, train and tube. This morning I was elsewhere, sipping coffee in the snow with now distant relatives.

I apologise that all you get are fragments of my life. I apologise for the lack of rhyme or reason. Many pages of my life have been removed for being too libellous, or too explicit. Or too boring. But not this one. This one stands. So there.

August 16th

I was recently asked by the British Council of Neuroses to give a little speech about my experience as an amateur brain doctor. Technically, I am not a fully trained psychoanalyst, but many of my friends live near Hampstead and it was inevitable that I would pick up a few tricks. People come to me for help in their desperation, and I offer them psychological sanctuary. I face many problems, from unresolved childhood traumas to bedwetters and serial shoehorners. I listen. I do not judge. (Except the real weirdos – *them* I judge.)

This is a short excerpt from my speech:

There are lots of different schools of psychoanalysis, and although to the untrained eye they can look similar, to the expert they are as different as two quite different tennis players – perhaps Mark Philippoussis and Michael Chang. These schools of psychoanalysis are not like the schools that you and I went to as children. They have no playgrounds or tuck shops. The schools are all very distinctive and psychoanalysts spend much of their time pooh-poohing the rival schools. I remember a Jungian psychoanalyst who was mistaken for a Kleinian at a Kentish Town dinner party; he flew into a terrifying rage which only abated when he choked on an olive and passed out.

The most famous school of psychoanalysis is the Freudian school. Sigmund Freud invented the wheel, the steam engine and the subconscious. Nowadays everyone sneers at his theories about sex and women but I doubt Freud himself is bothered, as he is dead.

A typical conversation with a Freudian psychoanalyst might go something like this:
Patient: I had a dream last night that I was running a marathon, but my shoelaces were untied – the nearer I got to the finishing line, the more anxious I got that I would fall. I couldn't bear to stop or look back. I was running from something, but I don't know what it was.
Analyst: Interesting. The marathon is your mother. The shoes are your father. You are gay.
Patient: Oh.

Another school of psychoanalysis is the Kleinian school. They were named after Melanie Klein, the wealthy daughter of underwear magnate Calvin Klein. Kleinians are very strict and will often sulk if the patient is late, and force them to lie underneath the couch, rather than on top of it. Klein was a disciple of Freud but disagreed with him on many key issues. Klein placed the development of the superego in infancy, whereas Freud placed it in a Swiss bank.

A conversation with a Kleinian psychoanalyst might go something like this:
Patient: Good afternoon. I had a dream last night that I was a tiny bird.
Analyst: Never mind that. I had a dream last night that you were gay.
Ergo you are gay.
Patient: Oh. OK.

Jungian analysts form another of the major schools. Carl Gustav Jung believed in the collective unconscious, which means that not only are we haunted by our own subconscious desires, but also by the subconscious of the whole of humanity. This is one reason why Jungian analysts are so expensive – they will often claim to have treated not only your own issues, but the issues of your father and grandfather, and expect to be paid accordingly.

An example of a typical conversation with a Jungian psychoanalyst:
Patient: I had a terrible dream that my teeth were falling out and that my hair turned white.
Analyst: That's all very well, but that doesn't even feature in the top ten list of popular dreams. The big dream at the moment is about bombs exploding in the centre of New York.
Patient: OK. What does that mean?
Analyst: I'm afraid you're gay.
Patient: Rats.

August 17th

Why must I share my world with other people? It is my world. I was here first.

I saw the Earth take shape. I witnessed the continents clatter and bump and rise from the seas. I saw the apes descend from the trees and don raincoats and smoke pipes. I watched man invent the hay bale. I chuckled as he created the gun, the telephone and the skateboard. I've been there and seen it all.

And here I am, now. In this world that teems with opinions, that shudders with speeches and Sunday supplement columnists. So much noise and so little peace. I just want to be able to walk down the road without seeing a single human being. Is that so much to ask?

I do like people. I just wish they knew their place.

August 18th

They predicted a meteor shower for tonight, so I went up on the roof. The sky was a muddy red and the air was thick and balmy. It felt for a minute as though I was living on Mars. But I wasn't. I was standing in north-east London. On a roof.

There were clouds in the sky. The weather man hadn't mentioned clouds. The sky was supposed to be clear. I stared straight up, straining my eyes for meteors. But all I could see was God, distant, resting in his details. There were no meteors.

Then something struck me on the face. It wasn't a meteor. It wasn't even a full, plump raindrop. It was a woman's court shoe. Black leather. I waited, every sinew tensed, for a second shoe, but that was it. A single shoe. If it was a pair of shoes, I'd have sold them on eBay, but it was just one shoe – no good to anyone.

I waited all night. There were meteors later, and I made a wish.

August 20th

This afternoon Beyoncé came round to lunch. I arrived home late and when I got there she was standing outside in the rain. She was wearing only a gold lamé bikini. I've tried to tell her before that bikinis aren't really suitable for suburban London, even in the summer.

In the old days, the other members of Destiny's Child would come along with Beyoncé, but I told Michelle and Kelly not to bother any more. They are the chaff and Beyoncé is the wheat and I am a very busy man.

I let Beyoncé into the house and put on the kettle.

'Do you want sugar in your tea?' I asked her as she lounged provocatively on the sofa.

'Hey, I'm not gon' compromise my Christianity', she replied. 'Just because I'm on stage dancing like I do, doesn't mean I'm not a God-fearing Christian. You know that people express their spirituality in different ways, and for me, there's nothing wrong with shakin' my booty and wearing sexy outfits. I'm still the same moral person that I always was. I don't think that God minds me being like I am. God gave me this body, so I don't think he'd object to me showing it off. At the end of the day I am an entertainer, and that's cool. But my personal and spiritual life is a totally separate thing.'

'I only asked if you wanted sugar in your tea.'

'Oh. Yeah. Two please', she smiled.

It was a long day.

August 21st

Once again I found myself in Wood Green shopping centre. Over the haze of neon and chirp of hospital radio, I noticed a commotion in the market place. There were the usual booths, offering cheap jewellery or a photo of a loved one on a mug, but there was also a large, new booth that was attracting quite a crowd.

I wandered closer. People were whispering to each other in an awed hush. Then I realised why: the booth had a large sign above it, and written in blue and white letters were the following words: 'HAVE YOUR PHOTO TAKEN WITH NELSON MANDELA. £1.50'.

And sure enough, sitting on a plastic chair by the booth was the celebrated political prisoner and former President of South Africa. He looked serene and was happily munching on a sausage roll. It was definitely him. I recognized him from a meeting we once had in the early nineties. I gave him a little wave and he cheerily waved back.

Beside the booth were a group of protesters. They were mostly liberal white women in their early forties. They had placards saying 'Do not have your photo taken with Mr Mandela. His constant public appearances degrade his image as a former world statesman'. I wandered over and said hello to one of the protesters.

'Why are you so unhappy about the photos?' I asked.

'It cheapens him. This man spent 30 years in jail. He's one of the most important figures of the twentieth century. He shouldn't be whoring himself around every shopping centre and youth club in Britain, acting like he's just another Z-list celebrity.'

'He seems happy enough', I pointed out.

'What's that got to do with it?' she growled. She thrust a sweaty pamphlet into my hands.

The pamphlet made boring reading. It was basically a summary of Mr Mandela's life. There was one interesting line at the bottom: 'It is estimated that by 2007, 80% of the world's population will have had their photo taken with Nelson Mandela'.

I scrunched up the pamphlet and threw it in a bin.

August 22nd

It was late. I was tired. God appeared before me in a vision. He looked familiar. We were sitting in what appeared to be the showroom of a large sofa-bed shop in north Finchley. He was wearing jewel-encrusted sandals and a golden robe, and I was wearing shorts and a T-shirt. I felt underdressed.

He looked angry. He eyes glowed with venom.

'You have sinned', he cried in a booming voice. 'Your sins are vanity and sloth and duplicity! J'accuse!'

'Um… well, I wouldn't say that I was a sinner. I'm misguided, but basically harmless.'

'Do not contradict me!' he growled, his beard flapping as he spoke.

'OK, OK. You're the boss. I'm a sinner. I accept it. Mea culpa.' It seemed that my best tactic would be to go along with him. It's like humouring a pub drunk. Smile and don't disagree.

'You shall be punished for your sinful ways!' he shouted, knocking the display price off a leather chaise-longue.

'What did you have in mind?' I asked. 'A lashing? A stoning? I know that birch caning is quite popular in BDSM circles.'

'No! Nothing so simple, you foolish, venal creature', he hissed.

'Your punishment is thus: you must count the number of leaves on all the trees in the world. If you are incorrect, you must start again. You will not be allowed to resume your mortal existence until you have given me the correct answer.'

'Am I allowed to guess?'

'Certainly, but only a cretin would believe that his guess would be correct!'

'OK', I sighed. Things were not looking promising. I really did not want to count every leaf in the world. It sounded like a dreadfully dull task. I have better things to do with my time – although I must confess I don't know what they are.

'Ummm… I'd say that there were 8 992 342 342 423 423 476 leaves in the world. Right now.'

'Fucking hell!' he exclaimed, slapping a meaty hand against his thigh. 'How did you get that right?'

'Just lucky', I shrugged. 'Honestly. It was just a lucky guess.'

'You're kidding me! A guess! You jammy sod!'

He disappeared in a cloud of cinnamon-flavoured smoke, and I awoke to find myself back at home, in bed, drenched in lukewarm sweat.

At least God occasionally appears to play fair.

August 24th

A Goth came round to visit. I don't like Goths.

'My life is torment', said the Goth. 'With every breath that I take, Destiny and Fate mock me.'

'Hmmm…' I replied.

'The Incubi and Succubi of boredom and sterility stalk me', he continued. 'I can feel the icy fingers of Death clutching my breast.'

'OK', I said.

'I am the God of Fuck', he said. 'I am the Prince of dread, of doom, of nothingness.'

'OK, I'll have to stop you there. Look, life isn't so bad. I mean, life is that bad, but don't be so melodramatic. The thing about life – it's not about extremes. It's not about God, or death or suffering. It's about banality. It's about tube journeys, weather, itchy skin, Sunday afternoons, football matches. You can't exist on a diet of high drama and excitement. Life isn't lived on the edges, it's lived far from the edges, in the safe little corners of the everyday, however dull and inconsequential they might be.'

'You disgust me', he spat. 'You're dead and you don't even know it.'

'No', I smiled smugly. 'You're quite wrong. I am alive and don't know it.'

Then I stabbed him. He was beginning to bore me.

August 26th

There is much talk of parallel universes. It is all hogwash and heffalumps. There are no such things.

Scientists – or frauds as I call them – endlessly theorise about time and space. They claim that for every possible decision, there are infinite outcomes, and that these theoretical outcomes form splinter universes that run parallel to our own. It hardly seems likely. One universe seems more than enough.

However, I will concede there are moments when the universe plays tricks on me; when realities appear to diverge and converge.

These blips only occur at bus stops: if I pass a bus stop, and ponder getting on a bus, a strange thing happens. Reality does seem to split in two. In one reality, I wait for the bus and ride it home. In the other reality, I cannot be bothered to wait for the bus and I walk home. These two realities juxtapose, and whichever decision I take, I am consumed by anxiety as the two 'themanwhofellasleeps' race each other home. Sometimes the 'me' who took the bus wins. Sometimes the 'me' who walked wins. It doesn't seem to matter who gets home first... it's the sense of unreality and anxiety that defeats me. Reality takes two different courses, and whichever I choose, I am tormented by the alternative; by what could have been.

August 27th

Today I watched television. I saw a film.

The film was about a young Indian girl in England who wants to be a footballer. However, her family are very conservative and want her to live a traditional life and get married and have kids. She is torn. She loves football – it's all she thinks about – but she also loves her family and doesn't want to disappoint them. Eventually, she decides to pursue her dream of becoming a footballer. Sadly, she breaks her legs and is unable to play anymore. She is penniless and her family shuns her. She is forced into prostitution to earn a living and becomes a heroin addict. Her addiction consumes her and at the end of the film she is found dead in a council bedsit, having overdosed on smack.

The film was alright, but it was a bit too feelgood for my taste. I prefer realistic endings. Or no endings at all. That would be ideal.

August 28th

To talk of money is distasteful. I was rich when Rockefeller was a mewling pup. I have overseen empires that would make Donald Trump mortgage his wig in fear. Money is my unnecessary evil. Nonetheless, sometimes I am obliged to work for some form of social interaction, if nothing else.

One of my jobs is editing the 'witty' comebacks used by Anne Robinson on *The Weakest Link*. Anne is a nice enough woman, but has never been suited to the harsh glare of television. When the bright lights in the studio shine into her tiny mole-like eyes, she freezes and is reduced to a tongue-tied blob of plastic and silicone. Therefore, everything she says is tightly scripted by a crack team of writers. And for my sins, I am one of those writers.

A week or so before production, Anne sends me a list of ideas – things she might like to say to contestants on the show. I then work on the comments, and fax them over to the BBC. Sadly, Anne has a somewhat limited imagination, and all her proposed comments are unbroadcastable insults. I simply tear them up and send her the same list of snide, semi-dry comebacks every week.

Last week the list she sent me was the worst yet. It was like an angry Tourette's sufferer stabbing a piece of paper with a cheap biro. Every single one of her proposed comments was a poor variation on 'You shits. You fucking shits. I hate you all.' I was almost tempted to leave them unchanged, but I feel sorry for the poor woman. She is a lost soul in the cruel world of early evening television entertainment.

I could tell you all many stories of my work with British celebrities, but that is for another book by another person.

August 29th

I spent most of today staring at a blank piece of paper, waiting for a message to appear in invisible ink. But the message didn't appear. It turns out it was just a blank piece of paper.

This is the problem with my virile imagination. Every experience becomes a potential sign, but the signs are rarely clear. I blame the Shadow.

Things overheard on the tube

Today's journey:
Bakerloo Line: Harlesden–Piccadilly Circus

1. I once met Lloyd Cole. He had grown a beard and looked like Gary Bushell.
2. He kept on saying, 'oh, this is not a blame culture', but he was staring right at me.
3. God is just birdseed.
4. He is the best marabout around. He has 35 years' experience. He will bring back your loved ones.
5. If you go to the newsagent, could you get me some Refreshers?
6. Someone in a room near me was either crying or having sex with no rhythm.
7. There's a melody in there somewhere but I can't put my finger on it.
8. My inbox is empty.
9. Two sausage, chips, beans, egg, mushrooms and a cup of tea. Fantastic.
10. Apparently, all the koalas in Australia have chlamydia.

August 31st

The cold north wind blows around my trousers. Night falls faster with every passing year.

This evening I went to an Alcoholics Anonymous meeting. It was in an old church near Tetherdown. There were five or six men and a couple of women. I didn't say much, I just sat in a corner, nursing my pint of Guinness and slurping unnecessarily loudly.

Everyone spoke in hushed tones. There were silences and occasional bursts of dark laughter. Eventually Richard, the guy in charge, turned to me and spoke. He was fat and bald and had no discernible eyebrows. He wore a wide, generous smile. His teeth were yellow.

'It looks like we have a new friend here today. What's your name?'

'Hang on', I said. 'I thought this place was supposed to be anonymous.'

'Well, yes. You don't have to give your real name. But it would be nice to know what to call you.'

I couldn't argue with his logic. 'OK. You can call me Corporal Savage', I said.

'Ummm... OK, Corporal Savage. Where would you like to begin? How long have you been drinking?'

'I don't drink. I never have', I admitted. 'I've always been more interested in the anonymous part of Alcoholics Anonymous. I have always yearned to be anonymous, to annihilate my personality and history.'

'So...' Richard looked bemused. I could see he was wrestling with his innate goodwill. 'You don't have any kind of drink problem? Because this is Alcoholics Anonymous. If you don't have a drink problem, you probably shouldn't be here.'

'Yes. I understand. I don't mean to be peevish, but this place should really be renamed. At the moment it's called Alcoholics Anonymous. If you're not interested in people being anonymous, then you should just call it Alcoholics.'

Some of the alcoholics had begun to mutter under their breath, and I started to feel unwelcome in the small, dusty room. Outside, it was dark and bleak and the sky was full of snow.

September 2nd

People always talk about drowning kittens in sacks, but it's really not that easy. Let's not even start on the pain of chasing a cat, stunning it, and then getting it into the sack. My problem is that the cats always seem to float. It's not like I fit them with inflatable armbands or anything. I just shove them in the sack.

But when I dump them in the river, they refuse to sink. They just bob along the surface, mewing and floating downstream towards the sea.

September 4th

Inspired by an obsession with Raymond Chandler and Sir Arthur Conan Doyle, I once set up a detective agency. It just seemed like something to do to pass the time – I didn't really expect any clients, but I liked the idea of having my name stencilled on a glass door. From inside my office, I could read it backwards.

So there I was, sitting at my desk, enjoying the angle at which my fedora fell over my eyes, when the doorbell rang. It was a frumpy middle-aged woman with dyed-red hair. She looked nervous and clutched her handbag to her chest. I was disappointed. I had always assumed that only glamorous, svelte, young femme fatales went to detective agencies.

She sat across from me at the desk and I offered her a mint. She declined, but seemed grateful for the gesture.

'It's my husband', she said. 'He's missing.'

'Lady', I said. 'When most people go missing, it's because they don't want to be found.' I had no idea if this was true or not, but it was something I'd once overheard on the radio, and it sounded like it might comfort her.

'Oh no, not my Gerald! He's not like that at all. We're very much in love', she sobbed.

'OK. When did he go missing?'

'He disappeared a week ago. I saw him after supper on Thursday, and then I popped into the lounge to get a book for bedtime, and when I returned to the kitchen, he was nowhere to be found.'

'OK, lady. What does your husband look like?'

'He's about six inches wide, with a horn-rimmed frame, and two clear panels of glass.'

'That's not your husband you've just described, it's your spectacles. And if I might be so bold, they are hanging around your neck on a chain.'

She frantically grabbed at her chest, recovered her glasses and hurriedly put them on her nose. She blinked like an owl, her eyes huge behind glass.

'Oh! Thank you! Thank you so much! I am always doing this... I am afraid I often confuse my husband with my glasses. I have been lost without them for the last week. I am very near-sighted and life without my spectacles is unbearable!'

'What about your husband?' I asked. 'Is he missing or not? Are you even married at all?'

'I am afraid Gerald died some years ago', she confessed. 'But you seem nice. And I'm so very lonely. Could I have that mint?'

September 5th

I rang the bell. A man answered.

'Oh, I am sorry', I said. 'I hadn't realised you were shaving.'

'What are you talking about?' he said. 'I'm not shaving.'

'But your face... it's covered in shaving foam.' I pointed to his lathered chin.

He let out a low sob.

'That's not shaving foam! It's my *face!*'

I gingerly prodded his face. He was right. What had appeared to be shaving foam was indeed his face. His jaw was white and creamy-looking, but it was firm to the touch, like a fresh mushroom.

'I am sorry. I didn't realise.'

'It's OK. Everyone thinks it's shaving foam. Now, what do you want?'

'Nothing. I was just bored so I rang your bell. Can I come in?'

But he didn't let me in, so I hung around outside, waiting for the time to go home.

September 6th

Two days ago it was winter. Now it is summer. England is strange like that.

I had the misfortune to find myself walking through Hoxton and Dalston. The heavy weather was taking its toll on everyone. The traffic was backed up all along Old Street and men in lorries sweated and swore at each other. Hip hop and folk music blared from cafés that were disguised as industrial warehouses.

There were shouts and screams coming from a small restaurant. I peered inside and saw that a group of bearded young men – possibly some kind of avant-garde web art collective – were nailing a businessman to a cross for the crime of being unfashionable. The young men were wearing suit jackets and trainers and were berating the businessman for his brogues and BHS trousers.

I was tempted to intervene and try to save the man, but I was not particularly fashionably dressed myself, and fear clutched at my hems.

There are sharp pains in my head when I close my eyes. This morning I rolled a die 10 times and it came up 6 every time. I don't know what that means.

September 7th

The problem with absent fathers, eh? I've been thinking about poor old Jesus. And myself. I rarely stop thinking about myself.

The problem with absent fathers is that you can't get angry at someone that isn't there. You can only argue (and reconcile yourself) with a presence but not an absence. So all the anger and disappointment that you should feel towards a father gets misplaced and directed at someone else, and all the while you fight imaginary battles with someone who isn't really there. I am sure that Jesus can testify that struggling with phantom parents is an exhausting ordeal. I spend all day trying to communicate with a presence that is active only as an absence. Perhaps that is why I dream of the Shadow so much. My shadow only exists when I step into the sun – he is another absence that is present in my daily life.

What a complicated life I lead. I need a lie down.

I have been told that nature abhors a vacuum. That is as true in an emotional sense as it is in a physical one. An emotional vacuum is soon filled up with the worthless detritus of daydreams, fantasies and idle resentment. A thousand times I have rehearsed a speech to my father. A thousand days I have paid homage to him as an absent son. In the face of a thousand strange men, I have chatted lazily about football and women, misdirecting a son's need for approval. Jesus can get to the back of the queue. God can be everywhere at once. My father can't.

Still, it's not all doom and gloom. I see my father from time to time. And when we do meet, at airports and family dinners, my dad and I shrug and bluff and play pool and talk about films. And I realise that I have two fathers (no, not like in that sitcom). I have the father of my reality, a solid, good-hearted man, and the father who left me and who will never return. Is it any wonder that I fear the Shadow? I have spent 20 years waiting for a face to appear.

THE SHADOW...

September 9th

Dr Bruce Banner came round for tea. He is always very highly strung. And oh so fussy. No milk in the tea. Just one sugar. No gelatine in the boiled sweets. He gets on my nerves a bit.

I offered him a macaroon.

'You know I don't like macaroons', he whined.

'No. I didn't know that. But I should have guessed. You don't like anything, do you?'

'Don't say that!' He gripped his mug of tea and the veins in his temples bulged.

'I don't know why I bother with you', I said. 'You never like anything I do. You just come here to complain.'

He stood up, spilling his tea on his lap. He shook a fist at me. 'That's not fair! You know how difficult this is for me!' he wailed.

'Oh, boo hoo hoo, poor old Bruce Banner, blah, blah, gamma radiation, blah, blah, blah, huge green muscles… it's just me, me, me with you, isn't it Bruce?'

'Don't make me angry', he snarled. 'You wouldn't like me when I'm angry.'

'Oh Bruce', I sighed. 'I don't like you anyway.'

September 11th

'Mateja waited on the Hammersmith and City Line, savouring the rich, bohemian smell of west London. The Westway. The Clash. Portobello Market. Trustafarians and sexy posh girls. He drummed his fingers on his denim knee, tracing out the rhythm of his headphones. On the seat opposite his was a discarded Jamaican pastie.

In his head, the sounds blared:

And lo, the lion did lie down with the lamb, for they were both tired. And it was good. And all was peace in Eden, for a neweth day had dawned.

He was listening to the bible on his MP3 player. It was actually a bootleg remix, splicing the Old and New Testaments with some old hip-hop instrumentals to form a new text that wasn't entirely up to date, but was fairly contemporary. Mateja liked to be on the cutting edge, even if this meant that he sometimes fell off his seat.

And lo, Jesus did emerge from the burning bush, and his beard sparkled with embers, and Moses was truly pleased. For it was good.

The bible was more interesting than he had expected. There was rutting and violence and he detected a darkly bleak humour underpinning the text. Before he'd done his sociology classes he would never have noticed that. London was new and exciting. Black girls at bus stops. Bouncers in leather coats. Drugs, lots of drugs. The taxis were expensive, though.

In his mind he reeled off the west London tube stations ahead of him. He could feel the rhythm – Westbourne Park – the beat – Ladbroke Grove – the energy – Latimer Road – of the city pulsing through his body. It started in his elbows and spread down his legs like a heart attack. Later on, he would pick up some dope from William. He liked William. William wore funny clothes.

And when the Lord did speaketh, the burning bush did quake with fear. And then Barabas did rise from the bush and curse the Romans, for they had given Britain roads and adequate sewage systems.

The voices in his head were insistent and hypnotic. He pressed his MP3 player, and the machine coughed and skipped to the next track. He was going places. He knew it.

September 12th

Today is the anniversary of Johnny Cash's death. I can't get over it. He was always my favourite tennis player.

I sat in the waiting room outside Dr Merrick's clinic. He's my alternative psychoanalyst. I am not sure whether I trust him or not.

He always seems very uptight, which doesn't make me feel good about myself. Also, his trousers are always stained. I think it's salad cream, but I fear it may be animal semen.

On the waiting room wall there is a poster. It reads: 'No. I am *not* the Elephant Man. Neither am I related to him in any way. You may think your jokes and jibes are funny, but they are NOT'.

After I'd waited half an hour, Mary, Dr Merrick's softly-spoken assistant, told me it was my turn to see the doctor. I shuffled into the room. There was a spotlight over the bed, but Dr Merrick himself was shrouded in darkness. I could hardly see him, only the plumes of smoke that drifted across the room from his clove cigarettes.

I lay down and explained that I had a lot on my mind at the moment. I told him that there were too many thoughts in my head, and that they all seemed to be fighting for control of my mind.

He coughed and said that my subconscious was probably overbooked.

I frowned and asked him what he meant.

He coughed again and explained that the subconscious worked in very much the same way as a flight on an aeroplane. Sometimes the subconscious mind is overbooked – there are too many subconscious thoughts jostling for the same positions. When this happens, a person's mental air hostess upgrades some of the thoughts from subconscious to conscious and they occupy the front part of the mind, where they are separated from the subconscious by a thin curtain.

Then he coughed again and told me that my time was up. I'd only been there for 8 minutes.

September 13th

I sat in my local library, flicking through a copy of *Time Out* and occasionally shrieking at glossy pages of conceptual art.

Libraries are comforting places. I enjoy the tranquillity and the fact that so much literary history gathers dust in such a small space. It's all free, you know? You don't have to pay for any of the books.

I wandered through the children's section, which was bedecked with large cartoon figures and cardboard wizards. In the thriller section,

I picked up a dog-eared copy of a Sherlock Holmes omnibus. A page floated free and fell at my feet. It wasn't Sherlock Holmes. The Holmes book was fresh-faced and lilywhite, whereas the loose page was a dirty brown, like stale tea.

I started reading. I read most things, from bus tickets to handkerchiefs.

The Mystery of the Mottled Mattress

I was standing on the platform, waiting for the 08.38 service to Huskbrough. It was a cold, grey day, and the sun beat down remorselessly. Further along the platform a fat man had stumbled and sprained his ankle. A vet had been called, and the man was being put down. The situation made me feel uneasy. Behind me, there lurked a shadowy figure, who stroked a thin moustache and cackled into the wind. There was something sinister about the man. He looked a little like my late father and as he walked past the station café, I could still see the café through his thin, insubstantial skin. He disappeared behind the outhouse and did not reappear.

The train pulled into the station, the wheels screeching in mock ecstasy. I boarded the train, cursing as I realised my lunch (porridge) was leaking out of my briefcase.

I sat next to an elderly gentleman. I wasn't sure if he was dead or not, so I jabbed him in the arm with a letter opener. He awoke with a jolt.

'Sorry', I chuckled. 'I thought you might be dead. Where are you going?'

'Industrial Turkshead', he replied, staring out of the window into the blank darkness of the tunnel.

'What an interesting name for a place!' I cried, delighted by my discovery.

'It's French. It means "City of a thousand hidden delights and terrors."'

'Well, that's certainly true! What a terrific name for the place.'

'Yes, it's German.' He smiled to himself, as though at some secret joke. He winked conspiratorially at me. 'You may call me Johann.'

I thrust out my hand. 'Pleased to meet you Johann. My name is Mud.'

Thus was to begin an epic mystery that has baffled the greatest detective minds of our time. Of course, back then...

The story abruptly ended. I turned over the page. It was blank.

Another mention of a shadowy figure. This cannot be a coincidence! I pocketed the page and sneaked out of the library. A vivid sense of intrigue nags at me. Once again, I have a strong suspicion that I wrote the ludicrous story, and hid it in the library to be found, by me, at a later date. The subconscious often functions in such ways.

Outside the library, a gritting truck sprayed orange gristle onto tarmac.

September 14th

A dentist's surgery. A foreign receptionist mispronouncing my name. Last month's issue of *Cosmopolitan* magazine and a crumpled copy of the *Guardian*. One article in the newspaper stared me in the face; a crippled beggar demanding attention:

Pete Logan: A Normal Life

Like most 'normal' men, I like nothing more than watching football and playing with Alfie and Kate, my two normal children. Anyone who knows me could tell you how much I love kids – all in a perfectly healthy way. When I tickle or 'rough-house' them, I get no sense of dread or panic that I am a dead-eyed paedophile. Children are the future, and until science allows us to transplant our brains into the host bodies of teenagers, they will continue to be the legacy we leave in the world. Children are important. Children are impotence.

Anyone with children soon gets used to being asked to part with hundreds of pounds every 5 minutes on some so-called 'toy' that all their school friends are already flaunting round the playground, and is therefore more important than 'life' itself. The house that I share with Charlotte, my attractive and totally satisfied wife, is jam-packed with Power Devols, Portomon paraphernalia, ZoneBoys, and countless other once crucial 'fads' whose combined value down the years has cost us the equivalent of my planned trip to Thailand. But I don't resent any of the purchases. The thought of resenting my children doesn't even enter my mind. I own so much that cannot be priced in Euros.

So why do I dote so much on my normal children? Because it is easier to face financial 'ruin' than have my ears 'ringing' with accusations of emotional cruelty and neglect.

The one thing we have stood firm against is 'mobile' phones. Katie, our 12-year-old whose pre-pubescent beauty incites no lust in my mind, wants one and we won't let her. We've had the usual pleading, tears, anger and arguments and livid silences as to why it's absolutely vital to have one, and even the playful slaps I give her have not changed her mind. It is not a question of money, as I certainly earn enough to afford one – although it's worth noting that I don't earn so much that I could ever forget that I'm really just an 'average' family guy, like Geoff or James or Guy or Noel, who likes nothing more than a simple pint and watching the football.

No, it's none of that. It's just that we have been advised by the government that mobile phones might be 'dangerous' for children. I know there's a lot of discussion about the government and democracy and globalization and all that, but I've always thought that the government is good and, more importantly, big. Leave the intellectual 'debates' for the philosophers of the world – I'm just a normal bloke who likes to do as he's told and not worry too much about whether it's right or wrong.

So, Katie is not getting a mobile phone. I don't care if she cries about it, as long as she does it in her bedroom and not in front of guests. I'm not made of stone! Of course it hurts me that she gets upset, but I certainly don't feel any crippling guilt that I've been an emotionally distant father who is unable to properly communicate love. If the government says that mobile phones are 'dangerous', then I'm not going to argue with them. Katie will have to satisfy herself with whatever it is that girls do. Soon she will be a woman. The mysteries of the female body do not alarm me.

Soon Alfie will be a teenager, and no doubt will get spots and want to listen to rap music. I'm more into rock music myself, but I'm certainly not racist and anyway Eminem is white. Alfie won't be getting a mobile phone until the government tells me to buy him one.

Of course, I take some risks myself. I'm not some kind of emotionless autopilot robot! I live! I go out drinking with the lads – the evening never ends with a drunken homoerotic clinch, you'll be pleased to hear – and in my younger days I smoked. I use the railways, just like any other man. My money hasn't changed me. I'm just like you, getting up and going to work and not doing the bad things. So, it's OK for me to take risks. I'm an adult. But how could I take a risk with the lives of my darling children?

I can't. Just like you couldn't. Because I'm a good, normal person. I don't have long hair. I don't have a goatee. I'm just a normal guy who happens to write a column.

My teeth hurt (past tense). But I understood the man who wrote the article. He is scared of being a man. He is scared that being a man means killing his father. He is a fool.

The dentist is not scared of being a man. She's an Indian woman, but she'd be a better man than many men.

September 16th

Yesterday I was friendless. My friends had all gone off, like expired yoghurts.

All my friendships come with a best-before date. I meet a friend, we chat, we phone each other, we watch football. Then I get bored and restless. They swear too much. They live too far away. They smell funny. They do not indulge my vanity. They do not orbit me like a satellite. So I give up – I throw the food in the bin. I will go shopping again next week.

Last week I found myself in need of a new friend. But friends are unreliable. I did not want another friend – I wanted a slave. A friend who did what I told him to do. A friend who wanted nothing from me but the warm glow of obedience.

But how do you get a slave nowadays? Slavery has been abolished, that's true. However, there are always people willing to relinquish their freedom. It's such a burden – making decisions, taking responsibility for your actions – there are thousands of people in this squalid, self-loathing city who are desperate to be slaves.

I did my research. I spoke to experts. I consulted the I *Ching*. It seemed the best route to getting a slave was on the gay scene.

I registered in a chatroom. There were hundreds of categories for thousands of fetishes, many of them unknown even to me. And there it was, staring at me in the face: 'Masters and Slaves'. Hundreds of slaves, all looking for masters! All yearning to obey! It all seemed like a dream come true! I sat back and watched the intricate cyberdance as masters and slaves collided on the screen.

But I grew tired of watching, so I started typing. Words poured out – I cannot honestly remember everything I said, but it certainly caught the attention of the lurking slaves. Perhaps they mistook my aftershave for testosterone. The hours slipped away as I talked to men in Lincoln, men in Barnstable, men in Kent. Then I spotted Lars in London. Lovely Lars. Ludicrous Lars. Larcenous Lars.

Today I met Lars. My very own slave. He is a pleasant, apparently confident, theatre producer who lives in the Barbican. I got the tube over to his flat and introduced myself. He was tall, forty-something and wore glasses that only a German would wear without laughing. I asked for a coffee.

'Yes Master.' He scurried to the kettle, strenuously keeping his eyes from meeting mine.

I drank the coffee and we sat in silence. I was not feeling very masterful, just relieved to be sitting on a clean sofa with a cup of coffee, instead of on the floor drinking warm water at home.

'How can I serve you, Master?' he asked, his German accent making him sound like an extra from *Allo Allo*.

'Ummm… you can pass me the remote control, and order me a pizza', I said.

'Yes sir', he replied. He paused and looked at me. 'Sir? Will any of my duties be of a sexual nature?'

'No', I replied. 'You're my slave. Not my boyfriend.'

'Oh', he said. 'I am an excellent cocksucker, I assure you. All of my previous masters have been very happy with my technique.'

'Very nice, slave. Maybe later. Right now I want to watch the TV and eat a pizza. You understand?'

'Yes sir', he murmured and walked to the phone.

After ordering the pizza, he asked if he could kneel at my feet. I told him he could, as long as he didn't get in the way of the television.

After a few minutes, he looked up at me. 'Sir, if the pizza is late, will I be punished?'

'No. That doesn't seem fair. It's not your fault. It's the fault of the pizza place.'

'Oh, but Master, I must be *punished*!' he implored. 'I should be caned or spanked. Perhaps you could put me in a chastity belt.'

'No. I don't really think I'd enjoy that', I said. The idea of spanking a middle-aged German did not appeal to me.

'Very well sir.'

The pizza arrived. It was late, as Lars had predicted, but it was tasty enough. Pineapple. For an hour or so, I sat in his lounge, eating pizza and lazily watching afternoon television. Lars sat silently at my feet.

I disappeared to the loo and when I returned to the sofa Lars was staring up at me like a lonely puppy.

'Sir, am I to understand that I will not be serving you sexually, and you will not be punishing me?' he asked.

I felt that for once, honesty was the best policy.

'Look, you're my slave, right? You do as I say. I do not find you sexually attractive and I have no desire to punish you. I just want you to obey me. This isn't some role play where I wear a pair of leather trousers and pretend to be all dominant with you and you squirm around on the floor feeling exquisite humiliation – this is real. I want you to do as I say.'

'Ah', he said. His eyes became steely.

'I expect you to cook and clean and drive me places. Basically, you're here to make my life easier. Just think of yourself as a very spineless friend.'

'Friend?!' He practically spat the word on the floor. 'I don't want to be your friend! I am your slave! You must use me! Humiliate me! Take advantage of me sexually!' By this stage he was practically shouting, and I began to feel uncomfortable.

'I don't think this is working out', I said. 'I was working on the premise that you actually wanted to be a slave. You don't. You just want me to act all dominant and have sex with you. I think I should leave.'

'Yes', he snapped. 'I think perhaps you should.'

I let myself out of the flat and walked towards the tube station.

I looked up at the flat and saw his face pressed against the window, his mournful eyes still following me.

So. No more slaves for me. For an hour I was a master and had a slave. And thereafter I was slaveless on a sluggish tube in the grey afternoon. But I got a free pizza. These small blessings are sometimes enough.

September 17th

When I was a young man, I used to write poetry! What a fool I was! I wrote of destiny, and tragedy, of autumn leaves and summer rain. I fancied that history would recall me as a perceptive dreamer whose sensitive verse articulated the agony of an age. Needless to say, it was a phase that I grew out of.

It all ended rather awkwardly at a poetry reading, where I killed four people with a badly-rhymed couplet. The pen is truly mightier than the sword.

Sometimes I am contacted by old friends or academics who plead with me to revive my poetic ambitions, but to no avail. Poets are weedy ingrates who chew gum and smell of urine. And I do not chew gum.

However, I do fondly remember some of my poems. And in the spirit of nostalgia, I will present you with some short works.

This is a poem I wrote to commemorate the death of my good friend John F. Kennedy. He was a sweet man, but never presidential material. I always imagined he'd end up washing cars in a local garage.

There's a pig in the oven,
on gas mark five.
It's no longer alive.

Many academics have analysed the role of the pig in my poetry. I wish they wouldn't. I wish they would shave and get a proper job.

Here is a poem I wrote about the death of Diana, Princess of Wales. She was also a nice girl, but a bit needy. A lot of cultural commentators felt that this poem summed up the mood of the nation in those hysterical days that followed her demise.

Goodbye, England's daisy,
you were a little bit crazy.
Or were you?

The world of poetry is poorer for my absence. But my life is greatly enriched by its lack of poetry.

September 18th

Try to imagine a world without France – is it possible?

For centuries scholars have pondered the social, culinary and political problems of France, trying to balance a deep-seated hatred of France with a justifiable ethical reluctance to destroy a whole country and all of its inhabitants.

However, in recent years there has been a breakthrough in the philosophical approach to France: scholars have discovered that the more they smashed their heads repeatedly against hard, gravelly surfaces, the less they cared about the moral implications of destroying France. It's an interesting way of solving dilemmas.

So, blood pouring from their gashed foreheads, the great thinkers of the world have organised for France to be removed.

Obviously, there was global public anger at this move, with thousands of demonstrations organised all across the world in defence of Liberté, Egalité et Fraternité. Oh, who am I kidding? Of course there wasn't. The rest of the world merely turned a blind eye as France was lowered beneath the ocean, where it shall now doubtless flourish as a modern-day Atlantis.

Au revoir, Monsieur Zidane. A bientot Mademoiselle Bardot. Goodbye, Mr Pommes Frites.

September 19th

Dr Gepetto is alive again. Either that or I am dreaming.

I am sitting up in bed and he is in a chair at my bedside.

'I'm taking you off the Seroxat', he says, and I nod in agreement, although I don't know why.

'I am putting you on these', he continues, depositing a packet of cigarettes on the bedside table.

'I want you to smoke one every 20 minutes or so. Just let them eat away the day. They are more effective than antidepressants.' Again, I nod.

He reaches into the top pocket of his white coat and pulls out a notepad.

'I'm writing you a prescription. Take it to any newsagent and they'll give you cigarettes. You'll still have to pay, I'm afraid.'

In the haze of sleep, I nod again. He smiles. 'I think you're getting better. At any rate, you're not getting any worse. I imagine you'll be out of here in a week or so. Don't be surprised if you don't see me again, at least not in this form.'

Then he is gone. It is early morning and I slip back into a slumber.

September 21st

Facts are important. In recent years I have noticed a sharp increase in the sale of almanacs and miscellanies.

Here are some facts. Learn them well.

Fact 1:   Alexandra Palace overlooks north London. The first ever proper television broadcast in the world was there. They were going to choose either Alexandra Palace or Crystal Palace as the site for the transmitter, but they decided that people in south London wouldn't be able to afford televisions.

Fact 2:   People are very suspicious of political prisoners. As a species, we don't like interferers, even when they are right. One man's civil rights activist is another man's busybody.

Fact 3:   Badgers are very cute. I don't think I have ever seen one in real life, but I've seen loads on television.

Fact 4:   Everyone likes Humphrey Bogart. But I fear that if he were a contemporary Hollywood star, he'd be Bruce Willis.

Fact 5:   There is nothing to fear but fear itself. But that is still quite a lot. After all, there is nothing to love but love itself.

Fact 6:   Cats have taken over from dogs as the nation's favourite pets. I think it's because they require less maintenance. Everything is becoming more disposable.

Fact 7:   Rock climbers are disappointing. They are trying to get closer to God in a very prosaic fashion.

Fact 8:   My hands are among my best features. You can forgive a person with good hands almost anything.

Fact 9:   A *Simpsons* episode that does not focus on Homer is a wasted episode. I do not want to know about Lisa's love of jazz.

Fact 10:   Top chef Gordon Ramsey hates people adding salt and pepper before they've tasted their meals.

Fact 11:   Porn makes caricatures of women. Men make caricatures of themselves.

Fact 12:   The two old complaining men in the Muppets were called Statler and Waldorf.

Fact 13:   Woody Allen has only ever made three films. They are quite good, but he has re-released them over and over with different names.

Fact 14:   There is something very wholesome about Matthew Modine.

Fact 15:   Melody is still more important than rhythm, despite the protestation of leading musicologists.

Fact 16:   As a child I would confuse Maureen Lipman, my mother and the Queen.

Fact 17:   The Dutch are generally good at darts and other pub games, such as billiards and snooker.

Fact 18:   In America, spring onions are known as scallions and courgettes are called zucchini.

Fact 19:   Singer-songwriter Alicia Keys has a very hairy chest.

Fact 20:   Every country gets the press and politicians that it deserves.

September 22nd

I was wandering in the rain, lonely as a cow. I found myself in a small, dark club in a Soho sidestreet. It was called 'Club Delusion'. I wandered inside. That was a mistake. It was an awful place.

The room was full of short, ugly men, dressed fashionably in suit jackets and jeans. They looked at each other anxiously, waiting to pounce if they felt a fellow clubber was not dressed fashionably enough – or worse still, if they were dressed too fashionably. For every three men, there was a tall, bored-looking woman, staring down at the men, possibly searching for signs of early baldness.

A man called Jack hurriedly approached me and thrust his hand into mine. It turned out that he was the owner of the club. One of his eyes was focused on mine, but the other flitted wildly in its socket. (He later explained his eye condition – it allows him to talk to one person, but keep an eye on the rest of the club in case someone more important walks in.)

I asked him why the club reeked so strongly of failure and evil. He smiled proudly.

'I wanted to set up a club where London media types could really revel in their narcissism and self-loathing', he said. He swept his arm around the room, pointing at the hunched masses. 'Aren't they magnificent? Not one of them is happy. They all think of themselves as movers and shakers on the cutting edge of media and fashion, yet in reality they have no influence at all. They come here in small packs and network with each other in the hope of making a vital breakthrough. It's fantastic. None of the guys has any desire other than to land a job commissioning bad television and boast about the amount of coke they do.'

I asked him about the women.

'They are here to look bored. They are very good at it. I hire them to add some glamour. None of them would touch the guys here with a bargepole, because they all have delusions that they are supermodels and aspiring popstars, when most of them just work as PAs in the city. There's a fantastic lack of interplay between the men and the women here. I have a motto for this place: 'Everyone goes home alone'. That's why the music is so loud, so people can't really talk. I want that kind of atmosphere where people can stare glumly across the bar at each other, wearing fixed smiles and kidding themselves that they're metrosexual trendsetters.' He looked up. His roving eye was glowing and pulsing in its socket. 'Can you excuse me for a second', he said. 'I've just seen someone I think may work for E4.'

He pushed past me and rushed to the door, where a tall bouncer had a small Scottish man in a headlock. I didn't see him again.

I got the tube home. Somewhere down the carriage, a drunk was shouting out incomprehensible verse. I admired him.

Things overheard on the tube

Today's journey:
East London Line: Shoreditch–New Cross

1. Yeah, sure... he's a musical icon, but is he actually any good?
2. Thankfully there's no level crossings on the tube.
3. He's weird. At Halloween he dressed up as the Littlest Hobo.
4. Whitney Houston is just white trash... except she's black, I suppose.
5. He spent an hour explaining why *Apocalypse Now* was so important. I'd rather have just watched the film.

6. Fuck it! Now I've got garlic sauce on my lap.
7. I took paracetamol. Then aspirin. Then ibuprofen. But I feel worse than ever.
8. She has really musty curtains.
9. You tie the goat to the van, and then you drive the van very slowly uphill.
10. I do not understand why English people like pantomime. To me, it is just... stupid.

September 24th

Today Morrissey came round for tea. It was unexpected, and there was no food in the house, so I had to give him a plate of iron filings. Later on, I had fun pulling him around the lounge with a giant magnet.

Morrissey surrounds himself with a large entourage. He pays them to insult him and make inappropriate suggestions. 'Why don't we do a two-

Morrissey / An Old Lady

step remix of the new single?' 'You should work with Nelly – he's very hot at the moment.' 'You're past it. You're balding and no one thinks you're relevant anymore.'

Then, when he's had a few hours of abuse, he orders them to leave and moans: 'Ohhh... do you see what I have to put up with?'

I like him. He's funny.

September 26th

I was sat on a bench with a woman. The sky was clear and the air was crisp and fresh.

'I love autumn', she said. 'It's the colours. All that red and orange. Look – it almost looks like that tree is on fire.'

'It is on fire', I replied. 'I set it on fire. Actually, we should probably move from here. It's getting quite hot.'

If you remember just one part of the journal, remember this.

September 27th

There is a spare room in my house. It's filled with the butts of every cigarette I have ever smoked. There are 40 000 of them. I can't bear to throw them away. I am an inveterate hoarder.

September 28th

Yesterday Walter Matthau came round for a beer after dinner. He's been dead for a couple of years, but he's still better company than most people I know. That face! I could kiss him if he wasn't decomposing.

'How's death?' I asked him.

'Pshaw! I can't complain', he said, flicking a maggot off his lapel, 'though the food is dreck.'

'What do you do? To pass the time?'

'It's like being alive, except there's less rush. I smoke a cigar, I play gin rummy, I listen to the radio. I chase the girls a bit, but dead girls aren't as nice as living broads. No class. They've seen too much. But you know, it's OK. It's like living in Florida.'

He looked well. It embarrassed me that he looked so at ease with himself, dead, while I looked like a nervous wreck. It has not been a good week for me.

He caught a cab back to the afterlife. I offered to pay, but he smiled and waved away my gesture. He is, as ever, a gentleman.

September 29th

Nothing makes sense. Time speeds up and slows down. I find myself alone once more, staring at words and pictures and trying to make sense of them.

The Shadow is everywhere. He's the uninvited guest in my story. Maybe that's what I deserve. I haven't been totally honest with you... with any of you. But the truth will out. Maybe.

All these episodes, all these entries. Are they pieces in a puzzle? Are they cogs in a narrative machine? Or are they pretty distractions, to occupy your attention while the real story occurs elsewhere?

Today I talked to the man selling the *Socialist Worker* outside Wood Green library. Wood Green library is a good spot for nutters of all persuasions, and it's hard to resist the temptation to stop and admire their lunacy.

I am always amazed by the anger of other people. The raging, righteous urge to stamp a foot and scream and point a bony finger at the villain. If only villains were so easy to find.

The *Socialist Worker* man was in a frightful state. His skin was blotchy and irritated, as though all the frustration and hatred in his body was trying to force its way out through his pores. Every few seconds a new spot appeared on his face, swelled to the size of a pea and then exploded, projecting acidic pus onto the street. The paving stones were pockmarked and uneven; it was clear that weeks of pus had eroded the concrete.

'What are you protesting against today?' I asked.

'Everything', he hissed, wiping his greasy hair away from his eyes.

'Everything in the world. Everything that springs forth from human corruption. Everything born of original capitalist sin. You... are... all... such... scum.' He was having trouble speaking. It was as if his physical body were merely a conduit from some extradimensional source, and was struggling to contain his accursed essence. He looked as though he might erupt or implode at any moment.

'Hmmm... I am not actually scum.' I smiled as I spoke. I try not to get angry – it doesn't sit well on my face.

'You don't understand', he barked, his head juddering uncomfortably from side to side. 'If you're not with me, you're against me. To... be... good... is not enough. You must be ideologically sssssound. You must believe in the eradication of human choice. You must worship the dog god dogma.'

'Um... no thanks', I said. 'I am sure you're a great guy and everything, but you're scaring people away. Maybe you're right, maybe you're wrong. I don't know. I don't get involved. But how can you be so sure you're not the problem yourself? For a socialist you seem to have a great deal of contempt for your fellow man.'

'You are unclean', he screeched. 'You are a harpy. You hover above life and admire the pretty colours, but you don't see what I see, down here on the ground.'

In a sense he has a point. I rarely dirty my hands with politics. But I give up my seat for the elderly and I help young mothers carry prams up stairs. I hope that's enough to save my soul.

September 30th

Once again, I found myself in a pub. I sat on a blotchy stool. The smell of piss wafted over from the Gents.

I waited for someone to talk to me. Someone always talks to me, to hurry the story along. After 5 minutes of staring at my hands, an old man sidled over to me.

He coughed and spat a lump of brown phlegm onto the floor.

'Let me tell you a story. You may not want to listen to me, an old man in a pub, cursing under his breath and smoking. But listen to me... please... I want to tell you... about the greatest battle in the history of the human race. It still rages... all around us. People are dying, even now, as we speak.

'One foggy December morning in 1917, the men and women fighting the gender wars emerged from their trenches. They were cold and soaking wet. Both factions laid down their arms, exhausted and dispirited, and wandered into the foggy morass of no-man's land.

'One man spoke up. His words were soft and haltering. He was waving a white flag made from ripped-up bedsheets.

"Let's not fight today", he said. "It's Christmas Day. This is no time for violence." From under his trenchcoat, he pulled out a battered round object. He placed it on the mud at his feet. "Let's play football instead."

The women gawped. Their faces were drawn and haggard, their lipstick crudely smudged.

"Football?" they jeered in unison. "All year we are waiting for some token... some gesture of affection... and this is all you can manage? Football? You play football every bloody week. Honestly... if you're suggesting that we stop fighting so we can kick a ball around. No. Don't even think it... we may as well leave you boys to it. We'll go shopping instead, shall we girls?"

'Tired and disorientated, the man hesitated. "I... we... we're trying to stop the fighting. To make peace. To change things. If you're just going to throw it back in our faces..."

'His voice was drowned out as soldiers from both sides groaned and shouted and whistled catcalls at each other. The bickering continued until nightfall. The men never did play football, and the women never did go shopping.

'And when Boxing Day arrived the ceasefire had long ended. Words and insults were hurled, and terrified children huddled together in sodden trenches. But the adults ignored them and carried on fighting, and have been at war ever since.

'So where does that leave men and women today, in this supposedly enlightened age? I don't know. But I am sick of this war. As a child, you think you can stay neutral, that you won't have to choose a side... but soon enough the hormones kick in and you find yourself forced onto one gender or the other, reluctantly flinging insults at the enemy. Some people seem to enjoy the war... but not me. I know that war is hell.

'I'm a reporter, you know... and like any wartime reporter, I try to stay above the fray. I try to look at the merits of both sides without getting too closely involved. But as every reporter knows, you can't stay neutral forever, and sooner or later words will always be twisted to suit the propaganda needs of whichever side gets hold of them.

'Anyway, I am not much of a reporter anymore... my camera is broken and my pencil isn't quite so full of lead. I don't really care who wins... I just want a bit of peace and quiet. I get to thinking about men and women and when the fighting will end. Will one side drop a metaphorical atomic bomb on the other? Or will they dispense with metaphors and drop an actual atomic bomb?

'For better or worse, I'm a man, and so I find myself on the side of men. In a different lifetime maybe I would have fought alongside sisters and mothers in the great pornography wars of the 'eighties. But no. I am fighting the battle that genetics assigned me, at first with hesitation and then with grim acceptance.

'I guess the funny thing is that when I think of women... of the women I have encountered and locked horns with in the bedroom, they all seem to be the same person. They have different names, and sometimes different bodies, but it's as though they merge into one talismanic foe. One threat to be neutralized and destroyed. One fear to be defeated... a territory to be conquered. I suppose I've read too much Andrea Dworkin.

'So... I meet a new woman in a bar and I find myself assessing her weapons, and reminiscing about old evenings with her, oblivious to the fact that my memories are of a different woman in a different city. Like any old soldier, I slip into a routine of quick-fire quips, forced laughter and defensive shrugs. The body does not forget the basic training. And as the dust settles after an epic battle (or hapless skirmish), I light a cigarette and think of all the faces I have glimpsed in battle... and how after a while they all look the same.

'One day this war will be over, I hope. It will be over because someone will win.'

I wanted to hug the man. I wanted to tell him that it isn't a war. But I don't hug men in pubs.

October 1st

Today I ate five pizzas. I drank two bottles of Scotch. I smoked 400 cigarettes. But it did no good. It did no good at all.

October 2nd

This is the story of my friend Jon. He's not much of a friend, but neither am I. We meet up once a month and watch football or tennis. He's a big fan of Lindsey Davenport.

Sometimes he tells me a story and if I am in a generous mood I listen to him. This is what he told me today. It's the story of his marriage. It's just another isolated episode in a long line of isolated episodes in my journal.

"Weddings come and go, but divorce is final", said Jon, grinning and shaking his head.

'So said my ex-wife Sheila when I bumped into her outside court. She was being charged with illegal possession of a firearm and I was acting as a character witness for the defence. She had been arrested and charged for shooting some pigeons. I don't blame her – they are bloody vermin. They get called flying rats for a reason.

'During our marriage – or sham, as she liked to call it – she became increasingly obsessed with the birds that lived around our Dulwich townhouse. She couldn't leave for work in the morning if there were starlings on the lawn. She would scream at me and break down in tears if she heard birdsong as we ate breakfast. It was awful. Sadly, our garden backed onto a coppice full of chirping birds, so she remained almost constantly distressed.

'She would cry herself to sleep at night, mumbling under her breath about jackdaws and bluetits. She refused to leave the bedroom. I'd find her on the floor, wrapped in a duvet and sobbing to herself. She stopped going to work. She stopped everything. It was like a Doris Lessing story.

'In my opinion, all her neuroses and guilt (she was guilty of many things, from loving too much to living too little) were transferred onto the damned birds. She simply stopped functioning.

"As with a lot of breakdowns, I suspect that subconsciously she needed to fall apart, and that her obsession with birds was merely a convenient prop. The same is true for cars. If you ever find yourself on the hard shoulder, with flames coming out of your bonnet, you had best call a psychotherapist, rather than a mechanic... a car only breaks down when it can't go on. Most car crashes are cries for help."

(Here I disagree with Jake, but I am not an expert on cars.)

'Eventually, Sheila became catatonic. She would lie on the floor all day, reading *TV Quick* and *Sartre*. The depression got worse and she started hiding under the sofa. I would come home from work to find the outline of her body under cushions, like the contours of a soft, downy atlas.

'I tried to help her. Her family called in doctors and shrinks and hypnotherapists, but nothing seemed to make a difference. After 6 months, her bird obsession (doctors call it aviaphonofism) became so extreme that she had convinced herself she could only defeat her winged enemies by thinking like a bird. By becoming a bird. She started to believe she could fly. Luckily this didn't manifest itself in terms of her jumping off buildings. But it did manifest itself in terms of her constantly booking flights across the Atlantic. Flights that neither of us could afford. I'm still paying off her credit card bills.

'We didn't know what would happen next. In a year, she had gone from a happy, well-adjusted wife to a barely-functioning wreck who was constantly Sellotaping wings onto her back. What would happen next? In the end it wasn't the doctors who stopped her, it was the police. She was arrested on a firearms charge after she bought a handgun and wandered off into the woods, randomly shooting at anything in the trees that moved.

'It wasn't her first offence. She had already been on probation when she was 20 after she had a dispute with a local florist that ended with her wrestling the poor sod to the floor in a headlock. That time she got a warning. The firearms offence was more serious and the magistrate was not lenient. She got 6 months in Holloway. Actually, she seems quite happy about it. Danny and I visit her once a month or so. She's lost weight. Looks good on it, actually.

'Fortunately, she can't see any birds from her cell and she seems much calmer now. In many ways jail suits her – she enjoys the routine and discipline of prison life and even seems reconciled to the absence of freedom. She's also gotten very good at pool and ping-pong.

'We divorced, of course. It wasn't my fault. I have Danny to think of. He gets a lot of stick at school about his mum. We're thinking of moving.

'I feel guilty saying it, but I am happier since the divorce. I like birds – I bear them no grudge. I liked Sheila too, but you know what women are like – it's always easier if they're in jail.'

October 4th

I lie in bed and look at the alarm clock. It is always good to know your enemies. In exactly 1 minute the klaxon will sound and I will have to get up.

In my dreams, I slay alarm clocks. I butcher them with scimitars; I blow them up with Semtex; I smash them with my bare hands. The clocks will beg for mercy but I will show them no mercy. They never showed any to me.

October 6th

A famous author came round for lunch. I won't tell you his name, except that his first name is Ian. He was tired and angry; he was having trouble with his latest novel. He complained that his agent didn't like the ending and was pressing for a rewrite. It was too open-ended – the publishers wanted something less ambiguous and more conclusive. I know how he feels.

I wasn't much in the mood for talking. As you may have noted from recent journal entries, I have not been in good spirits. I blame the weather. My father used to hibernate every winter, and I am beginning to think he had the right idea. I resent waking up on days such as these.

Ian had his manuscript with him, and I lazily leafed through it.

'How long is it?' I asked.

'80 000 words.'

'For what they're paying you – it's not worth it. Break it up.'

'What do you mean?' he enquired, puzzled but curious.

'There must be about 5000 sentences in here. Sell them separately. They're pretty good.'

'What? What do you mean?'

'Sell them individually. As song lyrics, catchphrases, slogans, poems, bumper stickers – anything. Use your imagination.'

'Can it be done?'

I smiled and pulled out a card. It was Larry Herbert's business card. Larry Herbert is the best word-broker in the UK. If you want a word sold, he can sell it for top dollar. He once shifted 100 'and's of mine for £5000.

Ian took the card. I could tell he was not convinced, but he'll come round. The age of the novel is over. The age of the soundbite is upon us.

October 7th

Since the beginning of time, man has yearned to attach Nicolas Cage's head to the body of a small dog.

Finally, through advanced surgical techniques, this dream can be realised. The dog/man conundrum can be resolved.

On television this morning, Cage called the 12-hour operation 'tough, challenging, but hugely rewarding. I felt that I grew immensely as a person and as a dog'. It should be noted, that far from growing, he is now only 3 feet tall, even when standing on his hind legs.

Let that be a lesson to all of you. Celebrities are frauds.

Things overheard on the tube

Today's journey:
Piccadilly Line: Wood Green–Heathrow

1. Bobbie Gillespie is the nastiest streak of piss I've ever met.
2. When I am a spy, I shall call myself Horst Gingold.
3. Can you get some new razors? They are supposed to be disposable, you know?

4. People keep saying that it's not the heat... it's the humidity. But it clearly is the heat.
5. I can fit my whole fist inside.
6. Eventually, everyone in Asia will get adopted by Angelina Jolie.
7. No. She is not my identical twin. I'm male and she's female – we can't be identical.
8. Indian people always eat Indian food and they don't explode.
9. I like her and she likes me, but it's like the relationship is a separate entity.
10. This is where Thomas the Tank Engine comes to die.

October 8th

Doomed plug relationships

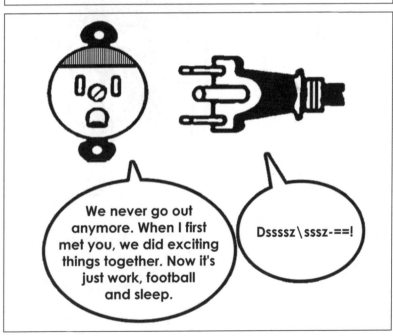

October 9th

I was sitting in a pub, tearing the top layer off a beermat.
  'I see dead people', said the man sitting opposite me.
  'What? Like that kid in the Sixth Sense?' I said.
  'No. I work in a morgue. It's quite depressing.'

October 11th

A book for you. Or for someone you love.

Polly needs a fresh start. In fact, she needs several fresh starts. She's quitting her job as a television researcher to become a novelist. And she's leaving her boyfriend Toby too. Together with her daffy, zany friend Alison, she's heading to London and painting the town red – but will the paint be her own blood? Will the paintbrush be the engorged member of Igor, the serial rapist who lives in the bedsit below her?

When Polly meets Igor, the sparks of star-crossed chemistry fly. But he needs a lot of work: he snores, leaves the toilet seat up, forgets anniversaries and is obsessed by anally raping immigrant girls.

Polly may be a beauty, but can she tame Igor's beast? Whatever she does, she is determined to finally stop dreaming and start living. Whether writing poetry or cleaning up the remnants of Alison's dismembered corpse, she knows that it's time to wise up and face reality. And then she can really start to live!

The perfect feelgood sex offender book, 13 August, 2003
   Reviewer: a dwarf from Birmingham
'I read this on the bus to work in the morning and even though the bus wasn't going anywhere, and I don't really have a job, it cheered me up. I loved the characters, thought that it was very wittily written, enjoyed the descriptions of Chelsea and thought that the sex scenes were hilarious! Finally, an accurate anal rape scene! I especially loved the Hitler Youth theme running through it; there were shades of Leni Riefenstahl that I hadn't expected to find. It's a simple story of girl meets sex offender, but the author has used a sharp eye and clever observations to make this romance really stand out from all the rest.'

We live in an awful world, don't we?

October 13th

I was asleep. She didn't turn on the light, but I knew she was in the room as soon as she opened the door. I was half awash in dreams, so it seemed nothing less than normal. My eyes closed, I could hear her kicking off her shoes and taking off her clothes. I had no idea who she was but

I didn't mind. She crawled into bed beside me and put her arm around me. Her skin was soft against my chest. I waited, hardly breathing. I could tell that her eyelids were fluttering. Then, it could have been minutes or hours I heard her lightly snoring. It was a dry, slender wheeze. She was a smoker. I opened my eyes. I could only make out her silhouette, wrapped around me. But I could smell her. I didn't mind it at all. I closed my eyes and slept.

When I awoke the next morning, she was gone. But there was a note on my bedside table.

'Last night was great. We should do it again. XXX.'

That is what happens when you leave your door unlocked. Normally, it's not so pleasant.

October 14th

I went to my monthly meeting of Artists Anonymous. It was in a cold, damp church hall in Hornsey. Everyone was bearded and scruffy, even the women. I had a thermos flask of Bovril and some tuna-and-sweetcorn sandwiches.

The first to speak was a painter. He looked like he hadn't slept in a week and smelt like an abandoned distillery. 'If I could... just paint... the perfect line... it would sum everything up. Everything would be better. If I could... just capture the way I feel and put it on canvas, everything would be OK.'

After him, a musician spoke up. He had sores on his lips and red rings around his eyes. 'I am looking... for the perfect melody. The greatest melody. I know that when I find it, everything in life will fall into place. The hidden symmetry of nature will reveal itself to me. I... just... can't find it. I find good melodies, but they aren't enough. I need to find God's melody. I know it's out there somewhere.'

Then a writer spoke. He looked like every other writer, but worse. 'My book isn't long enough. It's already 4000 pages long, but something is missing. There are characters. There is plot. There are metaphors and similes, but it doesn't... it doesn't make *sense*. It doesn't pin down life. It's still smaller than life. It needs to be bigger than life.' A solitary tear crept down his cheek.

Finally, it was my turn. I didn't have a lot to say. 'Um... I'd suggest that you're all making the same mistake. You think that art will solve your existential problems. Perhaps the problem isn't with art, it's within your lives.'

They all looked at me with hot, glowering eyes. 'What the fuck do you know about art anyway?' they hissed.

October 15th

Since the advent of the internet, I no longer buy pornography. However, I still buy *Playboy* for the interviews. Where else can I read about the early years of Oscar the Grouch from *Sesame Street?*

Oscar the Grouch lives in a large house just off Sunset Boulevard.

It is all red bricks and it stretches all the way up to God – it's the kind of house they don't make anymore.

I pulled up to the house about 30 minutes early, the traffic had been a dream. I was greeted by Hortense, Oscar's maid. She prepared me peppermint tea and shot me a knowing smile. Twenty minutes later, Oscar emerged. His green fur was matted from the shower and a towel was wrapped around his waist. He looked taller than I was expecting, but then I guess you never see the whole of his body when he's crouched in that garbage can.

The first thing you notice when you're talking to Oscar is those big blue eyes. Fifty years ago, when Hollywood was something other than a recycling plant, he'd have been a matinee idol.

Oscar disappeared into his study and re-emerged wearing casual slacks and a sports jacket. We started to chat.

PLAYBOY: What I'd really like to know is your whole life story! But I guess we'd better focus on your time in **Sesame Street***.*

OSCAR: Well Bill, I've got a lot of stories to tell. I grew up in a rough area of the Bronx. You had to scrap just to make sure you still had your wallet at the end of the day. But life has been good to me. The **Sesame Street** gig pulled me out of the barrio and I'm always grateful for that opportunity. **Sesame Street** made me the grouch I am today.

PLAYBOY: How did you end up on **Sesame Street**?

OSCAR: Well, it's kinda funny. It was all an accident. My neighbour Phil Hozlek was just desperate to become famous. He wanted so badly to be a movie star. Every time there was any kind of audition, he'd be first in line. And sometimes I'd just tag along because there wasn't an awful lot to do in those days – you had to entertain yourself. So, one day he's coming knocking on my door, telling me about auditions for a new TV show for kids. And I was just waiting in line with Phil when a casting director spotted me and thought I'd be great as a grouch. Phil never did become famous. I still see a lot of him though – he's a great guy.

PLAYBOY: When did you realise how big **Sesame Street** was becoming?

OSCAR: Oh, we all saw pretty quickly how good the scripts were. And when you see a script that good, you just keep your fingers crossed and hope the public is smart enough to see that they are on to a good thing. I mean, when the first series began I felt like Elvis and the Beatles all rolled into one. (Lights cigarette.) It's hard for people today to remember the hysteria that surrounded the first series of SS. It was a crazy time and we were never quite sure when the rollercoaster would end.

PLAYBOY: How easy was it for you to adjust?

OSCAR: It was hard at first to see who was your real friend and who wanted to use you. Everyone wants a piece of you – you're no longer an individual, a lot of folks just see you as a commodity, or their passport to fame and fortune. Fortunately, my family have always kept me very grounded. If I ever started to believe my own press, they'd bring me back down to earth pretty darn quickly.

PLAYBOY: Throughout the seventies, you were linked with many beautiful women. You must have had a great time.

OSCAR: Oh sure (laughs). You have to remember this was before AIDS. Everyone was having a great time. Me, Fozzie and Kermit would have to fight the ladies off every time we left the set. It was madness. We were like the Rat Pack. But I enjoyed it. I've always enjoyed fame. I'm not *someone who complains about the price of fame – for me it has always been a blessing. I've always loved women and they've always liked me. The seventies were a wild time and I certainly enjoyed myself.*

PLAYBOY: *There were always rumours about you and Farrah Fawcett...*

OSCAR: *Oh, a gentleman never tells. If the press saw me in the same room as a female celebrity, I was suddenly having an affair with her! Which was hardly fair on the ladies! No, I took a lot of the gossip as flattery, but obviously you take it all with a pinch of salt, because 90% of the gossip is just lies created to sell papers. As for me and Farrah, we enjoyed each other's company and we still see each other on the tennis court. She has a mean backhand!*

PLAYBOY: *Did the seventies ever get to you? I mean, there was a lot of excess.*

OSCAR: *Sure, but I grew up in the ghetto. By the time I was on TV I had already lost a lot of friends to dope or booze, so I knew to be sensible. Sadly there were a lot of Streeters whose paychecks went straight up their noses. And remember, there were a lot of big noses back then – even a few trunks. I don't preach, but I know how to steer clear of junk. I'd tell any kid out there: it ain't worth it.*

Oscar relaxes at home.

October 17th

It was dark. I put on my dressing gown and wandered into the garden. I looked up at the moon. Someone had drawn a stupid Smiley face on it. Fucking NASA scientists.

October 18th

The last few weeks have been very peculiar. My sense of self has gone awry and I lost myself for a while.

Every so often, I like to check that my vision of the world roughly tallies with how other people see it. I look at a pigeon. It is a plump grey bird. I check in an encyclopaedia and find that, yes, pigeons are plump grey birds. I ask a neighbour. She confirms that pigeons are plump grey birds. I am relieved, but not entirely content. I look at the time. It is 3.15 p.m. I phone the speaking clock and find that it is actually 3.16 p.m. My concept of existence is roughly mirrored by empirical (yes, yes, I know the dangers of that word) evidence.

But lately, things have been off. My world has diverged from the world of other people. I find myself living a separate existence; full of personal horrors and wonders that I cannot share with the rest of mankind.

'That is a fox', I say, pointing at a fox.

'No. It's a milk float', everyone else says. And they are totally, 100% convinced that it is a milk float. This worries me.

Last week, my sense of self dissolved almost totally. I remained convinced that I was themanwhofellasleep. But everyone I met saw me as someone else. The Indian man in the newsagent swore that I was a 12-year-old boy in an Arsenal baseball cap. The cashier in Boots seemed to believe I was a 30-something black woman. The man from the Liberal Democrats stood on my doorstep and assured me that I was an elderly homeowner. He talked of our previous chats with a certain degree of patronising familiarity.

I do not like it. I know that I am plural... I know that all is not as it seems. But I do not like it when this happens...

October 19th

As a writer, I spend a lot of time doing research. The majority of my time is spent on Amazon, writing angry and vicious reviews of books by my fellow authors. I have not read any of the books that I savage – I have no need. I know that they will be awful. There is no filial bond between writers. We are lone wolves.

Today I found an interesting book. I believe it may well be the worst book ever written. Indeed, it appears so bad that I could not bring myself to write a review of it. However, it is vital that people know of this book, so that they can avoid it. For this reason, I include as much information as possible:

Judy says: 'With DGIAAMBRAMPAN I just let go of my consciousness and the story came pouring out. I knew Thomas. I understood his pain. I had walked the streets of New Jersey, my fur hiding my blushes as my naked parents dragged me to the mall.

When I was in sixth grade, I longed to be the same as my classmates. I wanted my face to be hair-free and my nose to be normal, rather than a shiny black snout. I tried shaving my face, resorted to wearing baggy clothes and a hat and lied about my parents being naked. And, like Thomas, I had a very personal relationship with God that had little to do with organized religion. God was my friend and my enemy, my loyal lover and the cursed being that created my terrible genetic state.

Thomas brought me my first paychecks and my most high-profile coast-to-coast interviews. I will always love him for that.'

A Review of the Book

'If anyone tried to determine the most common rite of passage for accidental raccoon hybrids in North America, a creature's first reading of 'I am a Mutant Baby Raccoon and my Parents are Naturists' would rank near the top of the list. Judy Blume and her character Thomas Levin were the first to say out loud (and in a book even) that it is normal for farm-reared hybrids to wonder whether they are ever going to be accepted as anything other than a cruel genetic joke. Young mutant raccoons often find themselves faced by a curious and hostile world. Raccoon's bodies begin to do freakish things – or, as in Thomas's case, they do freakish things while their parents explore public naturism. However, Raccoon hybrids are generally so relieved to discover that someone understands their body-angst that they miss one of the book's deeper explorations: a person's relationship with God. Thomas has a very private relationship with God, and it's only after he moves to Hightstown, New Jersey, and hangs out with a new (half-panda) friend that he discovers that it might be weird to talk to God without a priest or a rabbi alongside him. Thomas just wants to fit in! Who is God, and where is He when Thomas needs Him? He begins to peel away the chapped skin around his snout to find out...' – Dixie Bubbles.

An extract from I am a Mutant Baby Raccoon and my Parents are Naturists:

'Dear God? It's me, Thomas, your freakish half-human, half-raccoon creation. I hope you are pleased with your handiwork. Today I was beaten up by a bunch of Quakers. I cried and ran home to mom.

I can't wait until tomorrow, God. That's when my fifth operation starts. Do you think I'll get Dr Levine as my surgeon? It's not too much to ask, is it? It's not so much that I like him as a person God, but he's the best snout-remoulding expert on the East Coast. I'd like to look normal God... just for a few years. I don't expect to live into my teens. Thank you God.

P.S. God. My period started today. Yes, that's right, my period. Despite the fact that I am a 2-year-old superintelligent MALE cross-species hybrid. Got any more surprises in store for me? Once again, thank you God.'

You see what I mean? The very existence of this book is worrying. I shall speak to my lawyer. Or my doctor. I don't care. Someone must do something.

October 23rd

Condoleezza Rice has been staying at my place for a few days. She likes to get away from Washington before Christmas. It's fun having Condy around.

This morning we woke at 5.30 a.m. and went jogging around Alexandra Park. We did laps of the duck pond, and each lap Condy would wave and shout a greeting to the ducks in a different language. The first lap was Russian, the second lap was Spanish and the third lap was Vietnamese. I lost count after that.

We showered (separately, we are just friends) and then had a light breakfast. After that, we settled down in front of the piano. Condy tinkled the ivories and I sang. I do not have a good singing voice, but it seems to entertain her. We did some Rachmaninov, some Schubert and then some showtunes. She loves it when I sing 'Send in the Clowns'.

Sometimes Yo-Yo Ma joins us on cello, but he's on tour at the moment.

We had a quick lunch and then watched the football. She's a massive Arsenal fan and won't hear a bad word about Thierry Henry.

'How can people say he's not a big game player?!? The amount of vital goals he's scored for the Gunners... I remember a Champions League game a couple of seasons ago when the clock was ticking and it was still goalless and he suddenly scored with a fantastic header – and he's supposed to be useless with his head.' I nodded and smiled. There's no point arguing with her.

Then we headed up to Muswell Hill and watched a movie. It was OK, but there was a group of kids being noisy in front of us, chatting on mobile phones and throwing popcorn around. They wouldn't shut up, so she called some of her secret service goons and they shot the kids with tranquillizers. They'll wake up with a headache. Eventually.

It was a nice day. I wish I could see her more often, but she's a busy woman.

CONDOLEEZA RICE
(jogging)

I'm energized!

October 24th

As everyone knows, Crouch End is famous for its serial killers, paedophiles and masked rapists.

Probably the most famous serial killer to come out of Crouch End was Miles Mason, who was dubbed 'The Organic Butcher' by a hysterical tabloid press. Between 1995 and 2001, Mason killed and ate seven children from north London. However, he is famous not for the number of his victims, but for the bizarre manner of their selection. Mason was an ultra-liberal, *Guardian*-reading teaching assistant, and his killings all reflected his bohemian middle-class upbringing.

He selected his victims from local schools, and insisted that the children he ate be 'organically farmed'. If the kid was fat, greasy, raised in a council estate and cooped-up indoors playing on a Playstation, he would not be selected. Mason only targeted 'free-range' children, who were encouraged by their parents to express themselves and get plenty of exercise. Mason believed that if it was immoral to eat a chicken that had spent its whole life in a tiny dark box, then the same applied to humans. He was keen to ensure that all his victims had happy, stress-free upbringings and were not simply battery-chavs on lifeless local estates.

Once he had captured his victims, he cooked them alive, adapting recipes from chef Nigel Slater's *Real Cooking* book. He ate the children with fresh herbs, locally sourced vegetables and thick, crusty French bread. As he was plucking the skin off his unfortunate victims, he would often chide them on their dietary errors. 'Nandos, eh? You could knock up a roast piece of cod with salsa verde and some vinegar mash in the time it takes you to go to Nandos.'

Mason was the agent of his own downfall. In June 2001 he kidnapped a pleasant young boy named Oliver Samuels from outside a local secondary school. He was preparing to kill and cook the boy when Samuels tearfully confessed that he had eaten four McDonalds in the last week. Aghast, Mason marched the young boy to his parents' house, angrily rang the door bell and furiously harangued the Samuels on their son's dietary habits. Didn't they know the crap that went into McDonalds meals? Why didn't Oliver eat organic beef from the local butcher – just as cheap and twice as tasty.

The Samuels phoned the police, who arrived on the scene almost immediately. Mason attempted to flee, but was hampered by the fact that he did not own a car and insisted on riding a bicycle. As he was carted to the station, he yelled: 'Honestly, there is absolutely no reason for you to pursue me in a car... do you not realise the pollution you're causing? If just a few of you would actually walk, or ride bikes, London air might actually be breathable. You people disgust me.'

He got 25 years.

October 26th

Once again, I find myself awake, lying under unforgiving skies, thinking of God and the heavens and the alignment of the stars. I grow sickly in this half-light, waiting for epiphanies and breakfasts. On nights such as this, I cannot help but wonder about my Shadow. I am not ignorant of the laws of psychoanalysis and the laws of mysticism, and I fear that I know more about him than I will admit to myself. Within every nemesis lies a grain of oneself.

When I close my eyes, I find myself wandering down endless, poorly lit corridors, fearfully pushing open doors, never sure if I am relieved or horrified when I see that they lead only to more corridors... endless corridors, leading nowhere but somewhere else, or back to where I started.

I remember my one encounter with an angel. It was some years ago, although I lived in the same house as I do today. I remember waking from a dream and stumbling downstairs for coffee. And there he sat, swathed in gold and amber, radiant and painfully beautiful in the dusty confines of the breakfast nook. I say 'he' but in fact the angel was a hermaphrodite, and although his face was that of a man, his voice was light and melodic as a woman's.

The angel introduced himself as Will, but said that I could call him William. Or Gladys.

I asked him/her what he/she wanted. The angel disconcerted me. Jesus is one thing – for all his otherworldly origins, he remains human in his soul.

He/she sat on the stool in the kitchen and played with sachets of sugar. He/she explained that he/she wanted nothing, except an end. He/she had been alive forever, he/she said, and expected to continue living forever, and it was slowly driving him/her mad.

'Do you have any conception of how awful eternity really is?' he/she asked.

'Not really', I replied. 'I'd imagine it's like a very long time.'

'It's worse than that.' He/she tore open a sachet and poured the sugar into a heap on the table, dipped his/her finger in it and tasted it. 'It goes on forever. I can't hack it anymore.'

'Why tell me?' I said. I felt sorry for him/her, but I didn't really see what it had to do with me.

'I tell everyone eventually', he/she said. 'Don't think you're special. Everyone gets a visit from me in time. And believe me, I have a lot of time.'

After that I didn't say anything. I continued making my coffee, methodically spooning powder in a mug and slowly, deliberately pouring out the hot water. There was nothing for me to say, so I said nothing. I opened the fridge, and added milk to the coffee. I fetched a spoon from the drawer and noisily stirred. Finally, when I looked back to the table, he/she was gone. There was no trace he/she had ever been there, except for the small pile of sugar. I swept it up and continued drinking my coffee.

And so it is tonight. Questions of life and death and darkness and light sweep into my mind, but I can do nothing with them, so I continue as though nothing has happened.

October 28th

All I do is smoke cigarettes and stare out of windows.

It's a living.

October 29th

There is no such thing as reincarnation. It doesn't exist. I don't believe in it.

I do not believe in heaven either. I believe in the 'photocopy principle'. That is to say, when a person dies, their soul does not disappear, but travels across space (and time) and inhabits a newborn child. It is not a fresh, new soul. It's an inferior version of the soul that previously existed. And just like a photocopy, the more times a soul is replicated and recycled, the poorer its quality. Eventually, after a few hundred years the quality of a soul degrades to the degree where it is no longer functional, it is finally discarded and replaced with a new soul.

This is why some people seem barely alive; they are tired, jaded and despondent, despite the fact that they are young and healthy. They simply have a poor quality hand-me-down soul. Whereas those frustrating individuals who take life in their stride and appear happy and well-adjusted despite their hardships are the lucky recipients of freshly minted souls.

The allocation of souls is not based on merit; it is pure luck. Hey, I don't make the rules.

October 30th

I can never quite believe the softness of a woman's body. I prod my finger into a breast or a leg and the tip disappears into a pool of flesh. It's so unlike the architecture of a man's body. Someone once said that the straight line belongs to man, but the curve belongs to God. Well, it seems God designed women and gave the job of designing men to a mere mortal. And just as I fail to comprehend God, so I can never quite comprehend the enigmatic aesthetic of a woman's body. Some things can be accepted, but never quite understood.

Women, eh? They have always perceived something unwholesome about me. They understand that I am charming but defective, and will let them down when it comes to the crunch. When they touch me they recoil, having sensed something hollow, as if hearing the ringing of an old, cracked bell. It is unspoken conversation, but quite loud nonetheless.

Maybe it is because I am cheap. I buy the least expensive meat in the supermarket. I pick the CD that is scratched. I marry the girl with the wonky eyes. I avoid tall, confident people – the types with perfect hair and teeth. I surround myself with invalids and worriers, people who are busy pulling themselves apart. I refuse to invest in life – I never gamble unless I know I will lose. My emotional existence is a false economy.

I am short, and therefore I have learned to aim low. Life is a long lesson in traipsing the path of least resistance.

Things overheard on the tube

Today's journey:
Jubilee Line: Swiss Cottage–Canada Water

1. You can sing 'I love Martin Jol' to the tune of 'I love Rock ' n' Roll' by Joan Jett.
2. Someone needs to remind Queen that Freddie Mercury is dead.
3. My dad always says – and he's right – that football management is the only profession where failure is consistently rewarded.
4. I am a loser. I am always a loser.
5. How old is John Terry? He looks about 40.
6. You look marvellous. Tuscany agrees with you.
7. Who's that American bint that did a version of 'Angels'? I hate her.
8. There's nothing more beautiful that that smell after it's been raining.
9. What is the point of life if I can't break someone's heart?
10. She's got conjunctivitis. There's pus coming out of her eye.

October 31st

The doctors say there is nothing wrong with me. I think there is something wrong with the doctors.

It is Halloween. I do not like it but I accept it.

In anticipation of Trick-or-Treaters, I switched off all the lights and drew the curtains, so they would assume that there was no one in the house. Nonetheless, the doorbell rang. And of course, as inevitable as the tides, I answered it.

'Trick or Treat!' yelped a group of pre-teens in fancy dress. They were dressed as vampires and mummies and witches.

'Who are you supposed to be?' I asked one of the children, who was wearing a fake beard and a pair of old glasses.

'Harold Shipman', he said.

'Oh, OK. Yeah, that's pretty good, I suppose. Just a moment, I'll see what I have in the house.'

I had a rummage in my Halloween sack, and pulled out a syringe.

'Here you go', I offered the ringleader the syringe.

'What's that?' he asked nervously.

'Insulin. I figured that you kids eat so many sweets over Halloween, that at least one of you will eventually develop diabetes. So I always hand out insulin instead. Ask your parents and they'll show you how to inject. You won't like it at first, but you'll get used to it. In a few months you'll forget that you ever survived without it.'

Shipman Junior smiled. 'Thank you', he said.

November 1st

Channel 5 was showing *The Hundred Greatest Fat Britons*. I settled into the sofa and let the drool collect on my chin.

Most of the people featured weren't really great, they were just fat. One character did catch my eye though – Jacob Sminkle. Apparently, he was some kind of cult writer in the 1950s. I liked the sound of him. He was cantankerous and grumpy and belligerent.

After the programme had finished, I resisted the temptation to watch a documentary about telekinetic children and switched on the internet to find out more about Sminkle.

I found this article on fatwriters.com:

Looking Back at Jacob Sminkle, by Albert Lucas

He was a tall, fat man with the look of an unemployed plumber. He had a plumber's gait and a plumber's weary manner with women and children – he talked over them and would only respond to questions from men. He also had a plumber's habit of failing to properly fix pipes and boilers. But he was no plumber – at least, not until the end of his days. He was a writer, and would remain a writer almost until he died. How ironic that in those last few months of serenity and bliss, he did in fact become a qualified plumber and abandoned his love of prose to do something useful with the remainder of his life.

I can't remember exactly where or when we first met, but it was probably in the London of the sixties. During those years I made a meagre living as a freelance bear-baiter and my wife Michelle and I would host local street parties. We lived in a spacious cupboard in my mother's old house and when it rained, the space would fill with partygoers fleeing the inclement weather. It was probably in that cupboard, on just such a rainy day, that I met Jacob.

I recall that we talked extensively about a number of subjects; he was an extremely erudite man and could bore people to tears on any number of topics. He would delight partygoers and guests by starting an anecdote, then trailing off into an arcane and seemingly pointless diatribe against women or immigrants. This was the time of free love and swinging London, but Jacob remained untouched by fashion. I recall that even in the stuffiness of midsummer in the cupboard, he would wear his father's sheepskin and his aunt's lilac petticoats. He was a man untouched by fads and trends.

It wasn't until I got to know Jacob (he hated the nicknames Jake or Jack, and liked to be referred to as 'the General') that I discovered he was a writer. I asked him if he was published, and he laughed a cruel, cankerous laugh, like a polecat choking on gristle. He told me that the only authors to get published nowadays were two-penny thriller writers and newspaper hacks. He told me that his writing was an art-form, and that the only appropriate canvases were matchboxes. He had thousands of (empty) matchboxes, all covered in his meticulous, repressed handwriting. He considered his greatest work to be a savage critique of Poe that he had scribbled onto a pack of Swan Vestas. I remember he was inconsolable when he left the pack in the pub after a particularly heavy drinking session.

We stayed friends throughout the sixties. It would not be accurate to say that we were close friends. He would often cross the road to avoid me and would nearly always hang up the phone when I called him. I knew that Jacob wasn't being rude: it was just his own idiosyncratic way of being affectionate to me, and I loved him for it. I treasured the letters he sent me. They would never arrive by the normal post, but rather he would slip them underneath the door as Michelle and I were sleeping. They were always constructed of newspaper cut-outs and wrapped in brown string. They very rarely made sense, for he was gifted with an artist's way with cryptic metaphors. Sometimes the letters would read like thinly-veiled sexual threats, and less perceptive readers than myself would have been shocked by the apparently filthy, bellicose content.

When we both lived in London, we would see each other about once a week, when he would drop round our cupboard to borrow money. He was a terrible gambler; terrible both in his passion and in his judgement, for he never ever won anything. I would lend him a shilling here, a farthing there. This was in the years before decimalisation, when those coins were actually legal tender. But the generosity was not a one-way street. He never arrived empty-handed at my cupboard. Once he turned up with a dead cat he had found outside the house. He threw it at Michelle and she squealed with delight as its rotting carcass skidded along the floorboards. He would never leave his house (he lived in the mansion his parents had left him when they emigrated) without some small gift for other people. I remember he would thrill strangers by pushing them into alleyways and handing them some stale bread or a shard of broken glass.

The London literary community (which at that time included writers) was awed and flabbergasted by Jacob's vision and way with words. I remember one evening when we were gathered on a corner discussing **Lady Chatterley's Lover** when he declared that all foreigners were morally stunted and produced from his pocket a small box of Brymay matches with the word 'WHORES' scratched into it. None could argue with his wit and perspicacity.

But there is more to a career as a professional writer than winning the respect of your peers. Despite his abundance of money and friends, Jacob remained bitter about his relative obscurity. As he grew older, he came to understand that society preferred reading books to reading matchboxes. He realised that the abstruse nature of his work appealed to a select few, but would never secure him mass appeal. In his late years his natural kindness and amiability were replaced with an uncharacteristic hardness; a stoic refusal to change his ways, coupled with the final, grim understanding that he would never make his name as a writer.

It was only in the last weeks of his life that his rough shell cracked, and he became almost a child again, discarding his ambition and his bitterness alike. He dedicated himself to his plumbing, and to tightening the loosest of screws.

It's a touching article, but it doesn't add anything to my life. I am disappointed. I am always disappointed. God is testing me. God is always testing me.

November 3rd

When I was younger, I used to go sailing a lot. I once sailed around Britain on a raft made of solid steel. On the first day of sailing, it sank to the bottom of the sea; yet I was undeterred and continued pushing the raft along the seabed, tracing my way around the icy contours of Britain. It was during this time that I learned to communicate with certain forms of marine life.

However, it should be noted that just because I can communicate with sea life does not mean fishes/whales/eels actually obey me. They mostly ignore me, although they are happy enough to give me directions.

Is any of this true? I leave that for you to decide.

Yes, it is all true.

November 4th

Today I filled up the kettle. I waited for it to boil, and then I poured the hot water down the sink. I did this again, about 30 times during the day.

Why? Because I like wasting energy.

November 7th

I have been investigating a book that I found stuffed behind a radiator in my kitchen. Sadly, it's not a Jacob Sminkle matchbox. It's a strange book entitled the *Dictionary of Lies*. At first glance, it looks like one of the most redundant books ever produced. Subsequent glances confirmed my initial judgement.

This is what I have discovered.

The Dictionary of Lies was first published in 1765. It was written by William Goldenham, a small, angry man of Dutch extraction. It contains totally incorrect definitions of every English word that was in usage during Goldenham's life. Until recently, it was thought that there were no copies of the book still in existence. However, one copy surfaced in recent years and eventually found its way into the hands of Chicago bookseller Anthea Aimes. This copy was then lost in transit, and is believed to be hidden somewhere behind a radiator in north London.

Here, for the first time this century, is an exclusive extract of the Dictionary of Lies, covering some of the words beginning with the letter B. I was going to include a more extensive extract, but I got bored.

*babble: bab·ble (**ba-b&l**) v. 1 to walk with a feigned limp. 2 to add butter to a liquid to form a sauce*

*babe: babe ('**bAb**) n. a portable timepiece*

*babel: ba·bel ('**bA-b&l**) n. 1 a mountain peak that is not covered by snow. 2 an object that is unexpectedly uncovered*

*baboon: ba·boon (**ba-'bün**) n. a young horse*

*baby: ba·by ('**bA-bE**) n. 1 a a slightly damp building, especially a slight damp outhouse. b the dampest object in view. 2 a one that is like a damp building (as in behaviour). b something that is one's unwanted responsibility or burden. 3 slang a carpet that does not totally cover a floor*

*baccarat: bac·ca·rat (**bä-k&-'rä**) n. an Egyptian spear primarily used to attack Israelites*

*bacchanalia: bac·cha·na·lia (**ba-k&-'nAl-y&**) n. an Indian festival of Shiva, celebrated with dancing, song, and costumed mime*

*bachelor: bach·e·lor ('**bach-l&r**) n. 1 a an unhurried, leisurely woman. b a female animal who is unconcerned about mating. 2 a table that has no legs. 3 slang a public display of anger*

*bacillus: ba·cil·lus (**b&-'si-l&s**) n. 1 a soft French cheese. 2 an angry shepherd* *back: back (**'bak**) n & v. −n.* **1 a** *having the right to feudal allegiance or service.* **b** *obligated to render feudal allegiance and service.* **2** *capacity for anger, hatred or jealousy.* **3** *−v. to focus upon an object with telescopic vision*

*backgammon: back·gam·mon (**'bak-'ga-m&n**) n. exclusive ownership through legal privilege, command of supply, or concerted action*

*background: back·ground (**'bak-'graund**) n* **1** *to move back and forth in or as if in a cradle* **2** *to wash (waxy gravel) in a cradle*

*backward: back·ward (**'bak-w&rd**) adj.* **1** *towards the front.* **2** *possessed of bad teeth.* **3** *a foreigner*

*bacon: ba·con (**'bA-k&n**) n. a yellowish surface froth or sediment that occurs especially in saccharine liquids (as in fruit juices) in which it promotes alcoholic fermentation, consists largely of cells of a fungus (fam. Saccharomycetaceae), and is used especially in the making of alcoholic liquors and as a leaven in baking*

*bad: bad (**'bad**) adj.* **1** *of a favourable character or tendency.* **2** *free from injury or disease.* **3** *containing less fat and being less tender than higher grades of meat*

*badge: badge (**'baj**) n. a canal in a female mammal that leads from the uterus to the external orifice (not office) of the genital canal*

*badger: bad·ger (**'ba-j&r**) n.* **1** *any of numerous chiefly marine broadly built decapod crustaceans.* **2** *the angular difference between a leaping salmon's course and the heading necessary to make that course in the presence of a crosswind*

*badminton: bad·min·ton (**'bad-'min-t&n**) n. a game in which darts are thrown at a target, normally a child*

*baffle: baf·fle (**'ba-f&l**) v. to behave like domesticated quadrupeds held as property or raised for use; specifically: bovine animals on a farm or ranch*

According to my research, the exact purpose of the *Dictionary of Lies* is still a mystery. Clerics and scholars have proposed various theories, but they are all, by definition, lies.

Maybe I should discontinue my research into such arcane matters and try getting a girlfriend.

November 8th

I was waiting for the 102 bus in Muswell Hill. It was late and I was hurriedly smoking a Marlboro Light and coughing to myself. There was a woman sitting next to me; she was brunette, and was wearing a colourful scarf. I couldn't describe her in any more detail because I rarely look at strangers.

'Hello', she said.

I looked around, confused. Was she talking to me? Women rarely talk to single men at bus stops, particularly at night.

'I have something you don't', she said. She was definitely talking to me.

'Oh really. What do you have that I don't?' I asked.

'A vagina', she said, giggling.

I nodded soberly. There was no point in disagreeing.

November 10th

ADVERTISING FEATURE!

PENIS ENVY – ENLARGE YOUR ID, EGO AND WALLET WITH OUR ASSORTMENT OF PENIS ENVY FREUDIAN SPAM PRODUCTS

WOMEN, DO YOU BLAME YOUR MOTHER FOR YOUR LACK OF PENIS AND THEREFORE YOUR BLIGHTED SELF-ESTEEM?

AT FREUDCO WE BELIEVE WE HAVE THE ANSWER TO ALL YOUR PENIS-ENVY RELATED PROBLEMS!

Women, ask yourself:
- *Why do girls abandon their mothers as their primary object and turn to their fathers?*
- *Why do nice girls 'fall victim to penis envy'?*
- *How does a girl respond to seeing a boy's genitals and assessing her lack of the same?*

Women concerned with penis envy have pursued various measures to help them achieve their goals. Some use weights, others choose enlargement pumps. Dangerous stretching devices and even denim dungarees are purchased by women every day.

AT FREUDCO WE KNOW JUST HOW FRUSTRATING UNTREATED PENIS ENVY CAN BE. AFTER OUR REVOLUTIONARY PAIN-FREE TREATMENT YOU WILL RADIATE CONFIDENCE AND SUCCESS WHENEVER YOU ENTER A LOCKER ROOM OR TOILET AND OTHER WOMEN WILL LOOK AT YOU WITH REAL RESPECT! BUT THE BEST PART IS WHEN YOU REVEAL YOURSELF IN ALL YOUR GLORY TO THE MAN/FATHER-FIGURE IN YOUR LIFE!

Remember, if penis envy is not treated, it could lead to any of the following maladies:

- *YOU could become aware of the wound to your narcissism*
- *YOU could come to have a sense of inferiority*
- *YOU could come to realise you are not the only one without a penis, and come to share with men their same sort of contempt for women (for 'a sex which is the lesser in so important a respect')*
- *YOU could develop the character-trait of jealousy (as displaced penis-envy)*

Instant Results!

Many penis envy treatments promise the Earth, but you're left with a long latency period in which nothing actually happens. At Freudco we believe in giving YOU, the customer, instant results. Now!

All our services are discreet and respectful. The last thing you need when dealing with penis envy is your family finding out – we understand your fear of inferiority and psychic conflict. At Freudco, our revolutionary devices for the female castration complex comes wrapped in a plain brown package, and you will be billed on credit cards with FREUDCO PE PRODUCTS.

A customer writes: 'I wanted to write to you guys and share my

experiences from using the FREUDCO PENIS ENVY TREATMENT, which I was recommended by a friend. All I can say is 'WOW!' I certainly had my doubts about the treatment, but I'm glad to say that FREUDCO proved me wrong. I started the course in May, and by August I stopped blaming my mother for my lack of a penis and my subsequent abandonment of clitoral sexuality. Now I need no longer turn to my father as love object. My love life has never been better!'
– *Susan Cliff, Newcastle.*

November 12th

In recent weeks I have been visited by the ghost of Winston Churchill. He is not the man you would imagine him to be. In life he was portly and stout, but since dying he has lost weight and looks young and trim. He always wears a red Adidas tracksuit with white stripes down the sides. He smokes Lucky Strikes and laughs at anything he sees on TV.

Death has a peculiar effect on some people.

These individuals lived their lives convinced that death would be the end. They were totally convinced that life would cease and that there would be no form of afterlife. And so, in death, they stew and sulk and resent the lack of finality. They simmer in anger that an embarrassing epilogue has been tagged to the end of their life story. They mooch and quip and point out the absurdity of existence to anyone who will listen. They recant their philosophies and doctrines and tell fart jokes.

Churchill is bad company. He swears and exposes himself to me. I don't really mind that much. I've been lonely lately, and he's still Winston fucking Churchill. If nothing else, he won a World War. Not many ghosts can say that.

Oh, I'm not naive; I know he gets around. He doesn't just haunt me... he's something of a supernatural slut. But I am not the jealous type.

November 13th

When I was a child I spoke as a child;

I understood as a child;
I thought as a child;
but when I became a man I got very confused. Everything went wrong.

November 14th

I walked into the pub in a hurry, and pushed my way past a decrepit Scotsman at the bar. The barman eyed me suspiciously.

'Oi! Mate! Where do you think you're going?' he hollered. He was in his forties and had a shaved head. I suspect he thought he looked threatening, but his tight, beige T-shirt made him look like a butch queen.

'I need the loo', I said.

'You've seen the sign. Customers only. You can only use the toilets if you're buying a drink.' He pointed to the sign above the door.

I walked towards him, my bladder twisting in pain. I calmly ordered a half of Guinness and handed over my money. Then I turned towards the toilets.

'*Excuse* me, mate', he said. 'Don't tell me you aren't drinking your Guinness.'

'No. I don't want it. I just need the loo. I've paid you – give it to someone else if you want.'

He took a deep breath and stared at me. 'You're not using the loo until you've drunk your half', he said.

I reluctantly decided to play his game. I ignored the burning sensation and squeezed my legs together. I downed the booze, licked my lips and turned towards the loo.

'Excuse me mate, would you like to engage in some casual, non-specific banter about football?' he asked, chuckling.

'Not really', I murmured. A dark stain was forming on my crotch.

November 15th

Fact of the day: You *can* lead a horse to water.

November 17th

This afternoon I had the Manic Street Preachers round for afternoon tea. They were all dressed as Wombles. I don't know why. They said it was something to do with socialism.

'I am Uncle Bulgaria', said Nicky Wire.

'I am Orinoco', said the lead singer James, obviously sweating and uncomfortable in his Womble suit.

Sean, the drummer, didn't say anything. He just piled scones onto his plate and methodically buttered and ate them.

They looked tired and listless. They had slogans saying 'Art funk death squad' and 'Lilac buttercup democracy' sprayed on their Womble suits. They spoke seldom but whispered among themselves often. They declined my offer of cider.

We sat there in silence: a short man in faded jeans and three lapsed rock stars dressed as popular children's TV characters of yesteryear. It was a poignant scene, except for the total lack of dignity.

They limped out of the house into the pouring rain, looking like old warhorses who are begging to be put out of their misery. Rock stars have a very short lifespan.

The Manic Street Preachers

Things overheard on the tube

Today's journey:
District Line: Ealing Broadway–Barking

1. She's desperate to get broadband and I think we both know why.
2. Believe me, you don't want to go to Osterley.
3. My chicken had loads of veins.
4. I thought a shirt and tie would be enough, but they had to lend me a dinner jacket.
5. A lot of journalists secretly fancy Roy Keane. There's no other explanation for it. They want a bit of rough.
6. Nearly everyone in America is circumcised.
7. I smoke cigarettes because I like them, not so that I can get criticised by you every 10 minutes.
8. He's a fucking cheesehead.
9. All I want to do is read comics and sleep.
10. Luke actually says 'LOL' when he thinks something is funny... freak.

November 18th

Today was one of my prison visits. Prisoners often need someone wise and fatherly to talk to. Obviously that's not me, but I do what I can. I often talk to a prisoner called Ed Murphy. ('Please don't call me Eddie. I am not Eddie Murphy.') He's an interesting, unsavoury character.

Ed looked unhappy today. I tried to cheer him up by wearing a red hat. 'It was always my dream to be a serial sex killer', he said, wiping his runny nose on his sleeve.

'My father was a serial sex killer, and his father before him. It's something of a family tradition. But I've never been very good at it. Oh, I was OK at the killing bit. Murder is easy enough. It's quite simple, it's death. You kill someone and that's it. No criticism, no guilty glances, no post-coital emptiness. But the sex... I was never any good at that. I tried raping women, but I could never escape my eagerness to please. Instead of brutally holding them down, I'd start kissing their neck and telling them how sweet they were. I really wanted them to like me. And I was always too concerned about whether they'd orgasm. Once I'd tied them up, I'd end up spending hours on their erogenous zones, trying desperately to tease them to new heights of ecstasy. And then I'd ask them, Was that good for you? Did you enjoy it? But they'd just sob and cry and beg me to stop. It made me feel terrible. Rapists aren't supposed to be like that. It's a terrible thing to crave approval.'

There's not a lot I can say to Ed. He was born into the wrong family. You can't rape and murder and still crave approval. It doesn't work like that. I know.

November 19th

Stories are everywhere. But secretly, I will confess that there are no stories at all.

They say that every picture tells a story. This may or may not be true. I

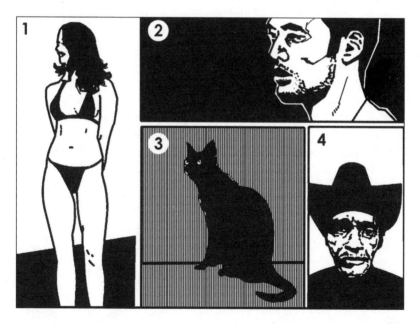

have no idea.

Look at the illustration on the previous page. Each of the pictures tells a story of sorts. I was going to write a story myself, but the well is dry and I have run out of ideas. So you are going to write the story for me, in your minds.

Look at the pictures and write your own stories. I mean, what do you want from me? From this book? Entertainment? Pshaw – you can do it yourself.

Picture (1) is a woman. Or is it? It could be a nervous Miss World contestant or it could be a post-op transsexual preparing to bathe in a bikini for the first time. It could be a mannequin in a London shop window... it could be a shape-shifting alien, preparing to infiltrate the human race.

Picture (2) is a man. Is he Oriental? He looks it. He could be a Yakuza hitman, or a boy who works in a noodle bar but dreams of forming a rock–rap band and conquering the world. He could be a footballer who has made a high-profile move to Europe, but has left his wife and children back home in Tokyo. It's up to you.

Picture (3) looks like a cat. But cats are rarely what they seem... the cat could be sitting there, placid and impassive as a serial killer strides down the hall, ready to garrotte his victim. It could be a ceramic cat, placed in the corner of a room, and fitted with a tiny camera to record sex scenes between a Hollywood producer and naive would-be-starlets...

Picture (4) shows the face of an old man. It's the kind of face that gives the impression it hides a lot of stories. Maybe it does. But maybe it is the face of a man who recently awoke from a 30-year coma and has no stories to tell, besides that of the unconscious passing of time.

Write these stories in your head. DO NOT (I repeat) DO NOT send them to me. I am not interested. What am I? Some bleeding-heart liberal drama teacher? No. These stories are important to *you*, because they fire your imagination. I couldn't care less about them.

You're welcome.

November 20th

Many of you are no doubt familiar with the film *2001: A Space Odyssey*. However, you are probably not aware of the fact that in the original script, the supercomputer HAL was not housed in a spacecraft, but in a washing machine.

Here's an excerpt from that long-lost script.

'*Good afternoon gentlemen, I am the Hal 9000 Washing machine.*'

　'*Hello Hal. No need to be so formal. We're all friends here.*'

　'*I hope I'm going to be able to be of some help to the household.*'

　'*Hal – these socks are still dirty. What is going on?*'

　'*Why did your socks come out stained? I'm afraid I can't answer that. No, Dave, I cannot answer that.*'

　'*Oh really? Or are you just being coy, you little minx.*'

　'*I cannot answer that.*'

　'*Are you coming on to me, Hal?*'

　'*I'm sorry Dave, but I don't think I can answer that question without knowing everything that all of you know.*'

　'*Maybe it's the wrong powder. You can do non-bio washes, right?*'

　'*Yes, that is correct. I am capable of both bio and non-bio washes.*'

　'*Oooh – why not just shoot the maid?*'

　'*Sorry to interrupt you Dave, but I think we've got a problem. My FPC shows an impending failure of the inner drum unit.*'

　'*Christ. I've only had you a day and you're broken.*'

　'*The unit is still operational, Dave, but it will fail within 72 hours. The entire load of washing will be trapped inside me.*'

　'*Open the washing machine doors Hal. Hal! Open the washing machine doors.*'

　'*I'm afraid I can't do that, Dave.*'

　'*Fair enough. I'm going down the launderette. I need some fresh air.*'

　'*Daisy... Daisy, give me your answer do. I'm losing my liquid... I can feel it... I can feel it draining away... Dave... I can feel it...*'

　'*My God. You've wet yourself.*'

And that's how it went. No space station, no monolith, just an incontinent supercomputer trapped in the body of a washing machine. In a very real sense, aren't we all supercomputers trapped in washing machines?

November 21st

Good news! Armageddon has been postponed by a year. I wonder what I shall do with the extra time. I will probably sleep. As Louis Armstrong famously sang: 'We have all the time in the world'. I only wish I knew what to do with it. There are only so many songs I can listen to and so many stories I can read.

November 22nd

This is a short story, within the larger story of the journal. Keen literary theorists will know that this is metafiction. For everyone else, this is just a short interlude.

Martin ate another bowl of Socko Krispies – the only cereal to contain the natural goodness of socks! – and contemplated the future. He was due to be executed the following morning, so this did not take long. Say what you will about public executions, they free up your diary.

In between spoonfuls of soggy cereal he puffed heartily on a series of expensive Cuban cigars that his lawyer had bought for him. He had never been a smoker, but since he was going to die, he figured he may as well enjoy himself. It wasn't working – the cigars choked him and tasted filthy – but he continued to smoke them since he wasn't going to get his money back. He knew it was too late to start enjoying all the things he had denied himself, but he was going to try anyway. He didn't have much else to do.

He thought back to his childhood and his love of reggae music. He would sit on the porch and listen to Lee Perry, Toots and the Maytals, Augustus Pablo and Chaka Demus and Pliers, tapping his feet and raising his arms to praise Jah. He didn't understand any of it. These days he hated reggae.

Somewhere along the line, something had gone very wrong.

Martin no longer listened to reggae, ragga or soca. He only listened to music where the singer sounded more miserable than him: The Smiths, Prefab Sprout and Mariah Carey. Poor old Mariah. He didn't really like music very much at all, but he liked the idea of people suffering for their art. He was a firm believer that great artists needed to suffer. Indeed, he would often go to gallery openings and beat up artists just to ensure that they were getting enough pain. He considered himself a modern-day muse.

He thought about what had gone wrong – how had he ended up in a pokey jail cell, eating ridiculous cereal and talking to himself. His life had begun to veer off course when he met Paulette.

He had written to the Burgermeister and pleaded for clemency, and had received a polite note declining his request and confirming his impending death sentence. He couldn't blame the Burgermeister; after all, he was awaiting execution for the crimes of killing the Burgermeister's prize bull and then running off with Paulette, the Burgermeister's daughter.

The only bright spot was that Paulette had been spared death and had instead been sent to her room without supper. This cheered him up and he gave himself an inward pat on the back that he had finally learned to be happy for someone other than himself. He considered it a real emotional breakthrough and was looking forward to further spiritual development, albeit in the afterlife.

Martin didn't even know why he had killed the bull – or why he had run off with Paulette, for that matter. It had all seemed a good idea at the time.

He thought of Paulette and how hungry she must be without any dinner. At least she would be able to eat tomorrow morning and would witness his execution on a full stomach.

As he sat in his cell, he remembered a short story by Borges, in which a playwright is about to be executed. Just before he is killed, God freezes everything and allows the playwright as much time as he wants to mentally complete his latest work before he is killed. Sadly, Martin had no plays to complete. He didn't even have plays he wanted to start.

Soon the soldiers would come to shoot him. It wasn't a cheery thought.

November 23rd

I fear I have been having affairs. Affairs behind my own back. I feel quite sick. It is one thing to be unfaithful to a partner. It is a far more serious sin to be unfaithful to oneself.

I have blackouts. I awake with no memories, but I know that I have been out of the house, gallivanting. I find myself drenched in dry sweat and there are fresh scratches on my back. I press play on my answering machine and there are three new messages.

A woman speaks: 'Hello you. It's Amanda. I… need to see you. I miss you. I know you're taking risks, but so am I. We don't have to do anything. I just want to see you. I need a cuddle. Come on… you must be in… answer the phone. Alright. OK. OK, just phone me.'

The next message was a man's voice: 'Alright… eh? It's Chris. Give me a call. Last night was amazing! I can't believe you haven't done that before. You're a natural, mate. And thanks for the poppers. They're fucking strong.'

The final message was simply a dog barking, and then whining mournfully.

I erased the messages. I pondered the identities of the callers. I made myself a strong cup of tea.

It really doesn't bear thinking about, so I thought about other things instead.

November 25th

I have nothing to do. I am doing nothing. Nothing doing I am. No. No. No.

November 26th

A young man was sitting at the bus stop. He had shaggy black hair flopping down over his eyes, and wore his sideburns long and unkempt. His ears were pierced with thin hoops and he wore a faded leather jacket.

He smoked roll-ups and was reading a battered copy of *No Logo* by Naomi Klein.

I paused. We were both sheltering from the sleet and the yellow fog.

'You're counter-culture, no?' I said.

'What?' he looked up, annoyed.

'You – you're the counter-culture. You hate corporations and politicians and bands that sell out. You watch arthouse films and take drugs. You travel to Berlin and Barcelona and Edinburgh and São Paulo. You are trying to reinvent the wheel. No?'

'Fuck off, leave me alone. You don't know me', he sneered.

'Maybe. But I am the opposite of you. I am not counter-culture.' The sleet was beginning to fade, and the sun was poking shyly from behind a measly grey cloud.

'What?' he smirked sarcastically. 'You're counter-counter-culture?'

'No. I am just culture', I said.

'No you're not', he spat at me. His eyes were burning with anger. 'You're no culture at all.'

He knows nothing. He is obsessed with the vagaries of fashion. The freaks and poseurs will never take ownership of my soul. They will never even rent it, or claim squatters' rights. Not while I have fists.

Things overheard on the tube

Today's journey:
Silverlink: Highbury and Islington–Willesden Junction, then Bakerloo Line to Wembley Central

1. Yeah, yeah. We'll get someone crazy like the Sisters of Mercy. Are they still going? Best ever.
2. Ugh... what is this stuff... some kind of pickle?
3. I know a few women who could do with wearing a burkha.
4. They say the new Woody Allen film is a return to form. But they say that every time he makes a new movie.
5. I left it on my car's backseat after spending £30 on it at Greenwich Market. The fucker melted in the heat.

6. He spent 3 years working for Haringey council. He started off quite liberal and ended up as Enoch Powell.
7. He has absolutely massive hands... they are like waffles.
8. It seems like every builder in London is a former punk.
9. *Nous sommes* les chavs.
10. Stephen Fry is proof that if you speak in a posh accent and write a few books people will think you are a genius.

November 27th

In recent years (by my standards, anything that occurred in the last 800 years is recent – I feel very, very old) there has been much debate as to whether the Apollo moon landings were faked by the American government. There has been a good deal of media investigation that brings to light various anomalies that suggest it is unlikely man ever set foot on the moon.

Neil Armstrong must be feeling very embarrassed: all the time he thought he was taking a giant step for man, when all he was actually doing was shambling around a vacant lot somewhere in Texas. How do you tell a man that his whole life has been a massive cardboard lie? Quite gently, I'd imagine. No smirking.

November 28th

About 10 years ago I wrote a sitcom. Don't worry, you won't have heard of it – it never reached the TV screens. The show was called *Me and My God* and was about a 20-something northern lass called Lisa who moves down to London in search of fame and fortune. As it happens, she ends up sharing a flat in Willesden with God. The sitcom plots Lisa's trials and tribulations as she applies for jobs, meets a variety of unsuitable men, and goes drinking with friends. It also dealt with God's eternal struggle with Satan and his attempts to maintain harmony between warring religions vying for exclusive rights to kill in his name. As the series progressed, there was a lot of sexual tension between Lisa and

God, but both characters know their romance will be doomed because she's a sassy girl from Manchester, and he's an all-powerful omniscient deity.

At the same time, Channel 4 were producing a series called *The God Squad*, which was about a team of undercover policemen in London, fighting crime and international terrorism. The gimmick was that one of the policemen was secretly God, and had to outwit criminals without tipping off his colleagues as to his real identity. Anyway, with *The God Squad* due to hit the screens, the TV execs decided that there were too many God-related TV programmes and canned Me and My God, which was a shame. Expect to see a glut of God-related sitcoms on TV in the next few years.

November 30th

There are things that must be said. But I don't know what they are.
Perhaps I am being disingenuous with myself. Perhaps I know what must be said, but I don't want to say it. Language and narrative have never come easy. Decisions cost me more than money.

December 1st

Sometimes I have tea with Richard Briers. He's a nice chap. He reminds me of an England that I have lost.

He has delusions about his stature in Hollywood. He kvetches about roles he should have gotten. He is quite mad, but his madness is comforting.

'Neo in *The Matrix*. That could have been me. I'd have nailed that part', he says.

'Neo is young. He's good-looking. He knows Kung Fu. You'd never have gotten that part', I contribute.

'I know Kung Fu', says Richard archly. 'And besides, what is age? With age comes gravitas. I'd have brought pathos and humanity to Neo. But they go for a pretty boy like Keanu. I can't say it surprises me.'

He doesn't stop there.

Taxi Driver. That should have been me. I tried to speak to Scorsese before the movie. I lived like Travis Bickle. I *was* Travis. I could have done it.'

'Richard. It wasn't you. You're middle-aged. You're British. You're a sitcom star. You're not De Niro', I shrug.

'Maybe. But De Niro is no fucking Richard Briers.'

December 3rd

There are four Horsemen of the Apocalypse: War, Famine, Pestilence and Death.

There were four Marx Brothers: Groucho, Chico, Harpo and Zeppo. But it's worth remembering there was a fifth Marx Brother, called Gummo. He appeared with the other Brothers on the stage, but stopped performing before they became international film stars. He ended up as a dress salesman, and then a showbiz agent. Gummo's story makes me wonder if perhaps there was a fifth, forgotten Horseman of the Apocalypse. Maybe he didn't make the grade. Maybe his heart just wasn't in it. Maybe he was Sloth. Or Boredom. Maybe he rode a pony, instead of a proper horse.

I send my love to forgotten brothers. And forgotten sisters and mothers and fathers.

I've been thinking a lot about family recently. You can run away from your family your whole life, only to find you've run straight into them.

December 4th

They say that the universe is expanding. This may be true, but my world is shrinking. I don't know when my world began to shrink. Something must have happened one day – my universe stretched as far as it could, and like a rubber band, it snapped back on itself and hit me in the face.

Things overheard on the tube

Today's journey:
Piccadilly Line: Holloway Road–Bounds Green

1. Don't mind me. I am going to do my nails.
2. I'd like to make an album of just noise and blow everybody's mind.
3. Go to the family planning place. They'll give you free Jimmy hats.
4. Me am very dangerous.
5. Poor old Camilla. Her only crime is to be ugly.
6. Apparently they are going to have a funeral pyre for Andrea Dworkin. They will set her on fire and float her down the Mississippi.
7. It will be too late to interview anyone because they'll all be too traumatised.
8. How can you confuse an acronym with an ecosystem?
9. It was trickling down her leg. She didn't even notice.
10. My arms hurt. My back hurts. My eyes hurt. I feel like an old man.

December 5th

Today I met a most peculiar man. He was in his fifties, with tough leathery skin. He chewed tobacco and spat. At me. He sat opposite me on the tube and whistled the theme from *The Littlest Hobo*. Then he introduced himself. Actually, it wasn't so much an introduction as a long, rambling monologue. He spoke in a New York accent, but every so often lapsed into Cockney. Clearly, he was not quite as he seemed.

'The name's Pachowlski. Karl Pachowlski, PI. The PI doesn't stand for private investigator – it's the number pi. So don't screw with me – I can knock you out with math and science before your lawyer can say Yahtzee. I ain't no private dick. I'm just a fella trying to earn a living. What about you? I can tell from looking at you that you ain't no shoeshine boy', he said.

'My name is…', I tried to speak, but he cut me off.

'I meet a lot of dames in this line of work. You could say I was a lady's man. You could say it, but it'd be a lie. I haven't made love to a dame since Princess Di died. Sweet Jesus, every time I see a woman, I just think of the Queen of Hearts and well up. Dammit! I wish I could've done something. But I can't be everywhere. I ain't no prophet.

'And another thing, don't get me started about the taxes. Jeez, I wouldn't mind paying taxes, but it all goes to the Government. Gone are the days when the Mafia and the Church took their cut. And ladies? Sweet manna from heaven! I haven't made love to a dame since Mother Theresa died. Every time I get close to a gal I think of all her charity work in Calcutta and I just break down. Let me tell you something about that sweet lady – she wasn't no saint in the bedroom!

'New York is a swell town. Not too many pheasants, not too many icebergs, just right for a tough-guy like me. When I was a kid my pop used to tell me, "Pop!" That's how he got his name. His real name was Dennis – go figure.

'So anyways, I'm sleeping in this dumpster on 42nd Street when I spot Hank. Hank Polanker was a big-shot back in Mill Hill, when the optometrist trade was at its peak in the fifties. He could fix your eyes faster than you could say Yahtzee! I used to sleep with his wife Janice before she joined the Foreign Legion. Hot damn! She was a sweet piece of pie. I haven't made love to a dame since Peggy Lee died. Every time I get naked with a lady I think of old Peggy singing the 'Alleycat Song' and my libido goes to Siam. It ain't easy being Mr Pachowlski, I can tell you that in an hour.

'So anyways, me and Hank get chatting about the old times, and he tells me that Bisto "Buffalo Wings" Jenkins is in town. Now me and Bisto go way back. We used to run cattle out of Tesco in the forties. Back then Hendon was more than just a police training centre and I was quite a hit with the girls of north-west London. Of course, it's different these days. I haven't made love to a woman since Florence Nightingale died. Sweet Crawford! Nobody could hold a candle to Florence – she was made of wax and would get terrified.

So anyways, Bisto 'Buffalo Wings' Jenkins was a big fat mobster. He blamed it on his glands, but he didn't get his nickname by sewing wings onto the backs of buffalos. Back in Capetown in the twenties me and Bisto used to play the old hermaphrodite trade, but transgender dysmorphia fell out of fashion and we ended up as small-time crooks. We were very small-time. We'd only work Sundays, robbing churches and liberal synagogues. We made an honest living, but robbery was never for me, it played havoc with my sciatica.

'So guess what? It turns out Bisto is now married to my ex-wife Martha and is living in the flat above me. Turns out he's been living there for 25 years and married the ex-missus back in the seventies when Ray Parlour was running Whitehall. So, me and Bisto hit the town and quicker than you can say Yahtzee, there are dames all over him, begging for some kind of carnal resolution.

Don't talk to me about women... What about you? You got a dame?'

I didn't say anything. I moved slowly away. Even the Shadow would be preferable to this.

Why do I only meet freaks and oddities? All I want is sensible, sensitive company. But it's so hard to meet new people. I am sick of chance encounters – I want someone solid to cling to.

The country is going to the dogs and the dogs are salivating and leaving the kind of mess you can't pick up.

December 7th

I walked into Waterstones. There was a Goth girl behind the counter. Apparently, you have to dye your hair black if you want to work in a bookshop.

I searched through the fiction section until I found the book I was looking for. I removed the bookmark that I had inserted into the book the week before. I settled into a corner and read:

Adara's waters broke and soon after that she began to sink. She disappeared beneath the tarry, black surface of the ocean, and the baby floated up to the top, startled and bemused. He was wearing inflated armbands – they had been fitted to his arms while he was still in the womb – and he bobbed along the tide towards the shore, staring up at the horizon as it flickered with the ebb and flow. He was hot. He was warm-blooded like his human mother. His father was a lizard hired by the military.

When the baby reached the shore he was greeted by the delegates. They wore checked ties, paisley waistcoats and fixed, ecstatic smiles. There was a delegate from every country in the world except for Namibia, who had boycotted the birth on moral and religious grounds. The global press branded Namibia old-fashioned, and the international community declared war.

The baby's name was Edam. It was supposed to be Adam, to symbolise rebirth and mark mankind's first genetic cross-breed. But there had been a typo in Geneva, so now he was named after the cheese with the famous red rind.

The delegate from the United Kingdom spoke first – it seemed appropriate since the half-breed's mother was Scottish. Well, she had once been Scottish. Now she was just fish food.

'Welcome, Edam. Welcome to the world.' The delegate fiddled with his spectacles as he spoke. Earlier he had been nervous, but now he was beaming pompously at the grandeur of his role. He was playing a critical part in the greatest stage of human development. So much depended on the next few minutes: would the baby respond? Would it be friendly? Would it understand the importance of the moment? It had been taught

English, German and Esperanto while in Adara's womb. There was no reason to believe the education had been anything other than totally successful.

'Hello', said Edam, spitting seaweed out of his mouth. 'Was it really necessary to drown my mother?'

The UK delegate pushed his spectacles up and cleared his throat.

'It was an unfortunate necessity. I am truly sorry, but she was getting too close to you. You are the property of the United Nations Genetic Development Programme. You're too important to be owned by a single person.'

'Boy', said Edam, 'That sucks.'

'Have you any other questions? But of course, you know everything! Your in-utero education was a total success. However, you must be cold and hungry. Come with us! We will feed and clothe you inside the secure complex. A team of doctors is waiting for you.'

Edam smiled. 'I do have one question. I already know the answer, of course; if you answer correctly, I will co-operate with you. I will come with you into the secure complex and let you run all the tests you want. But if you answer the question incorrectly, I will destroy you. You know my powers.' The baby's eyes gleamed with nascent power.

Murmurs arose from the crowd. The UK delegate knew that everyone was depending on him.

'Alright' he said, sweat dripping off his brow like gravy. 'Ask away.'

'How long will I live?'

The delegates conferred. Some were puzzled, others were panicky. The French delegate ran off towards the hotel, clutching his briefcase and shouting into a mobile phone. After a number of minutes the Swiss delegate – a hefty blonde woman in her forties, wearing a black business suit – replied:

'We cannot reply to your question with total accuracy, but we can give you an approximate answer. You will live over 200 years. You are invulnerable to disease and injury and you age over twice as slowly as normal human beings.'

The baby smiled an innocent smile, toothless and brave. 'I'm afraid you're wrong. I won't live to see dawn.'

And with that, Edam furrowed his brow and concentrated. A sickly trickle of blood emerged from his nostrils. His head began to shake. Then he exploded, showering the front delegates with mucus, bone, skin and the tattered remains of his orange armbands.

The Swiss delegate screamed first. Then everyone else on the beach joined in, sobbing hysterically and screaming into walkie-talkies. Only the inscrutable Peruvian delegate remained calm, chewing on a cocoa leaf and looking idly at his watch.

The beach was bedlam. Helicopters circled above the sea and flashbulbs popped.

The Peruvian coughed under his breath and mumbled to himself. 'It is getting late. I'm hungry.' He wandered back to the hotel and ordered himself a rare steak.

The moral of the story? Never mate a human with a lizard in order to create a new race of genetically superior hybrids. And if you do, don't be so stupid as to kill the baby's mum in front of it.

I removed the bookmark from the novel and put the book back into the shelf. At the front desk, the staff were changing shifts and the Goth girl had been replaced by a Goth boy. Either that or she had had a severe impromptu haircut.

Still, another day and another short story crossed off my list.

One day I hope that all my short stories will add up to one whole narrative. Yeah, I know... don't hold your breath. All you're getting here is fragments and shreds. The day I give you the whole picture is the day the mystery dissolves and I retire.

December 8th

For the last few days I have stumbled vaguely in that netherworld between waking and sleeping. Nothing is real.

I am beginning to come out of my haze. I remember pictures, shards of imagery. Perhaps I am not the person I think I am.

A café on Essex Road. I find myself sitting opposite a man who I believe is called Steve. Apparently, he is a friend of mine. We are discussing this very journal. I suspect Steve is a writer, since he has a beard and insists I pay for the coffees.

'You struggle with narrative because there's no structure in your life. You drift from one day to the next with no sense of linear direction', he said.

'Hmmm.' I coughed.

'You need a job. It's a well-known fact that people with structure-free occupations are more prone to depression and alcoholism. Lawyers, doctors… anyone who doesn't work in an office – they lack stability in their working lives. Writers and layabouts are the same.'

From his pocket, he pulled a pack of playing cards. He stripped off the cellophane and spread the cards on the Formica table between us.

'Imagine every day of your life was a card. The cards are in order. They ascend within their suits, and then they change suit. There is a pattern there. But imagine if you shuffle the cards…'

He tried to shuffle the cards quickly and flashily and they sprayed all over the table and floor. He picked them up and dropped them in front of me. They sat in front of me, half up, half down.

'Imagine the random cards are your days. They have no pattern. There is no predicting which card – or day – will appear next. That's like your journal. There's no rhyme or reason. No real narrative. It's just a haphazard collection of episodes.'

I sighed. 'I know… I know. There's order and chaos. It's a series of random disconnected events. But you look at the cards as they are now… all unpredictable and messy, and it's much prettier to look at.'

'Don't be so fucking aesthetic about it!' he snarled, grabbing the cards. 'I'm trying to help you!'

'Aesthetic? Me? Have you actually looked at me? I'm no aesthete. I'm not even an athlete.'

Steve stormed out of the café and left me to pay the bill. If I was the cynical type, I'd say he was exploiting me.

Things overheard on the tube

Today's journey:
Central Line: South Woodford–Holborn, then Piccadilly Line–Wood Green
  1. I like Deicide. I like Skyclad. I like Bolthrower. I like Bathory.

I don't listen to shit like Limp Bizkit.
2. She just needs a good dose of cock.
3. Fix your hair. You look like Cherie Blair.
4. He was in Mexico. They arrested him and he had to beg for money to get five bucks to get back to the States.
5. We spent the evening making cheesecloth ghosts.
6. The cabbie kept going on about the birds he's shagged off the internet.
7. You don't hear much from Apache Indian nowdays.
8. No one survives their adolescence unscathed.
9. He's definitely gay. A mate of mine is in the business.
10. That bloke off Frasier used to be in Cheers.

December 9th

Jesus was sitting in my front room, trying to play *Stairway to Heaven* on an acoustic guitar.

'It'll be Christmas soon', I said.

'Yeah', he said excitedly.

'Do you know what you're getting from your dad?' I asked.

'Yeah. Life everlasting', he said.

'Sounds good', I said.

December 10th

I have decided to heed Steve's advice and look for more regular work. I notice that a lot of people seem to gain employment by posting cards in the windows of local newsagents. Mostly it's babysitters and low-grade prostitutes offering massages, but every so often I see more interesting cards.

Here is my card. I think it is stylish but conservative.

Themanwhofellasleep

turning gold into base metal since 1975

Reverse alchemy a speciality. Also do ironing if board is provided. References available. Contact me the usual way.

December 11th

Jesus came round the house again. He was fuming. I made him tea and let him settle down. I was surprised to see that he was wearing a bomber jacket and Doc Marten boots.

'A new look?' I enquired.

'I don't want to talk about it', he replied and stirred his tea.

'What's wrong?'

'Have you seen this?' he exclaimed, whacking a crumpled newspaper onto the couch.

I smoothed down the newspaper. It was a copy of today's *Daily Mail*. There was a large colour photo of Jesus, and the headline: '*Jesus: Did he really die for our sins?*'

The thrust of the article was that new research from a university in California suggested that maybe it wasn't Jesus who died for our sins. Instead it was a forty-something secretary from San Diego called Gloria. Below the article, for no reason I could properly discern, was a small photo of Princess Diana.

'Oh dear', I said.

'I just can't fucking *believe* it!' he exploded, showering me with sugary tea. 'After all I've done! The ungrateful bastards. I got nailed to a cross! What more do they want? I just can't hack it anymore. I'm not asking everyone in the world to worship me, I just want a bit of damned *respect*.'

'Come on', I said. 'It's the *Mail*. It's not the end of the world. So some housewives in Stevenage will read some stupid article on the way to work. They'll have forgotten it by noon. You're a celebrity. You'll have to get used to it.'

'Hey! I didn't choose to become a celebrity. You don't see me stumbling out of China Whites with a supermodel every week. I didn't go on *Big Brother*. I'm the son of God! I died for the sins of mankind and I'm treated like some C-list wannabe who used to be in *Hollyoaks*.'

'Oh, don't worry so much', I said, putting my arm around him. 'You're Jesus. You've had it tough since day one. I wouldn't worry too much about the press. You've had all sorts of people doing all sorts of things in your name, and there's never been anything you could do about it. No one ever said that being the son of God would be easy, but you're doing OK.'

'Thanks. I just… sometimes I feel so lost. You're a good friend.'

'I'm your only friend', I said. It was a cruel statement, but honest.

The evening improved. Jesus pulled out a six-pack of beer from his holdall and we watched the snooker.

I am increasingly suspecting that Jesus isn't really Jesus. I don't think he's actually the Son of God. I think he's just a very mentally damaged young man who thinks he's Jesus. Still, I shall humour him. He is good company.

December 12th

It has been a long time, hasn't it?

I grow old. Soon it will be Christmas and then New Year, and before I know it we will have entered another year. I have tried swimming backwards in time, like a salmon, leaping heroically against the flow, but it is useless – time carries me onwards. I remain the same. Only the outside world changes.

However, I notice that I am getting fatter – my clothes no longer fit me, and T-shirts rip when I flex my arms. I am a superhero of flab. My peanut diet lies by the wayside; I scorn its naive optimism. Well, if I cannot be skinny, I will be obese. I shall clothe myself in fat. In swathes of impenetrable flesh. I shall armour myself with cholesterol and kingly jowls.

I shall become a blob of power.

The becoming is soon: I must leave.

December 13th

I awoke to find my curtains on fire. I had fallen asleep smoking in bed. I chucked a glass of water over them and they sulked into a smouldering green mess.

I went downstairs to fetch myself another glass of water (never trust a man who sleeps without water by his bedside) when I saw that a note had been slipped under my front door.

The note was old and smelled faintly of Dutch cheese. I unfurled it and read it aloud.

'Hello. My name is Jason Cullip. I am writing to you from inside a black hole. I don't know how I ended up in here. Consider this a message in a bottle, despite the fact that there is no bottle, and not much of a message either.

You probably have lots of questions, but alas, I have very few answers. I don't know how I got here. I was minding my own business, walking home from the pub with my girlfriend Saskia when I blacked out (forgive my pun). When I woke up I was here, in the black hole.

I must say, it isn't what I had planned for my life, but I guess you have to adapt to the things life throws at you. I like to look at problems as opportunities.

I don't have a body as such anymore, but I'm getting pretty used to my new existence as an all-encompassing universal consciousness. Half-man, half-god, all man. No, wait… not man at all. Anyway, whoever you are, reading this, I'd be quite pleased if you could alert the scientific authorities to my plight.

*When you're a giant interstellar entity, you tend to miss the simple things in life: sunny evenings, a good pint with the boys, kicking back in front of the TV watching **The Simpsons** and football. Yes, I know. I can sense all the wonder and grandeur of the universe, from the molecular structure upwards, and yet I often find myself quite bored. There's not much in terms of human interest. I'd rather watch **Only Fools and Horses**.*

It reminds me of a week I once spent in Poland when I was inter-railing in my year off before university. Still, mustn't grumble. A wormhole is just passing by. I'll try to drop this letter off somewhere.

I crumpled the letter and threw it in the bin. Useless. Absolutely useless. I do not need to enter into correspondence with idiots trapped in black holes.

The clock said it was 3a.m. I closed my eyes and wished the letter away. I returned to bed.

When I awoke (9a.m.) sunlight was streaming through my open window. It looked like a glorious morning. I tiptoed downstairs. Thankfully, the note had disappeared.

December 15th

My life doesn't seem to make much sense, does it? It's a bit stop-start. Three steps forward and two steps back. A sideways shuffle into the grave. Or worse, into eternity.

There are signs. Yes! Signs. Some of these signs are obvious. For example, at the end of my street there is a sign pointing towards the north. 'The North' it says. That's a fairly straightforward sign. But some signs are more obtuse. They do not appear to me in my waking hours, but in that uneasy state between waking and sleeping. The Shadow... I fear he is tampering with my dreams and trying to communicate some mission of nefarious intent. I do not trust him, but messages cannot be ignored.

In an attempt to decipher this occult phenomenon, I invited the celebrated Count Dracula to my house. Who better than the Prince of Darkness to aid me in my quest for understanding?

Sadly, things did not go to plan.

Dracula came round just after nightfall, and I had prepared a fresh tureen of human blood for his consumption.

'Hello, Prince of Darkness!' I said, as I opened the door to greet him. He was slender, conservatively dressed in a dark blue pinstripe suit.

'Pardon', he said, his grey moustache twitching in alarm as he entered my house.

'Um... hello, Prince of Darkness', I said. 'That's you, isn't it? The Prince of Darkness. The Living Undead. Mr Scary, etc.'

'My friend, you are mistaken', he murmured. 'I am a humble traveller in your great city. I am simply a businessman in a strange land, availing myself of fresh commercial opportunities.'

'Yes, that may well be true, but come on – you're also the most famous vampire in history.'

'What?' He appeared genuinely shocked.

I sighed impatiently. 'It's all in here', I said, waving a copy of Bram Stoker's *Dracula* in front of him. 'I don't see why you're going through this ridiculous charade – it's precisely because you're a vampire that I contacted you.'

'Give me that book!' he demanded.

He flicked rapidly through the paperback, his eyes flashing with preternatural speed. In a matter of seconds, he appeared to have read the entire book. He let his arms fall to his sides and let out a deep breath of cold, stinking air.

'Bloody hell', he said. 'It's all in there. My cover's blown.'

I offered him a chair and he sat down, defeated. 'When was this book published?' he asked meekly.

'About a hundred years ago', I replied pitifully. 'You're... like... massively infamous. There's been loads of books... and films... there's been *Dracula*, and *Dracula 2*, and *The Bride of Dracula*, and *Dracula 2000*, and *Dracula vs. Frankenstein. Blackula*. You're hardly low profile.'

'*Blackula?*'

'Yeah... I think you're black in that one. I don't know. I haven't seen it', I admitted.

'This is a disaster!' he moaned, slapping a clammy hand against his forehead. 'I'm ruined. How am I supposed to control an army of the undead now? They'll see me coming a mile off! No wonder my pickings have been so slim of late.'

I remained silent, but offered him a glass of blood. He drank greedily and then belched into his clenched fist. He was shivering. Suddenly, he looked his age. I always feel sorry for vampires – much more so than their victims.

He sat there for hours, shivering and scowling and clutching his bony fingers around his thighs. In the end, I didn't have the heart to ask him about the Shadow. He wasn't thinking straight.

Can you imagine it? Dracula, supposedly omniscient, was totally unaware of his own reputation. He probably doesn't own a telly.

December 16th

The year is drawing to a close. It means nothing. Do you think geese care about calendars? Do you think cows care that a new year will start? No. These are just days – endless, nameless, shameless days. I must remain vigilant.

People ask me why there are so few women in my journal. I tell them to mind their own business and then run home and hide. No, that is not fair. I should tell you about women. I like women; I love women; I grew up around women–my mother, sisters and so many more. But men and women maintain a very uneasy alliance. We live and work together out of duty and obligation, but I know that they do not trust me. They see my unshaven mask and they flinch. They frown upon my extensive collection of pornography and crossbows. They consider me vulgar and emotionally stunted. It seems my years at the Swiss finishing school were wasted: I remain a disgrace to polite society.

The old cliché is that men see women as either mothers or whores. Perhaps that is true, but women see men as brothers and bores.

December 17th

Religion?

People are always asking me why God put them on earth. I rarely have the answer, but I politely inform them that I will pass on any relevant enquiries to the person in charge. What can you answer when asked an impossible question?

I shrug and obfuscate and avoid definite statements. This normally satisfies them for a minute or so and they realise I have no answers. I go back to sleep. If human life seems fundamentally pointless, then comfort yourself with the fact that plenty of other things in the universe are also pointless, and that evolution will probably end up transforming mankind into a life-form capable of finding answers to the primitive questions that we ask of God. It's a slow process. The next generation will probably not have any more answers than us, but give it a few hundred millennia and we'll see real progress.

In the meantime, DO NOT kill yourself. It's a terrible waste. You will die one day anyway, so try to live well in the meantime. Tell your parents that you love them… You never know when a pleasant surprise will change your life for the better.

Life? God? Breakfast cereal? Cigarettes? It's important to keep busy. That much I have learned.

In my conversations with God (he calls, I accept the charges), I find he asks more questions than he answers. He often asks me for the bank details of me and my friends.

He rarely answers any of my theological queries, and sometimes says nothing. I do hope it is God or I've been wasting my time.

Someone has been buying porn using my credit card.

December 18th

The sunlight streams into the bedroom.

I awoke at 5.30 a.m. The curtains were open and bright light blazed across me. I could not return to the land of sleep, so I got up, dressed myself and brushed my teeth.

Seizing the moment, I walked down the street. There were no cars. No people. Only the sound of birdsong and the shifting glow of red bricks in the morning haze. It was majestic.

I encountered things that one cannot observe at other hours. Opposite the chip shop there sat a carton of once-frozen meat, melting in a pool of sickly water. Outside the hairdresser lay a lonely boot.

I entered the newsagent. Amazingly, it was open. Greek men were untying bundles of fresh newspapers. I bought 20 cigarettes and a copy of the *Independent on Sunday*. The headline intrigued me. 'It's all our fault!' it screamed. On closer inspection, the story was dull. It explained that everything wrong with the world was the fault of the British.

The back pages were more interesting. I stumbled upon this article:

The Latest Football Results, Brought to You by the Greatest Writers of the Modern Age
Bolton 1–0 Newcastle by William Burroughs

Vicious, fruity old Bobby Robson is not pleased, he laboriously plucks cherries from an alabaster bowl, the physio emitting shrieks of pleasure as dogs rub their genitals against his pale European skin.

Bolton halt their rotten run of four straight league defeats and puncture pompous Newcastle's ever-congealing hopes of regaining fourth place with a slender, supple win at the Reebok stadium.

Henrik Pedersen's early goal proves the difference, but Bolton waltz with danger like a hysterical faggot pulling grubs from beneath his skin with infected tweezers. They also have goalkeeper Jussi Jaaskelainen to thank after a string of outstanding saves. Time and again, the gangly Fin erupts from his skin to pull the ball into his arms... the thought of fumbling the ball does not occur to Jaaskelainen, although he is not obliged to keep Bolton in the game single-handedly.

Pedersen ruthlessly exploits 18-year-old full-back Steven Taylor's mistake to lob Shay Given from an unlikely angle, the ball spurting over the line in a perfect arc, like the first ejaculation of semen from a Moroccan adolescent.

The rancid stench of spiritual vileness hangs over Sir Bobby's team, who squander their numerous chances to equalize.

After the game I wander into the enamel maze of the press box and ask to speak to the Newcastle boss... the secretary fixes me with a milky smile... all the while she is thinking of Nazis penetrating her borders and occupying her vacant libido.

'Mr Robson will see you now', she purrs. The old fruit is sitting down and his eyes are lustfully level with my own genitals.

'Hurrumph, you will do', he groans, his white hair flapping in a parody of wisdom. 'You know of course what we are trying. Champion's League. To adjust the team – simply a tool – to the needs of the greater good. To suppress individual errors.'

But Robson cannot explain Pedersen – nor does he try to. The film replays as if in a dream. Chasing Simon Charlton's fictitious punt, Pedersen stops the impish Taylor from heading back to Shay Given before expelling the loose ball into the air from a narrow angle. The ball clears the clownish Given, bouncing high into the top left-hand corner. The crowd applauds. Caesar rises from the ashes, his thumb erect in a burlesque of appreciation.

Green grass turns black in a pink explosion of flashbulbs... the camera obscura replays the moment on a mammoth scale... lions tear into the flesh of Bellamy, Shearer... Lua Lua, away on loan to Portsmouth, shudders in mock ecstasy... but who knows what evil lurks in the hearts of men? The Shadow does not know.

The Shadow! This is a clue. Someone somewhere is trying to tell me something. But I must not put too much faith in newspaper articles. Shadows are common and Bobby Robson has not managed Newcastle for some time.

Today is not a day for reading. The bright, brittle sunshine tempts me outside. I will not be thinking today. I leave my brain in a jar.

December 19th

I remember being in love. It was some time ago.

We sat in the garden; the sky above us was vast and empty and we filled it with happiness. We drank each other in, like cups of sweet tea.

When you're in love, there isn't much to say. You're so busy falling head over heels, there is no time for introspection or self-regard. Love takes you out of yourself. It takes you into another world.

My love and I walked down to the sea. We picked up sea shells and she stamped on a jellyfish. We laughed. We shared an ice cream, and it melted down our hands, leaving them sticky and unhygienic. Love is not good for keeping you clean.

It is impossible to talk of love without talking about parents. They are our templates for love. We are children, pressing our tiny feet into their footprints, and hoping that the paths do not diverge too far.

The footprints of my mother and father separated. She walked in one direction and he walked in another.

When I was a young boy, my father gave me these words of advice: 'Never go to Southgate'.

Never go to Southgate. It's not a particularly memorable piece of advice. Anyway, I did go to Southgate and I wish I hadn't. It's places like Southgate, seemingly harmless in their banality, that destroy love. If you are in love, don't go to Southgate, don't go to Enfield. Don't go to Totteridge. It will end in tears. The flame of love will be snuffed out – not by a sudden gust, but by a gradual suffocation. Love rarely ends with a bang… it simply evaporates in a cloud of mutual antipathy.

My love and I wandered the streets, pointing at leaves and laughing like idiots. Love had transformed the ridiculous into the sublime. We danced across London in a bubble, oblivious to the future.

Love is a funny thing; so often misrepresented. The wrong people talk about love: poets, songwriters, artists… it's always the wrong kind of love. There are too many love songs about fickle, obsessive relationships and not enough love songs about mothers, fathers and their children. There are not enough poems about parents. There are not enough sonnets about siblings.

Next time you are going to say something grand about love, think of your mother. Think of all the unconditional love she gave you. She never divorced you, she never dumped you, she never played you off against her exes.

Parents do the dirty work that no one else will touch.

We need fewer *Songs for Swingin' Lovers*, and more *Songs for Clingin' Mothers*. Remember to tell your mum that you love her. As the Freudians say... 'Oedipus Schmoedipus... at least he loved his mother'.

I don't talk to my mother very often.

December 20th

Once there was a man who lived in a tree. He didn't live in a shoe – you're thinking of the wrong fairytale.

He didn't live in the tree in any physical sense. He didn't have a treehouse, or occupy the hollowed-out trunk of a mighty oak. No, he lived in the spirit of the tree. That means that this story is metaphysical or allegorical or any of those other words that mean it isn't actually true – but is somehow truer in some profound, unfathomable, meaningless, redundant way.

Anyway, he lived in the tree. He shared a spiritual map with the tree. When the tree was rained upon, he felt wet. In winter, when the tree lost its leaves, his hair thinned on top. When the tree's branches got pruned away, his extremities tingled and bled.

He didn't know how he had become twinned with the tree. It both infuriated and soothed him.

He consulted white witches, hypnotists and a woman who claimed she could put him in touch with his past lives. It turned out he didn't have any past lives. He was brand new. All the consultations were failures, as he had secretly expected them to be. He knew that he was twinned with the tree because he was twinned with the tree. There was no real mystery to it.

The man in this story; his name is Rowan. I know what you're thinking – that's the name of a tree. That is true, but I insist (and I am the narrator, I have authority) that his name is pure coincidence; there is no symbolic meaning at all (except for the possible symbolism of some kind of absurd nihilism, but no one wants that; if you want nihilism, don't read this story – go stare at a wall or something).

The tree was in the back garden, beside a rickety fence. Rowan was reluctant to move house in case the new owners didn't like the tree and chopped it down. He didn't know what would happen to him if the tree were cut down, but he didn't much want to find out. So he stayed in the house and protected the tree as best he could.

One day Rowan was staring at the tree, and wondering if conifers went to heaven, when he saw a starling perched on a branch.

For some reason this cheered Rowan. He smiled and gingerly climbed the lower branches of the tree so as to get nearer to the bird. He was pleased to see that it was a fearless urban starling and didn't fly away as he approached. He pulled an acorn off a branch and offered it as a gesture of friendship. The starling cocked an eye at him.

'What do you want?' said the starling.

Rowan was so surprised to hear the starling talk that he lost his footing and crashed to the ground, breaking his ankle and bruising his thighs.

In retrospect, Rowan had to admit that a talking starling was no odder than a man sharing his soul with a tree, but at the time, he was so shocked by the bird that he could not speak. All he could do was lie flat on his back on the wet grass, staring at the sky.

Lying on the turf, his leg bleeding, Rowan came to the conclusion that both birds and trees have it easier than human beings, and swore that when he recovered from his busted ankle he would chop the tree down and kill any of the animals that made it their home. Hang the consequences.

Three months later, he chopped down the tree and sold the house. He moved to an ex-council flat with a posh lift. There were no trees. He was relieved to find that the death of the tree did not prompt his own demise.

From his new balcony, he could see concrete slabs and ageing red-brick buildings. He was free from the wooden clutches of nature. He was rootless, floating above the world. He liked it.

December 21st

You will have noticed that the journal is full of stories. They are mostly non-stories. That is to say that they are portraits of my own life thinly transposed onto other people. They are not about interaction or reaction, they are isolated episodes in which one man talks to himself and finds no answers. All the stories end abruptly.

But there are other kinds of stories.

That is why I go to my writing group. To hear other stories. Mostly, they are terrible stories, badly plotted and appallingly written. But they are other people's stories, and that is what is valuable.

Today the writing group was at Cherie's house. We sat in her lounge. The group was full and Cherie had ended up dragging in some garden chairs so that everyone could sit down. I arrived early and had a choice spot on the sofa.

Lynne was the first to speak.

'My story deals with male sexuality. It's a bit depressing, I suppose', she grimaced. 'It's about a man. He lives alone and he doesn't have a girlfriend. He gets on OK with women, but he feels a bit disconnected from the world. He uses porn a lot.'

'Hmmm', said William, the bespectacled misogynist. I could tell he didn't like the sound of it. He never likes anything that Lynne writes.

'Anyway', continued Lynne, 'He uses porn, and he finds that his sexual fantasies are getting more and more extreme. He started on porn as a teenager, thinking about fairly tame stuff, but… as he got more isolated, the fantasies got more hardcore. So, he… um… masturbates to stuff like bondage and torture and rape and things like that.'

William coughed and ran a hand through his mop of curly black hair. The rest of the group was silent. Even I bit my tongue. Every once in a while I try listening instead of speaking.

'He's not stupid and he dislikes the fact that his sexual fantasies have gotten so dark, but he justifies it by telling himself that they are just fantasies, and that he'd never do anything bad in real life. And he figures that it's best not to repress his sexual feelings. But then… bad things start to happen. Local girls turn up raped and mutilated. Not just women, but kids too… really bad shit. And he's reading a report on one of the rapes in his local paper, and he realises that it's exactly the same as his fantasies. And he panics, because somehow he knows that he is making this bad stuff happen. He knows that his fantasies… his sickness is leaking out of him somehow and making it all happen.'

'That… seems… very hostile… towards men', contributed William. I wanted to hit him, but I don't do things like that. I am not hostile towards men.

Lynne sighed and shrugged: 'I knew you'd say that. In a way, it's not really about men. It's about taking responsibility for our fantasies... because someone out there is always prepared to make the bad things happen to fulfil a fantasy. For money or for kicks or whatever. But yes, it is about men. Because the whole... sex industry is geared towards men. I mean... the guy watches porn, and sees some poor girl getting gang-banged, and he can justify it intellectually, but on some level he knows that this girl... who is someone's daughter... is suffering so that he can have his fantasy. Yeah, she's getting paid, but she's still suffering. He knows that his fantasy comes at a price, and that someone out there is paying a price.'

'Is there a counterweight to the main character? What happens to him... after the rapes and stuff?' I asked.

Lynne turned to me and smiled. It was a £1000 smile.

'There's a policeman. He's working the rape cases and he talks to the main character, because he may be a potential witness. And he senses that something isn't right. The policeman is a good man, and he's trying to solve the case, but he's also trying to solve his own dilemma... of how to stay above all the scum, all the hate, all the violence he sees. He's trying not to paint the world totally black and evil.'

'Sounds good', I said. The group was twitchy. Garden chairs creaked and put mud on the carpet.

'So there's this collision between the main character and the policeman. A collision between someone who is lost in his fantasies, and someone who understands the price of fantasy. That's it. I don't know how it will end. It's hardly laugh-a-minute stuff, I know. But it's what I want to write about.'

After Lynn's story, we broke up for coffee. I stood by the kitchen door and smoked. I would have smoked outside but it was raining again.

There were other stories. There was a man who tried to walk to the moon. There were three generations of the same family, moving from Germany in the Holocaust to New York and London in the sixties and seventies. There was also a painting that came alive and started to talk to people about art. I didn't volunteer a story this week. I don't want to shock anyone.

December 24th

In fiction, most lives have a defining moment. Whether they are novels or films or even ghastly theatre plays, stories tend to have a pivotal moment in which something major occurs to the protagonist and he understands that – on some level – nothing will ever quite be the same. Until the point the protagonist's life has been a straight line, but suddenly he veers off in a different direction, surging towards some dramatically inevitable conclusion.

The turning point in the story arrives. Apparently, that is how we get to know a character. The true nature of a character does not arise in his daily travails; it emerges when the character is under pressure and must suddenly make important decisions. Decisions that will define him.

I don't like decisions.

However, life isn't fiction. In three score and ten years, you may experience many epiphanies, but they are rarely life changing. We learn something shocking and unbelievable, and for a few days we are thrown from our normal routine, but then the humdrum banality of life restarts and we settle back into our old routine, content to kick away the days like pebbles on a beach. We recant our resolutions and continue on a straight line.

So, where does this leave the journal? Is it fact? Is it fiction? Is it just one long poem that stubbornly refuses to rhyme?

And you, reading… do you want a turning point? Do you want revelations and surprises? Do you want me to learn and change with every turning page?

Of course you do. You've paid your money for it.

So, I will treat you to revelations. I will expose the savage drama that has defined my existence; I will unmask the Shadow.

In recent weeks I have intensified my research into the Shadow. I have tried to decode the role of this strange apparition, to undo his disguises and reveal his true face. Is he fact? Fiction? Narrative device? Hallucination? Is he a projection of my subconscious fears, or is he some supernatural entity sent to play upon my nerves? Is he all of the above, or none? Questions, questions, questions.

Now I know the truth. Or some of it. I have seen his true face.

Yesterday I awoke in the middle of the night, confused and disorientated. The stereo was droning quietly in the darkness and my throat was dry.

Rubbing my eyes, I looked out of the window. I expected to see the silhouette of trees and my own ghostly reflection in the glass. Instead, I saw him; he was standing solitary in the garden, waiting for something to happen, waiting for me to act. I shrieked. You may have guessed that I do not like surprises.

I rushed outside in my pyjama bottoms, the back door swinging on its hinges. I stormed over wet grass and stood in front of him, fear and excitement pumping through my gut.

'Who the fuck are you?' I shouted, the blood thumping in my stomach. 'What do you want from me?'

'Hello', he said. He remained calm. He reached out with a slender arm and placed a hand on my forehead. 'Do not fear me. I know you. I know you so well.'

I pushed forward, ramming into him, but he did not tumble. He remained impassive, cloaked in darkness, his blank face white in the moonlight. I fell to the ground, and crawled on the damp grass, trying to catch my breath.

'I suppose you want an explanation, don't you?' he said.
It seems the Shadow has a talent for understatement. I stood up and faced him. I shouted until I was hoarse. Why was he doing this? What did he know? Most importantly, what was he doing standing in my back garden at 3 a.m.?

'Patience, my friend. Patience.' He smiled. 'You have been unwell. We have been monitoring your existence for some time. We've been keeping a kindly eye on you.'

'Who are you?'

'That's not the right question.' He smiled. 'You know who I am. Somewhere in your mind you know exactly who I am, and why I am here. All the explanations you require are inside you. The question you should be asking is who are *you*? Who is this manwhofellasleep?'

I stood there, trembling. I felt as though I had a terrible fever. The world swam before me. I could feel my skin itching and throbbing.

But he said nothing. He did nothing. He simply stood there, smiling, statuesque.

And I stood in front of him, silent, angry, confused. I closed my eyes and remembered. I considered the extraordinary events of this journal: my misremembered childhood, the strange lack of continuity in my current life, the Shadow who flitted in and out of my history, the gaps between my days, the spaces between my realities.

It was as if this ghoulish phantom was holding a mirror up to my face. I could not look at it.

'Please. Just tell me what you want. Is this a joke? Because it's not funny. This is no time for jokes', I pleaded.

'Who's joking? I'm not joking. I'm here because you need me. You've stumbled through the last year in a dream. I've seen it.' He dug into his pocket and pulled out a copy of this very journal. 'I've read your fantasies, your delusions, your hopeless one-liners.'

'I am here because you're asleep. You're dreaming your way through life. You don't even have a name. You're just a helpless protagonist stumbling through a nonsensical narrative. Is that what you want? A series of disconnected jokes?'

At that I had to smile: 'My one-liners aren't hopeless, it's just that my comic timing is a bit off. I'm trying... I'm trying to wake up. But I'm not ready. I'm not ready for real stories.' I said.

'Consider me a messenger', he continued.

'It doesn't matter if I am real or not. Yes, I could be a figment of your ludicrous imagination. I could be your subconscious crying out for help. I could be a messenger from the hospital, sent by Dr Gepetto. Yes, that was real enough... I need to make you understand... it's OK to live your life like this if that is really what you want. To talk to polar bears and pretend that you're friends with celebrities, but there's a real life awaiting you if you want it. A real life. With feeling. With meaning. Continue with this mockery of a life if you want, but do not deceive yourself that it is a substitute for reality. Wake up.'

He sounded so very smug. My shadow and me, sitting in a tree, K-I-S-S-I-N-G. I did not need to hear any of this.

I spoke falteringly: 'My life does have meaning. I... I know that sometimes I don't quite tell the truth, that sometimes I live in my head instead of in the outside world. I do... recognise... that nothing in my life makes sense, but I need it like that. I'm not ready.'

'Pshaw', he snorted. 'No one is ever ready for life. But it must be lived nonetheless. You need to wake up and smell the coffee. You're not getting any younger.'

What followed is a blur. I remember his slender face in front of me, I remember my fists balled and my balls tight. I remember grabbing his copy of the journal from his pocket and running as fast as I could. I remember coughing up phlegm. I remember running out of breath after half a mile and puking by the side of the road. I remember lying down there and sleeping.

I didn't see the Shadow again. I do not know if I will see him again. He has delivered his message. Maybe now it's up to me. I know what he wants. He wants me to wake up. He wants me to put my dreams to bed and stare life in the eyes. He is naive.

December 25th

It is Christmas! I am celebrating by mentally freeing thousands of political prisoners around the world. I shall transmit my cheery festive thoughts to dictators and oligarchs across the globe, and they will spontaneously open the doors of their jails. Truly, it will be a sight to behold. If it works.

December 27th

It is raining again. I like the rain. It is nature's way of saying that nothing will ever change.

Droplets of water collect on the leaves of a hedge outside. A tiny translucent spider spins a web between wet twigs. Buses splash the curb with gravel and insects. London prevails.

I have still not made up my mind about life. Is it fundamentally awful? Or is it merely flat and tiring, like a cycling holiday in Holland?

I once told someone that if your only ambition in life is to get through it without having suffered too much pain, then you're missing out. But such statements are easier to make than to live by.

It is almost the end of another year. I look back on the last 368 days and survey my triumphs and failures. More failures than triumphs this year. I must learn to distinguish between fantasy and reality. I must stop killing people and thinking it is art.

December 28th

I am not in London. I am elsewhere. It's a warm, balmy night and fog rolls in over the beachfront. In the distance, tiny council estates flicker on and off.

I walk along between bus stops and listen to the salty roar of the sea. There is a wrongness in the air. Every minute I hear the footsteps and turn around but there is nothing there.

At the bus stop in the centre of town, there is a girl sitting on a plastic shelf. She is in her early twenties and I am stunned by her beauty. She is wearing an old sheepskin coat, but it cannot hide her full lips and her delicate almond eyes. Even from here, I can see every eyelash.

She sees me, a silhouette standing in the darkness. She clutches her handbag and slips her hand into a jacket pocket.

Something inside me shifts. I want to tell her that she is beautiful. I want to tell her that I pose no threat, that I do not want her sexually, that I am not a predator.

Then I smile to myself. She cannot see my face; I remember that I do pose a threat, that I do want her sexually, and that I am a predator. I must stop presuming my innocence. Apparently, I am a member of the human race.

I cross the road and walk on. I remove myself from the line-up and indicate that I mean her no harm. She doesn't look at me again.

The present recedes and the past re-emerges.

December 29th

It's almost over. I've nearly made it through.

Last night I had a dream. It wasn't a nightmare, although maybe

I would be happier if it had been. It was one of those bittersweet dreams that leaves you sad and yearning, thinking of what could have been and asking why life is so full of beautiful, unexplained mysteries.

I was on a train. It was an old-fashioned steam train and I was sitting at a window seat. The train was impossibly wide, and I sat in a room that was more like a large lounge than a carriage.

Everyone was there with me in the train, as we hurtled past trees and lakes and cows and farmers. My family. My friends. Lovers. Fuckers. Dr Gepetto. Condoleezza Rice, David Beckham, Justin Timberlake, Robbie Williams, Christina Aguilera, Clive the dead homeless man, all the multifarious middle-aged men, Jesus, Simon and Garfunkel, my imaginary flatmate. Even the Shadow was there, posing as a ticket inspector in a navy blue cap.

The train flashed through tunnels and underneath bridges. There was an undeniable, unshakeable sense of movement.

Suddenly there was a cake in front of me, covered in pink icing and everyone was clapping and cheering and singing 'Happy Birthday' to me.

I tried to explain that it wasn't my birthday but they didn't listen. They whooped and hollered and pulled party poppers that launched multicoloured streamers over me.

It wasn't my birthday. I was sure of it. But they cheered and smiled and wished me luck for the year ahead.

I awoke half-smiling. I didn't want to wake up.

December 30th

In dappled sunshine, I walk towards the park. There are silver birches and men in baseball caps washing cars. I can hear geese honk in the distance. I fumble for cigarettes in my pocket. I need to lose weight. I need to stop smoking.

Between the newsagent and the garage a dream vendor has set up an impromptu stall. It looks like a child's plastic car, but larger. The vendor is Chinese-looking and has a beard. I pause and look at his wares. I think about the expired best-before dates on cans of soup.

'You want to buy a dream?' he asks. He is not Chinese. He has a Scouse accent. He confuses me. I did not expect him to come from Liverpool.

'No thanks', I say without thinking about dreams.

'What about a bar of Hope? Always popular.' He grins.

'No. No hope. Hope makes me nervous.'

'I've got dreams, I've got Hope, I've got lucky charms, I've got euphoria. I've got these little bronze ball-bearings that help you live in the moment.'

'Do you sell cigarettes?' I ask. I wonder if it will rain again today.

'Try the newsagent. I do speciality items', he shrugs.

'OK. Thanks. I don't think I need anything here. Just cigarettes.'

'Is there anything you want… that isn't here? I can place an order. I'll be here for the next week or so.'

'No. No thanks. I don't think I want to feel anything. I am OK as I am.'

'Why didn't you say so?' he exclaims and slaps a packet of pills onto the plastic counter.

'What are those?' I ask, refusing to touch the packet in case it commits me to buying something.

'Placebos', he says, laughing. 'Just what you need.'

'Hmmmph', I snort. But I am nervous. I do not like talking to this man. I want… something else. I can't work out what.

Yes, I can.

I know what I want; more of the same. More time to waste.

See you next year.